A Puhaka Books Selection

puhakabooks.com

Cubo Zoan

W. B Martin

Also by W. B. Martin

A Sports Fantasy

To Zoe Sophia

Chapter 1

Melbourne, Australia

The hot January sun blazed over the stadium as the Australian Open continued its competition. Being summer in the Southern Hemisphere, the tennis players all struggled to adjust to the extreme conditions.

Melbourne was noted for its inclement weather during the summer. For protection from stoppages in play that had plagued the Australian Open in the past, a new retractable roof had been installed. But with the fine clear Antipodal sun baking the court, the roof was open to the elements.

"We certainly have hot conditions today for our finals matchup between Number 2 in the world Svetlana Trenschenko from Russia and the Number 5 ranked player from France, Dominique Richard. This looks to be a battle of survival today. Both these players have fought their competition as well as the heat the whole tournament," the television announcer said.

"We certainly do, Hugh. Not only have these two women players had to deal with the heat, but both of them have endured three set matches in getting to these finals. With the number 1 player, Selena Roberts, out with injuries, this field is set to establish a new number 1 player. It will be a fight today," Karl Mahr, color announcer for ZBC Sports Network added.

Karl Mahr was a former professional tennis player from Germany who ZBC Sports Network had signed to partner with their top announcer, Hugh Godley. Being a recent start-up founded by European businessmen, ZBC Sports Network was seen as the new competitor to the American-dominated ESPN.

Hugh Godley, a British celebrity in his own right prior to moving to announcing sports, had seen the new network jump leaps and bounds in the ratings race for cable customers. The network had just recently extended Hugh's contract with a substantial salary increase.

"Well, Karl, without Selena in the mix, this has been a wide open tournament with no clear favorite. The roster of Russian players certainly gave us some moments where we could have seen an all-Russian Final. Dominique pulled off that amazing upset in the semi-finals, though. After playing for over three hours in the heat, it came down to four match points before she finally won. We'll have to see if she has anything left today."

"You're right there, Hugh. But don't forget that Svetlana also had to battle in the semi-finals. She had to beat a feisty opponent in a three set match. I think its anyones game today," Karl added.

The two competitors took the court to rousing applause and the players settled into their warm-up routine. Fans settled into their seats in anticipation. Water bottles and sun hats were evident in the boiling stadium.

Celebrities from all disciplines had choice seats, led by the Prime Minister of Australia, known as a huge tennis fan. With a box at center court, the Prime Minister adjusted his hat for protection from the sun. Sitting beside him, a deeply-tanned man sat with just a visor. His thick dark hair flowed down over his shoulders.

"Well, I see the Prime Minister has a guest with him today," Hugh observed.

"Yes, it's none other than Mr. Zoan, of the World Anti-Doping Commission. It would seem that he is out celebrating his recent success in dethroning cycling legend and four-time Tour de France Champion, Neil Aldrin," Karl said.

"We can be sure that all eyes are on him and his Commission here today. The situation between Neil and the Commission continues to be very controversial, to say the least," Hugh offered.

The World Anti-Doping Commission had raised many critics by banning Neil Aldrin from bicycling and taking away his four Tour wins. The controversy swirled around Neil's continued defense that he had never failed any test administered by the WADC.

The ban was solely based on testimony offered by Neil's teammates and competitors that they had seen Neil use performance-enhancing drugs. Considering the jealousy involved in professional sports, many thought such accusations were bogus at best.

No hard evidence was ever offered in Neil's investigation. Many thought the WADC was out to 'get some scalps' to establish its dominance over sports. And that attitude was certainly enhanced by the demeanor of its President, Cubo Zoan.

Cubo Zoan was a Brazilian who had been named head of the St. Moritz, Switzerland-based agency. Mr. Zoan brought a controversial reputation with him to the post and many in the sports world thought the Board of Directors of WADC had purposely chosen Cubo for his ruthless reputation.

Born to an Albanian emigrant and a Brazilian woman, Cubo had the tall, dark good looks of his Brazilian heritage. That Cubo's father had been a notorious European hater after his escape as a child from Albania seemed to come out in the son.

A victim of Mussolini's invasion during World War II, Cubo's Albanian family had suffered greatly at the hands of the Italians. Then the family had been subjected to German occupation for the remainder of the war.

That the British made moves to invade the Balkans but never did added to Cubo's father's rage. By the time of the family's escape after the Communist takeover of Albania and their subsequent journey to South America, the seeds were set for a lifelong venting at the father's European tormentors. Many thought the son had inherited all of his father's grievances.

That the WADC chose Cubo to head up its anti-doping efforts set a tone that was surely noticed in many European countries. And now he and WADC had taken out America's greatest cycling hero. The United States seemed to be joining Europe in their adverse opinion of Cubo Zoan.

"If WADC goes after some tennis players on the kind of flimsy evidence that they threw at Neil, it will reinforce what many now consider a rogue agency," Karl said.

"But as long as the individual sports federations continue to give them the power over each of their sports, the WADC will be in the driver's seat," Hugh rejoined. "So we'll see if the ITF jumps on the WADC bandwagon."

The ITF, or International Tennis Federation, was the governing body for professional tennis in the world. They continued to provide their own anti-doping program and had not joined the WADC.

Hugh was famous for adding the kind of sports info that drove his ratings. "Karl, I can only tell our viewers what the talk around the sports world is of Cubo and his organization. He has earned a new meaning for the acronym WADC, now referred to as 'What A Dick'."

"You have that right. Mr. Zoan has not made many fans. Especially when he ignores the talk of rampant cheating coming out of the Chinese athletes these days. Mr. Zoan had better be careful and expand his scope of scrutiny," Karl injected.

The program producer cut off his announcers with an ad before they stepped any deeper into touchy issues. While the ads were running, he told them to stay on topic when they were back on camera. And he reminded them that the topic was tennis.

Chapter 2

Somewhere over Nepal (3 months later)

The passenger intently watched the scenery out the window. In the window's reflection, he could see the person next to him pull her ear buds from her ears. She turned her head toward the plane window where the passenger sat transfixed by the sights outside.

"Dad?" she asked.

No acknowledgement.

"Dad?" Francine said louder. She added a tap on the shoulder for good measure.

"What? What is it?" came the startled response. But the passenger continued to look out the plane window.

"Dad, tell me again."

A frustrated father finally gave up on looking out the window and turned his attention to his daughter sitting beside him.

"Tell you what again?" he asked.

"You know. What's going to kill me here?" Her voice showed concern.

"Nepal? Just the normal stuff. Avalanches, buses rolling off cliffs, snow leopard attacks, yeti kidnappings."

"Dad! Be serious," Francine demanded.

At twenty, she wasn't a kid anymore. Dewey had to remember that. It seemed just a short time ago that she was swinging her bat in 'T-Ball'. He missed those days of uncomplicated joy in watching his daughter tear through any sport she wanted to master.

Francine had been the terror of Kidsports. Whether it was soccer or volleyball or softball, she would lead her team in all categories. Dewey still remembered working with his daughter on her volleyball skills. The first time she did a jump serve for an 'ace' was in third grade. The other kids were still mastering getting an underhand serve over the net.

And now here they were escaping all of that. Sports had turned into a nightmare for her and he was once again the dad coming to the rescue.

"Be serious. What might kill me here in Nepal?" Francine asked.

"Honey, we've been over this a million times. Stop focusing on it," Dewey admonished his daughter. He was tired of her fixation on things that might kill her. He supposed it was partially his fault. He should never have read those excerpts from Bill Bryson's book on Australia. She'd been focused on all the deadly things in Australia and now associated foreign travel with brushes with mortality. Dewey added, "Nepal is pretty safe."

"Define pretty," she demanded.

"Like I told you when we started planning this trip together, when the yak trains are coming up the trail at you, move to the uphill side of the trail. That's the biggest thing you need to remember."

"Are yaks mean or something?" she asked.

"No, yaks are yaks. They act like cows, just bigger. And wider. They'll have packs strapped to their sides. If you step out of their way downhill, there's a good chance

15

they'll knock you off the trail. And trust me, we will be on some trails where being pushed off the trail won't be good for you," Dewey said.

Dewey thought of the cliff face rock cuts barely wide enough for two people to pass that he had experienced. A knock off the trail meant a five hundred foot fall onto rocks below.

"Oh," was all Francine said.

Dewey kicked himself. He had done it again. Without even mentioning the five hundred foot fall to certain death, his daughter was now imagining even worse. Even though after the first hundred feet of fall, the rest didn't really matter. The results were all the same.

Dewey decided to get her refocused on the positives of Nepal. "Honey, just look out the window. The Himalayan Mountains are just outside. Aren't they spectacular?"

But it wasn't working. The thoughts of a likely early death on the trail was the only thing on his daughter's mind. He watched as consternation settled onto her face. She returned to her music.

Maybe this trip was a mistake, he thought. But after her experiences in her first year of college, he had to try something.

Francine had decided to focus on tennis and volleyball in high school. Things had gone well as she was named All-State in both sports as an underclassman. But as a sophomore she had come down hard on a middle blocker's foot in volleyball practice, breaking her ankle.

The operation to repair the damage had gone well, however the nerve block used was not done correctly and her right foot had taken much too long to develop feeling back in it.

To this day, Francine still had cramping in her right foot and her big toe continued to be numb. Although the rehabilitation had gone well, at 5' 6" in height, Francine had lost just enough of her jump to take something out of her game.

Francine's dream was to be an outside hitter at a Division I university. At her height, that was a big order. Typical outsides were 5'10" minimum, and 6'2" was more typical. Dewey had done his research as Francine played through high school. There had been short outsides in Division I, but they were in schools back East. And they were schools that didn't usually win many games.

Even her club volleyball coach had tried to explain the challenge of being short while playing a tall girl's game. But Francine took that as a personal challenge to succeed.

Along with the African-American genes she had inherited from Dewey, her workouts in the gym impressed all that saw her. The combination of quickness and power overcame much of her height limits. As a short outside hitter, Francine knew she had to maximize all the muscles she had been blessed with.

Her strength combined with the fire that she had displayed helped her lead her high school team to two state championships in her final two years. Each year, the school picked the play of the year and Francine was instrumental in being in both of them. As a senior, she had been named MVP of her Championship team.

After high school graduation, Francine had been excited to head off to college on a volleyball scholarship. Although it wasn't the college of her dreams, the community college that gave her an opportunity was the only offer she had received.

Unfortunately, high school was turning out to be the high water mark of her sports career. From the very beginning at community college, Francine ran into trouble. The head coach was driven to have her team succeed to the point where volleyball lost all its fun for Francine.

Dewey thought back to all the phone calls he had dealt with over those three months. He had dreaded the calls. They came about every three days, a distraught daughter crying on the other end of the call. She had hated every minute of it. Dewey finally had enough midway through the term.

Realizing that his daughter was suffering severe depression, he convinced her that the stress wasn't worth the scholarship she received. He assured her that her sports were too important in her life to let one person destroy her passion.

Taking his pickup truck to see Francine, she had decided to leave college. They packed up the truck and had left for home

Now this trip was the consequence of that action. Francine sat around for the winter struggling with her emotions. She had lost her fire for sports and had given up her personal workouts. Gaining weight just contributed to her depression as the cycle built on itself.

Finally Dewey proposed a change of scenery. Encouraged by the mom, they started planning an adventure. Dewey had proposed a trip to Nepal, a place he knew well from two previous trips. Francine reluctantly agreed to her dad's idea, although not before lobbying for a trip to Europe.

A quick run through the finances squashed any lengthy trip in Europe. Even with relatives in Europe, Dewey had no desire to be tied to his wife's family. Nepal was substantially cheaper and would allow the length of trip he felt necessary to swing his daughter's attitude to a more positive tone.

And he had an ulterior motive. Nepal had mountains and trails through them that would condition both him and his daughter. At 52, he still felt he could handle the rigors of trekking in Nepal. He had accomplished two previous trips to Nepal, but those had been when he was in his twenties. This would be a test for both of them.

The Royal Nepal Airlines jet circled Kathmandu as it came in for a landing. Dewey was anxious to see how much had changed in the last twenty-five years. He looked at his daughter, she was just anxious.

Chapter 3

Kathmandu, Nepal

The smell was the first thing that hit them when they stepped outside the airport terminal building. The pungent odor of something burning mixed in with the normal smells of a Third World country attacked their noses.

"Ohhh. What's that smell?" Francine asked.

"Honey, that's the smell of the Third World. Nepal isn't a rich country. Poor people burn wood for cooking."

"Dad, I've smelled wood smoke before. That's not wood burning. It smells like old gym socks burning."

"It's not very pleasant, is it? Well, things will be different here. I told you that when we planned this trip. We'll just have to adjust, won't we?" Dewey offered.

Francine looked at her dad with a certain disgust on her face. It was the look of 'there's a limit to how much I'm willing to adjust'.

Carrying their luggage, the two travelers stepped out onto the sidewalk beside the waiting taxis. They were met by a crush of humanity as chaos engulfed them

Dewey noticed the man standing with a sign that read 'McDowell'. He approached him and said, "I'm Mr. McDowell."

"Ah, very good. You may please follow me. I can take your luggage, sir." Heading across the paved area in the front of Tribhuyan Airport, a black sedan sat waiting. The man opened the back door and motioned his charges inside. He loaded the luggage into the trunk. Climbing into the front beside the driver, he motioned for the car to head out.

Dewey scanned the scenery. It was much as he remembered it. The greenery, the crowds, the hawkers, the mayhem of humanity, all trying to capture tourists as they entered the country. The car squeezed through the throngs and drove away from the airport.

The car moved slowly along the road toward the city. Reaching a hill that would take them down to the Bagmati River and a bridge crossing, the driver switched off the motor. The car sped up as it succumbed to gravity.

"What's he doing Dad?"

"Saving gas," Dewey answered. "Gas is very expensive here, so they switch off the engine while they're going downhill."

"Isn't that a little dangerous?"

"Their cars don't have power brakes and steering like ours do, so it's pretty safe."

"There's that 'pretty' again. I wish you would define that for me," Francine said.

By the bottom of the hill the car was moving at a good clip. The driver kept the motor off while he maneuvered onto the bridge. At the far end, as the car was slowing to a crawl, he popped the clutch and the engine fired back to life. They climbed the opposite hill in second gear.

"Why's he going so slow? This hill isn't that steep."

"It's the gas again. If he floors it up this hill, he'll lose all the gas he saved coasting down the other side," Dewey said.

Francine reverted to her 'whatever' face and turned on her music. Dewey sat and watched the view as they headed to their hotel.

The sign announced 'Nippon Guesthouse' over the entry as the car stopped on the narrow crowded street. Tourists and locals moved around the car as Dewey stepped out on the cobble stone street. It was just as he remembered it.

'Freak Street' was an institution in Kathmandu. Along with 'Pig Alley', this was the heart of the hippy haven that had once defined Kathmandu in the 60s and 70s. The drugs had been outlawed years ago, but the area still held the flavor of those times.

Dewey had spent time hanging out eating from the sweet shops that plied their cakes and cookies. The diet was very limited while trekking and anything sweet was a rarity in the mountains. After extended treks into the mountains, everyone craved sweets when they returned to the city.

"*Namaste'*. Welcome Mr. McDowell." The Japanese owner bowed and clasped his two hands together as his two guests entered the foyer. "We have everything arranged for a most enjoyable stay."

"Thank you, Mr. Matsui," Dewey said, returning the bow while bringing his two hands together in a traditional Nepali greeting. "It's been a long flight. We did have a reasonable stop in Tokyo but the overnight in Hong Kong really added to the trip. I think my daughter and I will just check in and relax the rest of the day."

"Very good. We have hot water all day. Please, if you may, just sign in and leave your passports. I'll see to everything," Mr. Matsui said. Turning to Francine, Mr. Matsui offered, "and *Namaste*, Miss McDowell."

"Thank you," Francine said. Then she addressed Mr. Matsui in Japanese.

The startled guesthouse owner stopped and stared in disbelief at the American. He said something back in Japanese, but a little faster than Francine could handle.

"I'm sorry, but my Japanese isn't that good, Mr. Matsui."

"Oh. It was very good. And such a pleasure to hear. I will be most happy to speak Japanese with you. I'll go slower next time," Mr. Matsui said.

Francine bowed to her proprietor and he returned the bow. Dewey gathered up their bags and headed up the stairs to their room. Once inside their room, he placed their bags on the table and began to unpack when Francine caught up.

"Well, at least I can practice my Japanese while we're here."

"And Nepali. I'm relying on your gift for language to get me through our visit. We'll pick up a phrase book when we get out sightseeing. All I remember is 'khoti pice diede'," Dewey said.

"'Khoti pice diede'. You got me there. What's that mean?"

"How much, Ma'am? Sorry. That's about all I remember," Dewey said.

"Oh Dad, I think we can do better than that," Francine retorted, a tone of exasperation in her voice.

Dewey had always been impressed with Francine's gift for language. She would hear a phrase once and could speak it again with perfect inflection. Whether it was Spanish in grade school or Japanese in high school, she was gifted. *It probably was a result of having an Italian speaking mother in the home,* he thought.

Anna Maria d'Alessandro was the most beautiful woman Dewey had ever seen when they first met. That had been twenty-two years ago in Venice, Italy. He was there working on his Graduate Degree in Architecture and she was a young college student.

They had met by the Rialto Bridge on a warm spring day after a long wet spell. It seemed the entire population of the city's young people were just hanging out on the bridge soaking up the sun. Dewey had been the determined American on his way to make sketches of the 'Salute', the large church built after the plague had devastated Venice.

He was trying to weave his way through the Italian youth, all on their cell phones, when he accidentally stepped on Anna's foot. The reaction to his misstep was immediate and vocal, typical Italian. He apologized profusely in his broken Italian.

When she realized that Dewey was a foreigner, she calmed down. With the crowd watching, Dewey had offered to buy Anna a cappuccino for his thoughtlessness. She accepted and the rest was love, Italian style.

Dewey never did get to sketch his church that day, or the next. Before he knew it, his school work was done and he found himself married and living in Rome. Anna's family lived in Rome and Dewey got a job in the family business. When Francine had come along, the three of them enjoyed the Roman life until Dewey needed a break from the now-smothering extended family.

He missed home and after much persuasion, convinced Anna to try America for a while. Dewey had grown up in Colorado, outside Denver. The three settled into a typical American life raising an energetic daughter while Dewey worked designing buildings.

When the economic slowdown hit the building trades, Dewey found himself out of a job with few prospects. Housing had collapsed along with commercial construction and he had wondered what work he could find.

Luckily, Anna Maria had returned to work upon Francine's graduation from high school. She had started working part time while Francine finished school and then had switched to full time. Alitalia, the national airline of Italy, had hired Anna Maria for her language skills but mostly because of her family connections. Her father was Chief Executive Officer of Alitalia.

That left Dewey able to enjoy his semi-retirement and his important task of recharging his daughter's fire for life. His disgust at the thought of the damage bad coaches did to young people and their dreams drove him to hope that Francine would once again have the drive to live her dreams fully.

* * *

"Let's go. The day is young and we have some sights to see." Dewey shook the bed where his daughter lay, buried under the covers.

25

"I'm tired."

"If we don't get moving we'll never adjust to the time change. The long flight shocks your body, so we need to get in rhythm while the shock is still in effect." Dewey knew about jet lag and adjusting to new time zones. The more you tried to adjust, the worse the jet lag was. One just had to force oneself to operate in the new time zone. *Nothing part way*, he thought. "Come on, time to move."

"Alright. Alright, I'm up, sort of," Francine answered.

Thirty minutes later they were eating breakfast served by the Nippon Guest House staff. Both travelers were famished and cleaned two plates. Dewey could see his daughter respond to the energy boost, and after her third cup of tea she was acting frisky.

"This tea is good. How come we don't have this at home?"

"We do. It's English Breakfast Tea. I have it frequently at home," Dewey answered.

"Well, it's sure good. Can I have another?"

"Let's hold off. You'll be floating through Kathmandu today as it is. The good part is the sugar and milk they put in it. Luckily they serve this everywhere we'll be trekking, so you'll get your fill of it," Dewey said.

"OK. What's first?"

"I believe Mr. Matsui has a guide for us today to take us to see the sights. How does the 'Monkey Temple' sound to start?" Dewey asked.

"Sounds like 'Indiana Jones and the Lost Monkey Temple'. Let?s go." Francine was up and heading to the stairs to their room to get her things.

Well, that might be the sugar speaking, but she seems excited, he thought. They both grabbed their day packs, loaded up cameras, and headed out. Mr. Matsui had a car and guide waiting.

Swayambhunath Temple was located on a hill to the west of downtown with a commanding view overlooking the entire Kathmandu Valley. Francine jogged up the stairs toward the Buddhist Stupa. Dewey followed along behind with the guide.

Reaching the top, Francine sat and waited for the others. The monkeys seemed to own the place and she found out from the guide that, in essence, they did own the temple. He explained that Hindus and Buddhist both valued all life and would not harm any of their fellow creatures. That was true of the 'holy cows' meandering through downtown Kathmandu as well as the 'sacred monkeys' here at the temple.

The monkeys certainly were entertaining to the tourists as they slid down the long stairway. Francine had her camera out capturing the action.

"My Facebook page is going to be busy these next few weeks."

"While we're in the city. There won't be access when we're out trekking. And no electricity either, so you can leave your electronics with Mr. Matsui," Dewey said with a certain satisfaction. Francine looked at her dad with a less-then-agreeable look.

She'll just have to get used to life as the Middle Ages knew it, Dewey thought. As an architect that had studied the history of buildings, he knew what the Middle Ages held for humanity. Nepal, especially up in the Himalayan Mountains was pretty close to Medieval.

The guide next took them to Patan, an ancient city to the south of Kathmandu. The buildings around Durbar Square were great examples of 15th Century architecture. Dewey loved it all, but Francine was notably bored.

They headed northeast to Boudhanath Temple. As a center of Tibetan culture in Nepal, the area was more interesting to Francine. Tibetan women wrapped in handwoven blankets walked around the chorten spinning the prayer wheels. The four sets of eyes on the spire overlooked all the worshippers as they made their circuits.

"What are the little wheels for?"

"Those are prayer wheels. You spin them as you walk around the temple. Each spin sends the prayers printed on each wheel up to heaven. Increase your prayers and you'll be reincarnated at a higher level next time," Dewey explained Tibetan Buddhism in the simple terms as he understood it.

"You mean if I spin them enough, I could come back as a 6'3" Outside Hitter in my next life? Let me at it!" Francine walked briskly toward the prayer wheels, but unfortunately headed in the wrong direction. The Tibetans all stopped as she walked up to the first wheel facing the wrong way.

"Stop!" Dewey yelled. Francine froze. She suddenly noticed everyone was watching her, all facing in the opposite direction. Her dad walked up and gently excused his daughter's intransigence to the locals, and gently turned her around. "Always spin the wheels clockwise. And always walk clockwise around the chorten."

Francine spun the wheel the correct way and everyone around her smiled and began walking again. Dewey fell in behind her spinning the prayer wheels. He knew he needed all the help he could get to get his daughter focused on life again.

After two circuits around the temple, Francine stopped and stepped off to the side. Worshippers moved by her chanting and spinning little prayer wheels on a stick in their left hand while spinning the Temple wheels with their right.

"So the little prayer wheels in their left hand are the same, right?" she asked.

"Yes. All going to heaven, building their karma."

"What would have happened if I'd gone the other way?" Francine asked.

"Spinning or walking counter-clockwise does the opposite. It reduces your karma."

"Oh, we certainly don't want that."

The driver was waiting when they left the temple area. For the final stop of the day they pulled into Pashupatinath Temple. Located on the holy Bagmati River, the sprawling Hindu complex of temples covered a vast area. Dewey led his daughter on the walk down and across one of the foot bridges over the river. From here they could sit in the shade and study the temple across the river.

"We aren't Hindus so we can't go inside. But you get a good view from here," Dewey said.

"Monkeys again," Francine pointed out. Walking across on the sides of the foot bridges was a large group of monkeys. Baby monkeys rode on their mother's back's as they jumped onto the walkways around the temple.

"Yes. They can get aggressive so keep your distance," Dewey warned. The monkey clan moved on to another group of tourists who seemed happy to have them near them.

"So Dad, what are these smoky piles over there to the left? And what are those men doing?"

"Those are the body pokers. They poke at the burning bodies to make sure that they are fully consumed."

"What? You're telling me there's humans in those fires?"

"Dead ones. It is part of the Hindu faith to be consumed by fire and then have your ashes sprinkled into the holy Bagmati River. In India, a Hindu would scatter the remains into the holy Ganges River," Dewey explained.

"And those people swimming just upstream?"

"Washing in the holy Bagmati River cleanses them in a religious way," Dewey said.

"Oh, and the women washing clothes opposite the burning bodies improves the clothes' chances for Heaven?" Francine quipped.

"Don't be smart, miss. Other people's beliefs are to be respected. They may seem strange to you, but it has been part of their life for longer than Christ has been with us," Dewey said.

As a Westerner things could seem decidedly different. Especially to a modern Westerner. That people threw dead body remains into the same river that people were bathing and washing their clothes in didn't set well when compared to Western standards of sanitation. *I guess*

I won't tell her where Kathmandu's drinking water comes from, he thought.

That night he went over again how to take a shower and brush teeth without using tap water. Treated water would be the only water to touch their lips and Dewey worked each evening with his membrane water filter to refill their personal water supply.

"Dad, are you going to be doing that every night?"

"It's very important that we stay healthy while we're here. Clean water is our first step. So only let treated water get near your mouth. And remember, keep your mouth shut tight when you shower," Dewey advised.

He hoped that his daughter could avoid his past personal experiences. On his first trip to Nepal he had caught some bacteria that laid him up. The explosive diarrhea had confined him to the hotel for a couple of days. He had finally resorted to taking Lomotil from the first aid kit.

Even cutting the medicine tablet in half, it had plugged him up for about five days. When he could finally go again, it was an extremely painful experience. He had stayed away from Lomotil ever since.

The next day in Kathmandu consisted of general sightseeing around the city. They walked through the city taking in all the wonderful exotic sights. There was the cobra snake charmer with his horn straight out of the movies. There were the constant beggars with all sorts of ailments, some real.

But the one that stunned Francine the most was the leper begging on the street corner in downtown. Even the locals crossed the street to avoid him. Dewey did the same.

"A real leper. Right out of Ben Hur. Wow. I can see why people shunned them and forced them to live in caves," Francine said.

"When I was here years ago I ran into an American doctor. He had come here to go trekking and decided to spend some time in a local hospital helping out," Dewey explained. "He told me he saw diseases that no longer exist in the West. What others only read about in text books, he got to observe and treat."

Eventually they found themselves in the Thamel section of Kathmandu. The change was amazing. Big western style hotels and shops catered to tourists. Western style restaurants lined the streets with crowds of visitors shopping.

"Hey Dad, how come we're not staying here?" Francine asked as the rock and roll music spilled out of restaurants and bars.

"This isn't Nepal. This is home suspended in Asia. I like where we're staying just fine. We came to experience the real Nepal," Dewey answered.

He remembered Thamel the way it first started. Back on his first visits there were just a few small four story hotels located here. With more open land than downtown, each hotel had some green space surrounding the building with an eight-foot cinder block wall for solitude. It was quiet and almost rural back then.

KC's restaurant had been the main place where travelers had all hung out. Dewey remembered getting real steak dinners which were usually followed by a visit to

KC's sweet shop across the street. But the big hotel chains had changed Thamel.

Now, he would only visit the place to get equipment for his trek into the mountains. With so many visitors traveling to Nepal to trek into the mountains coupled with all the mountain climbing expeditions leaving behind all their used gear in country, equipment was plentiful and cheap.

He and Francine had only brought personal equipment for their trck. The rest he would purchase with the help from the guide Mr. Matsui had arranged. But that would start tomorrow.

They found an Internet cafe and hooked up Dewey's laptop computer. Francine loaded up her photos and set about posting on her Facebook page. When she was done, Dewey sent off pictures and a long email to Anna Maria.

Chapter 4

Jiri, Nepal

The last couple of days in Kathmandu were hectic as Dewey and the Sherpa guide made sure everything was ready. Mr. Matsui had arranged for a guide that took on the task of obtaining the necessary trekking permits from the government.

Dewey and Francine would be their own party rather than joining a large trekking group. By arranging things locally, the cost was much lower and they had the flexibility of moving at their own pace. Dewey had experienced trekking both ways; having a Sherpa guide with porters and traveling solo while staying in lodges.

With Francine along, he wanted to make sure that they stayed as healthy as possible. That meant carrying food with them that wouldn't be available in the mountains. Freeze-dried fruits as well as meals would supplement the local diet. A means of assuring that food was sanitized properly would contribute to their health while trekking.

Dewey and Francine would stay in their own tent. This allowed some privacy from the communal lodges. Dewey had learned that the lodges and guesthouses were often infested with unwanted 'friends'.

Everything had finally come together as they left with their Sherpa guide in a four-wheel drive vehicle for the start of the Mt. Everest trek. The seven hour drive went smoothly for the first part as they made their way out of the Kathmandu Valley heading east. Reaching the Sunkosi River, the paved road followed the river valley toward Tibet.

Then the road turned to a rough dirt track as it crossed the river and headed up into the mountains. After a bouncy ride, the trekkers came to the end of their ride in Jiri.

"Well, we walk from here," Dewey announced as they climbed out. Francine stretched her legs and arched her back to get some blood flowing.

"Good. Walking sounds good right now. Which way do we head?"

"Well, tomorrow we'll get the porters loaded up and Ang San will lead us up the trail," Dewey said. "But right now we need to get the tent up and get squared away for the night. I have water to run through the filter."

Francine bent to the task of setting up the tent they had brought from home. It was a small dome tent her Dad had purchased in New Zealand a few years back. She was familiar with its operation and had it staked and ready in no time. She gathered up their pads and sleeping bags and got them settled inside.

It was a pattern they would follow for the entire trek. Francine was responsible for setting up camp while her Dad ran the water filter, using the safe water to brush their teeth and have ready for tomorrow.

"Ah, Dad? Where's the bathroom?" Francine quietly asked.

"Just like hiking at home," Dewey answered. "Find a quiet secluded spot and do your business."

Francine looked around and saw nothing but houses. They were camped in a school yard on the edge of town, but the houses continued out toward the fields.

"Could you come with me and help me find a spot? And then stand guard?"

"Sure kiddo. It will become more natural as we go along. But it's how it's done here," her dad offered.

Finding some large rocks a little ways out of town, Francine excused herself and went behind them. She soon emerged looking relieved. Dewey asked her to stand guard while he did his thing. They headed back to camp and the wash bucket they had for cleanup.

Dewey knew that the month of March was not the best month to trek in the Himalayas. It would be cold higher up and there was a risk of snow. Fall was the typical trekking time in the Himalayas while summer was the worst season as the monsoon rains from the Bay of Bengal took over.

While you could certainly hike in the rain, the constant downpours obscured any mountain views. And the leeches were everywhere. Just walking down the trail would result in leeches attaching themselves to any leg passing by, with the resultant blood loss. Dewey knew their spring time trekking would require watching the weather a bit but they had brought enough clothes to handle the cold.

The next morning found the sun just breaking the tops of the distant mountains when the three porters arrived. They had been hired by the Sherpa to carry the extra equipment Dewey and Francine would need. Dewey and Francine would only be responsible for carrying their personal things for the day; a camera, water, a wind shirt, warm fleece, wind pants, and a little food.

After breakfast, the tent, sleeping bags, foam pads, food, stove, fuel, extra clothes and many sundry items were all loaded into large wicker baskets. These were then hoisted onto the porter's back and a head strap pulled over each porter's forehead. The other half of the strap wound under the basket to hold the load.

Ang San got on the trail early, setting off while the sun was just over the mountains. It would be about five hours of hiking to their next stop in the village of Bander. The trail immediately began the up and down pattern it would follow on its way to Mt. Everest.

As they walked through a rhododendron forest, Dewey educated his partner on trekking. "Before the road was extended, the rule of thumb for people trekking to Everest Base Camp was that you would climb fifty thousand feet and descend forty thousand feet along the way. We have that many mountain ridges to cross to get to the Khumbu Region."

Francine listened but didn't say anything. The sweat was already pronounced on her face as she worked with her pack to find a comfortable stride. As they rounded a turn, Ang San announced that they would have a long descent now.

Dewey stopped the group and motioned to the porters to set the baskets on the available rock shelfs. These rock shelfs were located frequently along the trail for people to lower the loads off their backs while not having to drop them all the way to the ground.

Reaching in the basket, Dewey grabbed his heavy boots. Then he pulled out Francine's hiking boots. "We change to boots now. Just like we do in the Rockies. Sneakers on the uphill parts, boots on the downhills."

"And why is that again, I forgot?"

"Because five pounds on your feet is equal to twenty five pounds on you back. It has to do with how many times you pick up and lower your foot for each time you move forward. We conserve energy for the big climbs this way. And the heavy boots going downhill protect our ankles from injury," Dewey explained.

"And I'm all for protecting my ankles," Francine exclaimed. She had broken her right ankle in volleyball practice two years before and still had residual problems. Whether or not her ankle could handle the rigors of Himalayan trekking had been the big concern when they had planned this trip.

The exertion of the early start and the rising sun contributed to both of them stripping down. Off came the fleece tops and wind pants. Underneath, nylon shorts and shirts would suffice for the rest of the day. They laced up their boots, put their sneakers in the porter's basket, and threw on their day packs. The group all headed down the grade toward the bottom.

Nepal had very little flat area. Along with the towering mountains of the Himalayan range, the highest peaks in the world, large ridges descended down toward India. It was these small mountain ranges--giants if they had been in any other country--they were now crossing.

Hiking from the road head to the main village in the Mt. Everest region consisted of seven days of either a four thousand foot climb up or a four thousand foot descent. Dewey and Francine had just started their first large descent.

They would have four more large climbs followed by four large descents just getting to the last major climb into Namche'. Along the way, they experienced rural Nepali life, small villages attached to the sides of hills with terraced fields waiting to be planted.

This lower area would grow rice, a mainstay of the diet for the locals. Combined with a stringy leafy green vegetable that grew locally, the trekkers ate large plates of food to get the caloric intake needed to combat the hills. Sometimes eggs could be purchased for a morning treat. For a change in diet, they would pull out a freeze dried dinner. Otherwise it was rice and vegetables.

Lunch was similar for the porters and the Sherpa, but Dewey and Francine luxuriated with peanut butter on pan fried bread made each day by one of the porters. Using a cast iron skillet with fire ash as a lubricant, the bread was cooked without grease. The resulting chapatis were quite good with peanut butter smeared on and rolled up.

"These are good!" Francine announced at the first day's lunch stop. "But they'd be even better with some jam."

"You'll start having sugar withdrawals soon. Not much sweet stuff up here in the mountains. Now you'll understand why all those cake shops in Kathmandu do a roaring business," Dewey offered.

"And what's with that stringy vegetable we had last night? It's like eating twigs with small leaves on them. I end up pulling most of it out of my mouth because I get tired of chewing it."

"Soon we'll be in the cabbage growing region. And potatoes. When we get up higher," Dewey announced. He remembered the stringy vegetable from his times in Nepal, and agreed it wasn't very palatable. He didn't want to complain though in front of Francine. *She needed to experience the whole adventure and learn how to adjust,* Dewey thought. *That was an important part of traveling in exotic lands.*

"Cabbage. It's never been my favorite Dad."

Dewey smiled inside. *You'll appreciate it very soon,* he thought. Eat enough stringy vegetables and the alternative seems like heaven on earth.

"Time to start again, memashib," Ang San said. The porters were busy putting away their pot and plates from lunch. The baskets were made ready and the group headed for the next ascent.

Dewey and Francine had changed to sneakers during lunch for the uphill climb. They crossed the river on the swaying suspension bridge, stepping over flat stones placed on the bridge as they walked.

"What's with the stones?" Francine asked.

"Typically people from the Peace Corps or some other Western volunteer group build these bridges. The locals add some labor, but the money and expertise comes from the West. Then the volunteers leave and the locals are responsible for maintenance. But unfortunately there isn't the money or expertise to properly maintain the bridges," Dewey answered.

"And the rocks?"

"Well, when a pony or cow steps through the boards on the bridge deck, the locals cover up the hole with a flat rock."

"You're kidding! That's how they fix a hole in the bridge?" Francine asked. The look on her face said a lot to Dewey.

"That's how they fix the bridge kiddo."

As they wound their way up the valley paralleling the river, they came upon an old bridge. This suspension bridge was no longer suspended, but lay in a heap against the side of the valley. The tower closest to the trekkers was standing very alone with broken wires and a short section of collapsed bridge.

"Oh my God!" Francine exclaimed.

"That's what happens to the bridges once no maintenance catches up with too much weight on the bridge. Gravity takes over and the whole lot goes into the river."

"Do you think people were on that when it collapsed?"

"I'm afraid so," Dewey offered. They hiked along in silence thinking of the fate of whomever happened to have been unfortunate enough to be crossing when the bridge broke. The trail turned a corner and started uphill again. Everyone leaned into the exertion needed to put one foot in front of the other as they climbed the stairs provided.

Sometimes the trail would wind through the forest and fields much like trails they had experienced in Colorado. Trails throughout the Western U.S. had been standardized by the U.S. Forest Service to accommodate horse packers. Limited to an easy grade, the triais gently climbed the steepest grades through the use of switchbacks.

Francine and Dewey had backpacked over many a mountain range, the whole time never breaking stride. The trails of the western U.S. were designed so that any hiker could maintain a steady walk without resorting to physically lifting one's feet in a climb.

But Nepali trails were a mix of steady walking parts and climbs. When the trail had to go up, long sets of stairs were built into the hillside. Often these rock stairs would take on endurance climbs of a length that would begin to punish any hiker. Either climbing or descending, the constant steps took concentration and concerted effort.

As Dewey and Francine slowly climbed the long set of stairs, a pack train could be heard above them. Pack trains had to endure the same stairs, this train on the descent.

Here in the lower elevations, ponies were the main pack animal. The small Tibetan ponies were hardy animals used to the rigors of the up and down load carrying.

Dewey warned Francine again about the pack trains as the sound of the bell on each animal announced their arrival. Dewey watched to make sure that Francine climbed off the trail on the uphill side. The lead pony didn't even slow down as it carried past Dewey's group.

The ponies were very familiar with people on the trail and the lone herder at the rear would make sure the train would continue moving. Using his voice in a 'tsk tsk' sound along with his small long stick and the occasional small pebble thrown at any laggard, the congestion soon passed. The trekkers climbed back onto the stairs and resumed their climb.

Each day brought a similar routine. The trek took over their lives as chores were accomplished by each member each day. Hiking the four to five hours each day combined with a steady diet of rice and vegetables started to do its work.

On the end of the fifth day as Francine was pulling on her pants for the evening, a startled Francine exclaimed, "Dad, my pants arc way loose. I just moved up a notch in my belt."

"Me too. That's the Himalayan Weight Loss Program kicking in. 'Move more, eat less'," he said.

Dewey offered his standard response that he often had told his daughter in response to her past complaints on gaining weight. He then added, "But with the Himalayan Plan it's 'Move a whole lot, and eat as much as you can, but it still will not be enough',"

He had learned from his two previous trips that Westerners couldn't eat enough rice and vegetables to give them the calorie load needed for the extreme work of trekking in the mountains. Each meal Dewey and Francine would complain about their extended stomachs as they stuffed as much rice in as they could hold.

But always, soon after, they would be scrambling into any nearby forest to deposit a large mound in the form of fertilizer. The food seemed to move through their bodies so rapidly that it barely a stopped in their stomach. The peanut butter seemed to stick with them more, but the rice just added to the mounds they left behind.

Their waste would join the piles of other human and animal waste along the trail. They learned early to always leave their boots and sneakers outside the tent because they were always encased in fecal matter collected along the trail. It was impossible to hike in Nepal and avoid the stuff. Yaks, cows, ponies, dogs, chickens, humans: all left their droppings to be walked through. It was unavoidable.

The end result of eating rice combined with huge mountains to cross was weight loss. And the pounds disappeared as they grew closer to Mt. Everest.

"That's one of the reason you wanted to bring me here. To get in shape, right?" Francine asked.

"The lowest weight I've ever been since middle school was the three months I spent here years ago. Even binging on cakes and pies in Kathmandu in between treks couldn't make up for the weight that dropped off in the mountains," Dewey answered. "It's a combination of epic scenery and extreme conditioning."

"Hey, they should do a TV series here. 'Extreme Makeover - Himalayas'. Kind of catchy don't you think?"

"You might have an idea there honey." Dewey smiled as he winked at his daughter. He was glad to see she was starting to really enjoy their trip.

Chapter 5

Thyangboche, Nepal

The final hill up to Thyangboche Monastery was a killer. But the view made up for the effort. The group all set their loads down in the large field surrounding the Tibetan Monastery. Ama Dablam, often considered one of the most beautiful mountains in the world, towered over them to the right.

At twenty-three thousand feet, it was a relatively small peak in the Khumbu. Off to their left, Mt. Everest peaked over the shoulder of Nuptse and Lhotse. Lhotse at 27,890' feet tall stood in front of Everest. As the fourth highest mountain in the world, it was overshadowed by Everest, the world's highest peak at 29, 028'.

From Thyangboche, Lhotse hid all but the very top of Everest. But the sight was still spectacular. The small pyramid portion of Mt. Everest visible was a foreboding black compared to the white capped mountains in front of it. A plume of windblown snow highlighted the highest spot on Earth.

Francine had seen a glimpse of Everest from the bottom of the hill before the climb into Namche. Namche had been as Dewey remembered, but only more so. As the largest village in the area, it was full of guest houses catering to the Western tourists that flocked to the region by the thousands. An airport nearby in the village of Lukla could fly anyone to the area. A two-day hike from the airport would take them to Thyangboche. Dewey and party had spent nine days reaching the same monastery from the end of the road.

"How come we didn't fly in?" Francine had asked when they ran into people on the trail near Lukla looking clean and refreshed.

They had even taken a day hike from Namche to the nearby Everest View Hotel. Located at over 12,000', some would even fly right into the small airstrip at the hotel and avoid any strenuous exercise.

"What? And miss 'Extreme Makeover- Himalayas'? Are you kidding me?" Dewey teased.

"Oh, Dad. Really!"

"The truth is that these people are risking death from pulmonary or cerebral edema. When you don't acclimatize to elevation change, a quick change can cause fluid to form in your lungs or brain. Too much fluid and you're dead," Dewey said.

"Like friends and family that come to Colorado and can't move. I remember Grandma coming from Italy. It took her all month to be able to just walk around the yard."

"Exactly. But we're about seven thousand feet at home in Evergreen. We're already over 11,000 feet now and we've got more to go. People can get edema in Colorado, its just that usually they're in a car and aren't trying to stay up at the higher elevations. They drive to the top of Mt. Evans, barely get of the car and then drive down," Dewey said.

"So if they stayed on top of Evans, they'd die."

"Possibly. It's happened. But here it happens frequently."

The next day found them in Pheriche and the mountain aid station located there. Both of them got checked out by the British doctors manning the Aid Station. Francine sat still as the doctor listened to her lungs to make sure they were clear.

Next he took a lighted device and looked into her eye. The light opened up her iris so the doctor could see the back of her eyeball. Any cerebral edema would show up as enlarged blood vessels.

"Well, a clean bill of health. You're right for continuing up," the doctor announced.

Francine smiled and watched as her dad received similar treatment. He was announced fit for higher elevation.

"Well, that's good news. The last time I was here, I developed pleurisy. I couldn't go any higher," Dewey admitted.

"Must have been difficult just getting back to Namche," the doctor stated.

"What's pleurisy? Is it like edema?" Francine asked.

"An inflammation of the lining between the lungs and the stomach. Makes breathing very difficult. It's different than edema," the doctor answered.

"Francine, when I walked it felt like I had a large knife stuck in my left lung. We had to hire a yak to carry all my gear, as I couldn't even lift my pack," Dewey explained.

"Daddy! And you wanted to come back here? I think I would have taken that as a sign or something. Like you didn't belong up here."

"Superstitious. I didn't think you went for that kind of stuff. But I'm good to go now. You heard the Doc," Dewey reassured his daughter.

The next day found them hiking to Gorak Shep at 16,929'. Dewey and Francine labored in the thin air. Luckily Ang San had replaced the lowland porters with fellow Sherpas from the Namche area. Even the locals from the lowlands suffered at the high elevations..

Two days were spent doing day hikes from Gorak Shep, the climax being a trip to Everest Base Camp. The camp was where the numerous mountain expeditions staged their attacks on the world's highest mountain. Being the spring, the camp was quiet.

Because of weather, fall was the prime climbing season. Spring was the dangerous time in the mountains due to threat from avalanches. Not that the Himalaya Mountains were safe at any time. With an average ten percent death rate for Himalayan climbers, Dewey knew the serious nature of life up on the high slopes.

But at 18,192' above sea level, this was the highest elevation they would reach in their time in Nepal. Considering that all around them was towering snow-covered mountains, it made the elevation seem routine. Their labored breathing announced to them that it wasn't routine.

Returning to Pheriche on the way back down the Dudh Kosi River, they again stopped at the aid station. Again the doctors checked them out.

"Francine, you have a slightly enlarged vessel in your right eye. Nothing to worry about since your heading down now."

Francine shot a glare at her Dad.

"What?" Dewey responded.

"Pretty safe huh? You didn't mention my eyeballs popping out in our discussion of what would kill me in Nepal," Francine said. Her look said a lot.

The British doctor noticed the look. "Oh no worries. You eyeballs won't pop out. Cerebral edema is like getting drunk. Your brain slowly loses motor function ability and you just fall asleep. Unfortunately, you never wake up."

Dewey rolled his eyeballs. *Great, thanks for the help,* he thought. *Now Francine had a vision to put with the name. Things would really be better now.*

* * *

The trip down was uneventful. Yak trains were the only immediate threat but the trail to Namche' was wide enough not to cause any problems.

Dewey made sure they stopped in the small village before Thyangboche. It was famous as the location of the man with the Yeti skeleton. Or at least a skeleton of a Yeti hand.

"So explain what a Yeti is exactly?" Francine asked.

"An Abominable Snowman. Like a Sasquatch out in the Pacific Northwest. A large man-monkey creature. The locals call them Yetis," Dewey tried to explain.

"And this is a Yeti hand?" Francine asked. "Ohh, how gross."

Two more days found them saying goodbye to Ang San. They were sitting on the grass that made up the small airstrip at the Everest View Hotel. Three hotel guests waited with them by the small building that acted as the terminal. It was more of a shed.

At over twelve thousand feet, only small STOL, or short takeoff and landing planes, could even think of landing here. And to call it a runway was being very generous. It was more a yak pasture that slopped at about a fifteen degree downhill slant to the edge of a cliff. And the STOL feature would be tested on the very short runway that did exist.

Suddenly, everyone perked up to the strain of a plane climbing up the valley heading to the airstrip. The sound increased till finally someone spotted a very small plane dwarfed by the surrounding peaks. The plane's engine revved as it banked to line up for its landing.

The plane was a Pilatus PC-6 Porter; a 550 HP single engine, Swiss-built, nine-seat, high-wing marvel. The pilot raced the engine as he adjusted the wings to line up with the short runway. The plane came in over the cliff and immediately sank down onto the runway.

The engine backed off as the Pilatus ran uphill to the waiting passengers. The pilot gunned the engine one last time to reach the top of the airstrip and pivot the small plane around to face down the runway. The engine died as the pilot locked the brakes and switched off the motor.

"Wow!" Francine exclaimed.

"Impressed? Well, you make a beeline for the co-pilots seat and you'll really be impressed," Dewey advised.

The arriving passengers disembarked and almost keeled over. The five Japanese, three women and two men, obviously were not acclimatized to their new elevation.

The Japanese were the biggest customers of flying in and immediately heading up high. They often died for their efforts.

The ground crew helped the pilot roll out fuel oil barrels that would run the generators for the hotel. Other supplies were offloaded and placed into the nearby shed.

Finally the pilot motioned for the waiting passengers to line up. Dewey helped Francine get to the front of the line. Checking off his manifest, he took the tickets and allowed each passenger to climb up into the plane. Since the pilot flew solo, Francine grabbed the co-pilot's seat.

Dewey grabbed the seat right behind Francine. The other passengers climbed into the plane as the luggage was stacked in the back behind the last seat. The pilot climbed in and adjusted his seat.

"Everyone buckled in so we can take off?" the pilot asked. He was European and seemed to have a German accent.

"Are you Swiss?" Dewey asked.

The pilot stopped in his preflight check and turned to answer. "Why yes. I'm from a small town near Basel."

"Well, years ago I got to fly with Captain Wick," Dewey said. The mention of the infamous Captain Wick stopped all flight operations.

"You met Captain Wick? He was the original pilot sent by the company that builds these planes. He was to teach the Nepal Airline pilots how to fly them."

"But he never left. Yes, I got to sit in the co-pilot's seat for a flight from Kathmandu to an airstrip three days hike below Lukla. The most amazing flight I've ever had," Dewey said.

"Yes, Captain Wick did some amazing flying here. Rescuing mountain climbers in places no one thought a plane could fly, never mind land and take off," the Swiss pilot said.

Dewey began telling his experiences with Captain Wick. Years ago, he and his friend had been trying to fly to Lukla for days, but the overcast weather had prevented them each day. Returning to Kathmandu Airport on the fourth day, the airlines offered that a small airstrip lower down might be clear. Dewey had jumped at the opportunity to get moving.

Claiming the extra front seat, his friend had ended up in the rear seat. Taking off from Kathmandu, the Pilatus used maybe 100' of the paved runway. Reaching altitude, the plane leveled off heading east. Suddenly, Captain Wick asked if Dewey had seen Dhaulagiri yet, an 8,000 meter mountain, laying about two hundred miles to the west.

The plane quickly stood on its wing and was now headed west toward Dhaulagiri, the Captain explaining in broken English how he had landed on the shoulder of the mountain to rescue an injured climber. Then, just as suddenly, he stood the plane on its other wing to swing it around on its original heading.

Dewey continued his story. His friend was looking rather green by now from the whip affect in the back. As they cruised east, a large ridge that lay ahead poked out of the clouds that hung over the valley. The captain was busy entertaining Dewey with his exploits in the mountains and was paying little attention to the looming threat.

Dewey estimated that the plane was fifteen hundred feet below the approaching ridge. The solid wall of trees and rocks offered no relief as the plane flew straight and level toward certain death.

"We jump this one," was the only response Captain Wick offered as he gunned the engine, stood on the pedals and pulled back on the yoke. The powerful plane leaped into the air in an almost vertical climb, the engine roaring.

Dewey watched the ridge whiz by just beneath the plane. Then just as suddenly, the captain threw the plane into a steep dive returning to its previous elevation. Unfortunately the next ridge laid dead ahead, just visible above the cloud cover.

Again, at the last minute, Captain Wick jumped the ridge, only to reveal another ridge further ahead. A third jump was executed to arrive over the valley that held their desired airstrip. But the cloud cover continued its grip on the valleys. The huge mountains and their side ridges were all exposed, but the lowlands were obscured

Captain Wick put the Pilatus into a slow circle while he looked for the airstrip. Miraculously, a hole in the clouds opened up and far below, a small straight line appeared glued to the side of the steep hill.

At the command 'We go down quick now', Captain Wick killed the engine, pulled full flaps and dropped the nose into a vertical dive.

Dewey's seatbelt strained to keep him from falling through the windscreen as he stared at the airstrip quickly growing in front of him. The plane shook from the speed of the dive and Dewey continued his stare at the small airstrip that was growing larger each second.

Realizing that Captain Wick was lining up to go nose first straight into the ground, Dewey braced himself for impact. Instead, the airstrip flew by on the left side of the plane as they screeched down into the valley below. The locals that had come out to greet the plane all ran to the edge of the runway to watch the plane continue descending deep down into the valley.

The captain pulled back on his yoke and threw the plane into a wingtip turn that brought them around perfectly lined up on the runway. Except the runway was now several hundred feet uphill from the approaching plane. The captain hit full power as the Pilatus closed the distance towards the people lingering on the edge looking down.

The plane buzzed the crowd at a hair-raising height, scattering people and cows in all directions. The plane flew the entire length of the field at top speed and at no more than twenty feet elevation.

When the plane had done its job of clearing the runway of moving obstacles, the captain cut the power and hit the rudder, putting the plane on its wing again. The 180 degree turn at no more than fifty feet had lined up the plane for landing. Caption Wick killed the power and dropped the plane onto the grass strip before the crowd could return.

As he switched off the engine, the clouds closed in the hole that they had just plummeted through for their landing. Captain Wick had not left till the next day.

Dewey described the adrenaline rush he had as he jumped out of the plane. His friend in the back was immobile. Keeping her stomach contents in place was the only thing she was focused on. Dewey let her linger on the plane until she felt like moving. But he was pumped. He had just experienced the most incredible flight he'd ever had.

Francine listened intently. She had heard her dad's tale many times before. Now she was sitting in the chosen seat, but she didn't have Captain Wick to worry about.

The Swiss pilot thanked Dewey for his Captain Wick story and fired up the engine. Dewey sat back and glanced at his fellow passengers who had patiently waited through the story. They had an ashen sheen on their faces as they stared back at Dewey.

The Pilatus began to roll down the field. Dewey watched for his daughter's reaction. Many years ago he had flown out of this same airstrip and knew what was coming. He saw Francine's initial reaction to the realization that the strip was suddenly very short. She was also reacting to the airstrip being noticeably downhill toward the cliff and not flat like a typical airstrip.

As the plane increased power, its speed toward the cliff edge increased. At this elevation, the STOL aspect of the plane took a lot longer to take affect than at lower elevation. The plane didn't become airborne till just as the field ended.

But that didn't matter, because at the end of the field was a five thousand foot drop off, and Francine reacted as Dewey expected.

"Holy Mother of God!" she screamed. The plane sank several hundred feet in the light air before it roared back up to a steady flight. "Oh my God. Oh My God," she continued.

Dewey looked to his side. The ashen faces on his fellow passengers were now white.

"We will stop at Lukla and pick up some more passengers," the pilot announced.

The plane circled and lined up for Lukla Airport. But this was a paved runway that sloped uphill on the side of a mountain. Larger, twin engine STOL planes routinely operated here so it was a cinch for the Pilatus. Again, the uphill nature of the landing added to the experience. The plane spun around and stopped, heading down hill.

The crowd of waiting passengers surged toward the plane. Obviously the weather was at it again and planes had been unable to land recently. With the majority of trekkers walking into Everest and then flying out, the pile-up at Lukla could become extreme. Dewey had learned from his past trip to grab a seat at the Everest View Hotel, ahead of the crowd.

Francine turned to her dad, anxiety showing. The crowd was getting unruly as an airline clerk tried to figure out which two people would get the spare seats.

"Just don't undo your seatbelt. Stay in your seat. If you move at all, you'll be out of the plane in no time by the looks of this mob," Dewey advised. He had seen it before.

"Dad, what are those planes over there?" Francine asked.

"You mean the crashed ones?" Dewey answered. The wreckage of more than one plane were piled beside the runway, opposite the crowd. "Those are the ones that didn't make it. It's easier to just shove them aside then cut them up and pack them out."

"Pretty safe, huh?" was her only response. After another exciting takeoff over a large drop off, the flight back to Kathmandu was uneventful. There was no ridge jumping and no cloud holes to drop through. Which after the takeoff from the hotel, Dewey noticed, seemed to be just fine with Francine. Looking at the Himalaya Range laid out before them however made up for a lack of adrenaline from the flight.

"So point out where we're going next?" Francine asked.

Dewey leaned forward and pointed toward a large mass of mountains lined up east to west. "That's the Annapurna Massif. It's the tenth tallest mountain in the world. We'll be hiking around it if the weather cooperates. Off to the west is Dhaulagiri, of Captain Wick fame. To the east is Manaslu. Those are number seven and number eight in the world."

"And we go in between them all?" she asked.

"Ah yes. That's where you'll see the trails I told you about. Remember, pretty safe?" Dewey answered.

Chapter 6

Chame, Nepal

"Dad, can we stay here a couple of days? This feels wonderful," Francine asked. The warm water of the hot springs washed over their sore bodies. Dewey had to admit that it did feel divine. It was the only hot springs he had run into while in Nepal and he was glad it was still here.

Located just outside the small Tibetan village of Chame over the bridge on the opposite riverbank, a small stone pool had been built beside the river. After numerous cold mountain stream showers over the last few weeks, this was special.

The trick of open air showers in Nepal was that you had to take them with your clothes on. The locals did not abide public nudity, so Dewey had shown his daughter how to wash with their hiking shorts and shirt on. That was why all their hiking clothes were quick-drying nylon. *The advantage of clothed showers was that your clothes got clean too,* Dewey thought.

The break from their Everest Trek had been brief. After a couple of days in Kathmandu recuperating, eating and gathering gear for their next trip, they boarded a bus for Pokhara with their new Sherpa guide and replenished equipment. They had both climbed on top of the bus and hid ridden with the luggage. Francine had balked at first, but soon learned the advantage of life on top of the bus with the locals.

Dewey had explained that the view was fantastic, the smell was better, and the people friendlier on top. Dewey hadn't offered that the big reason life on top was better was if the bus went off the road and fell over the numerous unguarded cliffs, one could at least jump off. *A little chance at survival was better than none* Dewey thought.

Getting off before Pokhara, in the small town of Dumre, they had caught a four-wheel drive ride on a gravel road. They picked up porters in the village at the end of the road and set off hiking.

The hike felt easy after their conditioning from the first trek. The 'Extreme Makeover - Himalayas' continued its work. Both Dewey and Francine gathered the extra pant material in bunches as they cinched up their ever-shrinking belt length.

"I'm going to need a new notch in this belt next," Francine said. She pulled out the long tail of leather that now hung down her front.

"I've got my Swiss Army knife so we can go as small as you want. It might not be pretty though."

"If this keeps up I'm buying a whole new wardrobe. I wouldn't be caught dead in these things out in the world," Francine said. "But I'm liking the way my legs are looking. Look at the definition here." Pulling up her pant leg, she flexed her thighs and watched the muscles tense.

Dewey looked down at his own legs. They hadn't been this ripped since the last time he was in Nepal. He liked the springiness in his legs. They felt ten years younger.

"And my butt. Man, give me a volleyball court now. I bet my butt muscles are as big as Selena Roberts now," Francine joked.

"That's saying something," Dewey offered. Selena Roberts was the most physically intimidating professional tennis player on the planet. As an African-American player, Selena had muscle definitions few of the men's tennis players sported.

As her dad, Dewey had noticed the increase in his daughter's backside from all the climbing they had done. And all those descents had added to the front of her thighs. *She will be ready for volleyball when we return home,* he thought. *The trip is working.*

The trip had almost ended in tragedy two days earlier. They had been hiking along the most dangerous stretch of the trek into the Manang Valley. Where Annapurna and Manaslu, both over 8,000 meters, came the closet to each other, God had placed a river. The gorge that ensued was roughly 19,000' deep. It made Hell's Canyon in Idaho a piker by comparison.

The trail through the gorge was cut into the side of the canyon wall. Barely eight feet wide, the trail only had a six-feet height clearance in many places. And off to one's right was a drop of about five hundred feet into a tumbling crashing torrent. Not that anyone would survive the fall to have to worry about drowning.

Dewey had warned Francine about the day's hike prior to their reaching the dangerous stretch. But things had still happened so fast. One minute Dewey and Francine were creeping along hugging the cliff, bent over from the short ceiling cut in the rock.

Dewey just noticed the jingle of a bell before a yak train loomed around the blind corner just ahead of them. The yak train's human driver was far behind. Francine did what she was told and moved to the uphill cliff side. But in the tight confines of the cut, the six-foot-wide yak would clear all before it.

And the lead yak had continued its plod straight at the pair. Dewey grabbed his daughter's pack and yanked her backwards, quickly backtracking along the exposed trail to a small open ravine. More a rock chute cleft into the side of the canyon wall, the gap had been spanned with boards.

The small bridge was constructed of sharpened logs with one end pounded into cracks in the rock face. A rudimentary log frame was tied to the log supports and rough sawn boards offered a level walking surface

The long drop to the river was visible through the cracks in the boards. The two trekkers leaned uphill into the chute gaining valuable separation from the approaching yak train.

On both sides of the open chute were similar cuts in the solid rock wall. Like a tunnel with one side open to the drop off, these tight man-made cuts offered some protection from falling rocks.

The place where Dewey and Francine found themselves huddled against the cliff face was fully exposed. Above them towered the open area that acted as a funnel for any debris falling off the cliff.

It was the only place in the long stretch of cut-out rock where one could be more than six feet away from plunging over the edge. The two waited as the yak train grew closer. Dewey pulled his daughter tight to his body to help protect her from any falling rocks, both of them tight to the rock face.

A medium-sized rock dislodged beside them. It bounced on the wooden bridge that spanned the chute.and plunged into the air. As the bridge bounced from the rock's impact, both trekkers watched as the rock hit the cliff face repeatedly until it smashed into the rock pile by the rivers edge. It had taken the rock mere seconds to reach the bottom.

Suddenly the boards bounced violently as the first yak stomped onto the crude wooden bridge. Dewey looked down at the debris knocked loose from the bridges movement. That was when he realized that the only thing holding the bridge supports in place were some wooden supports pounded into the cliff. They groaned under the load as each yak crossed.

Finally the 'tsk tsk' sound of the yak herder announced his arrival. He smiled at the pair as he ambled by as though this happened all the time. *At least we were smart enough to beat a hasty retreat,* Dewey thought. *The man probably smiled the same way at those who were pushed off the edge by the yaks. All in a days journey. Life in the Third World could be unforgiving.*

Dusting off the dirt that had landed on them from the bridge shaking, the two intrepid travelers moved quickly into the relative safety of the rock cut. Not until they were safely past the cuts did they stop and catch their breathe. It was where the Sherpa had found them.

When he saw the look on Francine's face, he asked. "Memashib OK?"

Just another day on the trail for him but a 'life flash before your eyes' moment for us tourists, Dewey thought.

The bad stretch of trail was behind them now. The canyon between Dhaulagiri and Annapurna was nothing in comparison. In fact, a four-wheel-drive road had been built along the river that Dewey had hiked so many years before.

After safely reaching Chame, Dewey agreed to spend an extra day there. It gave them a chance to do a day hike up to a high spot to get a clear view of Manaslu. The only other view that they had seen of the mountain was partially blocked by the intervening canyon. Another evening soak in the hot springs finished out a splendid day.

The weather was holding, which was necessary for them to complete the circuit. Thorung La, a seventeen thousand foot pass lay ahead and any bad weather would force them to retreat back upon the route on which they had come. Another pass through the gorge and the rock-cut trail didn't inspire Dewey.

The next day was clear and bright and they made good time to Manang. A walled village, Manang's stone buildings with their flat roofs were stacked atop each other up the side of the hill. With the animals housed on the first floor, each family, lived above. Then another family with their animals lived above them, stepped up the hill.

This part of Nepal was Tibetan. The massive mountains to the south allowed little rain to make its way over the high peaks. Consequently, the landscape was very different than the Everest region. With few trees, firewood was hauled up from the low lands on the backs of humans and animals.

Higher up still, yak dung was dried and burnt for fuel. Francine had noticed this when she commented on all the buildings with crap smeared on the south-facing walls drying.

"At least we're not walking through it. That's a relief," she commented.

After Manang the trail gained elevation quickly. The group spent two days ascending the pass, camping in small villages located along the trail. The weather continued to hold but the cold increased as it had in the high Everest area.

After a day's climb, Dewey and Francine were relaxing by a small stream flowing out of the pass. They watched as the sun set behind the Dhaulagiri Massif. As the shadow of the retreating sun crossed the valley floor to where they were sitting, the instant cold hit them.

The little atmosphere at this elevation offered no lingering solar energy. As soon as the sun disappeared, the invading cold was brutal. The two hikers sat and literally watched the stream freeze over before their eyes. Francine commented that even in the cold of Colorado, she had never seen that before. Dewey said that he'd seen it before, near Everest one trip.

The next day, they rose and made ready for an early start for crossing Thorung La. With their headlamps cutting through the early morning darkness, they joined two other parties heading up the trail. Even with their acclimatization from the previous trip, the climb was slow and hard. As they approached the top of the pass, the sun met them.

Sitting on a rock at the top of Thorung La with her water, Francine took in the view. While not as high as Everest Base Camp, the view from Thorung La was ten times better. Snowcapped mountains scrapping the sky were all around. The drop from the pass on either side accentuated the feeling of great height.

"You know, I never got to cross this pass," Dewey said. "I got snowed in down in Braga, the village next to Manang. A good three feet of snow fell in a March snow storm. After two days, I hired two locals to break trail and carry my pack for me. It was an all-day slog through hip deep snow till we got down to where the snow ran out."

"No snow plows Dad?" Francine quipped.

"Human ones honey. Hard working human ones," Dewey threw back. "The locals I hired were interested in breaking a trail because there were about fifty people from their village waiting to come home. So the next day they all got to follow our trail back to Manang."

"Lucky them."

"Well, there was a party a couple of days ahead of me that was on the pass. They got caught when the storm hit. They weren't so lucky," Dewey said.

"What happened?"

"They all died. Froze to death probably," Dewey answered.

"Pretty safe, huh? I'm starting to think your idea of 'pretty' isn't the same as mine." Francine motioned that they had spent long enough taking pictures and relaxing on the pass. She grabbed her pack and indicated to the others that it was time to leave. By the time they reached Muktinath, even the Sherpa was tired. Hiking ten thousand feet of elevation gain and loss in a day was demanding. The two tourists collapsed that night and dreamed of the hot spring back in Chame.

* * *

Slowly moving tired bodies the next day, Dewey decided that a layover day in the Holy City of Muktinath was warranted. They would take in the sights that many Hindu pilgrims traveled from India to see. Housed in the temple was the sacred 'Burning Rock'.

Dewey paid the holy man the entrance fee as he and Francine watched the priest part the curtains to reveal a rock with a blue flame burning on it. Next to that in a different curtained box was the 'Burning Dirt'. Again a blue flame wavered from a piece of bare ground.

"How's does that work?" Francine asked.

"Well, this site is a very old traditional pilgrimage site for Hindus. But I would guess that some underground natural gas reaches the surface here and sometime in the past it caught fire. Been special ever since."

As they settled into their tent for the night, Dewey's excitement for the next week rose. The Kingdom of Mustang had not been open to travelers when he had last been in Nepal. Even now it was difficult to gain permission to travel to Lo Mustang, the main city. Dewey had worked with Mr. Matsui in Kathmandu to assure their trekking permit included Mustang.

Dropping down from Mukinath, they traveled through a desert landscape. Turning north after crossing the Kali Gandaki River, they headed toward Tibet. The entire area was close to China and had limited food, hence the reluctance of the Nepali government to allow hordes of trekkers into the area. But Dewey had planned ahead and had their food for the trip ready and waiting near Muktinath. They would not eat any of the local food while they were in Mustang.

Dewey was growing concerned because Francine was developing a hacking cough from the perpetual dust blowing. The thermal effect of the warmer low lands with the cooler high country created strong winds. Dewey had remembered the problem from his previous trip in the area and had packed dust masks for both of them. The masks did their job and Francine was soon breathing normally.

Their next challenge was the first real Tibetan bridge they had to cross. It almost ended their excursion when it stopped Francine in her tracks. "I'm not crossing that thing," she announced.

They had seen various bridges in their time in Nepal. Some were sturdy suspension bridges and others more rickety wooden ones. Even Dewey had to admit he had a similar response to Francine's the first time he had seen a real local bridge.

Before Westerners came with their suspension bridges, the locals had built rudimentary bridges each year. Knocked out with each spring flood, a new bridge was thrown together for the rest of the year.

It was surprising that Mustang was the first place they had encountered one. Western bridges had dominated the rest of the trails they'd been on, but this one was a challenge.

A traditional Himalayan bridge consisted of logs stacked on each other, each one sticking out from each bank a bit further than the other. Piles of stones were loaded on the ends to counterweight the whole thing. Eventually, some light weight boards were stretched across the gap between the two sides. While limited in length, it got the job done, at least till the next flood washed it out.

But the bridge sitting in front of them had a certain twist to it. The spring flood had shifted the piled logs so that now they had a decided list to them. For the locals, the bridge still worked. To a Westerner, it looked like a pile of debris ready to give way at any moment.

"We'll send the porters over first. You can see how they manage," Dewey said. He motioned to the Sherpa guide to start out.

With the Sherpa guide leading, the four loaded porters crossed one at a time using both their feet and their hands. Balancing as they slowly climbed the twisted logs, they arrived on the other side. The porters sat down after placing their loaded baskets on the stone shelf.

Still Francine didn't move. The Sherpa dropped his pack and returned across the bridge. He took Francine's pack and encouraged her to try crossing unencumbered.

"Memsahib, perfectly safe. I cross with you. You see," he said.

"At least he didn't say 'pretty' safe," Francine complained. With encouragement from the watching porters, she stepped out onto the first logs. There was a certain unsettling bounce to them as she moved out over the rushing river below her.

The Kali Gandaki flowed out of the surrounding mountains carrying the Himalayas to the Bay of Bengal. Soil erosion was a huge problem in this part of Asia and the brown murky waters of the river was proof. Millions of tons of soil particles scoured off the peaks above rushed toward the gigantic delta country of Bangladesh.

As she watched the water rush past below her, Francine crawled forward using her hands as support as her feet searched for flat secure places to step. Without her pack, she felt light on her feet even if that was not an attribute one wished for in this situation. Slow and careful was required.

Reaching the middle of the ramshackle native bridge, the rushing river just below her crashed unexpectedly and spray hit Francine. She froze. She stared at the brown torrent beneath her and couldn't move.

"Don't look down!" Dewey yelled. "Look at the porters."

Francine looked up while holding on for dear life. Another wave crashed and more spray hit her. She looked back down at the thing that was tempting her to fall.

Dewey dropped his pack and ran to the bridge. He slowly climbed up onto the shaky structure and inched his way out to where the cantilever started. Afraid to go further and cause the bridge to begin shaking, he again yelled, "Francine, its OK. I'm right here behind you. Look at the far end. Fix your eyes straight ahead."

She did as she was told.

"Now take your left hand and reach ahead for a good hold." Dewey waited till she had grabbed something solid. "Good, now move one foot ahead and plant it."

Again she did as she was told. Her eyes focused on the far end of the bridge, just a short twelve feet away. The advantage of native bridges were that most weren't very long.

"Good, now move your right hand," Dewey instructed. Francine followed each instruction as her dad directed. Slowly, keeping three points in contact with the bridge at all times, Francine gained the far side.

Once over the abutment that held the weight of the cantilevered bridge portion, she stood up and scrambled to safety. The Sherpa and the porters all cheered their approval. Dewey went back to retrieve his pack and quickly crossed the bouncing bridge.

"Well done. I thought we were going to have to throw rocks at you to get you moving. I've seen that technique work from the yak herders."

"Very funny," Francine fumed as she was unhappy with the situation. She normally had the nerve to handle anything. "Well, lets get going."

Dewey knew her well enough that she wanted to move away from any site where she had shown weakness. She had never displayed weakness easily in her life and Dewey knew that this site was now a sore spot for her.

"Just remember kiddo, we have to come back this way," Dewey teased his daughter.

Francine didn't respond. She just threw her pack on and headed up the trail.

The rest of the journey to Lo Mustang was uneventful. More bouncy native bridges were crossed but luckily they hadn't been affected by any flooding. Francine handled them with growing confidence.

By the time of their return, Francine was ready for her nemesis of a week earlier. She didn't even wait for the porters to cross first but charged ahead. With her pack, she scrambled expertly across to the opposite shore. Dewey and the natives rewarded her with rousing applause.

Francine glared at the outpouring of support. As her dad, Dewey knew that she wanted no reminder of her previous weakness. She had always been very feisty and he loved seeing her get that fire back. That fire that had driven his daughter had almost been crushed by bad coaches over the last year.

He hoped that she could rekindle that determination that had made her such a force in any sport she attempted. Francine had always possessed three important traits that helped her excel in sports.

First, she was extremely strong. She had received Dewey's African-American genes in the lottery of life. Dewey's father had been black and his mother white. He luckily ended up with a mixture that produced a tall athletic body.

The genes had worked overtime on Francine and she had been blessed with a very strong body. Not tall enough for her tastes, considering Dewey's six-foot-two height. She never let him forget his failure on that part.

Her second attribute was an incredible hand-eye coordination. Dewey had seen her reaction many times and was simply amazed at her quickness.

Once Francine was walking along on a tennis court when a player on the adjacent court hit an errant ball. The ball changed direction practically beside Francine and within fifteen feet of her. She simply turned her hand and caught the ball; no babble, no extra bounce, no anything. The player who had shanked the shot just stood there and stared at the quickness, at least until Francine tossed the ball back.

The final gift she possessed was a fire of determination. Her competitiveness was unmatched by any player Dewey had ever seen. He had attributed this trait to Francine's mother's Italian heritage.

Dewey often told the story of Francine when she first started tennis lessons. As an eight-year-old, she had already been competing in sports for a couple of years. During tennis practice, her competitive attitude showed up when players called their own lines. Francine was too competitive as shots that were in, she called out.

Her instructor, a twenty-one-year old man from the local university tennis team, called her on the bad calls. Her reaction was immediate. Walking over to the instructor, Francine got in his face arguing the call. Since she was only about four feet tall, the 'face-to-face' aspect was a little lopsided.

Dewey watched in amazement while his eight-yea-old went toe-to-toe with a grown man arguing her case. Finally, the instructor noticed the time and called an end to lessons. Francine stomped off muttering to herself.

Dewey had walked over to the instructor and asked him jokingly how he liked coaching John McEnroe's daughter. Dewey would always remember his response. "No. I love it. She has fire. I can't teach fire. You either have it or you don't. And she has it."

To watch his daughter lose that fire had been the hardest thing he had ever experienced in his life. *What coaches do to young people is almost criminal,* he thought.

Reaching the village of Jomsom, Dewey sat down with his daughter. They had a decision to make. Jomsom had an airstrip and they could fly out to Pokhara. There, a bus could take them back to Kathmandu. Or they could hire a four-wheel-drive to transport them to Pokhara.

"Dad, can we continue hiking? I'm liking this 'Extreme Makeover - Himalayas'. Look at my legs."

Dewey looked down at her dark legs as Francine squatted slightly to accentuate her muscles. He was impressed by the strength that she had worked back into the legs.

"And check these out." Francine pulled up her shirt revealing a flat stomach and a slight 'six pack' peeking out. "I've never had these before." She slapped her stomach to emphasize the tightness.

Dewey knew the feeling. His pants were determined to fall off him as he cinched up his belt each night. He too felt the strength in his legs.

"If you want. I'm sure our guide and porters will be glad to work longer. The trail out to Pokhara has been open a long time so we'll have no problems with supplies. And the best part will be stopping in Marpha," Dewey answered.

Dewey considered Marpha the most beautiful village in Nepal. And that's saying a lot considering the setting that surrounded all the villages. But Marpha was different. With the buildings painted white, like the famous Greek island villages, Marpha took on a clean image that most Nepali villages lacked.

The cleanliness was attenuated by a small channelized stream that had been diverted down the main street. With only about twenty feet separating the twin row of houses, a cobble stone path through town lay adjacent to a three-foot-wide rock-lined stream.

Acting as a fresh water supply, waste removal and clothes washing feature, the stream added to the uniqueness of the setting. Large stones had been laid over the stream to act as entryways to the walled houses that made up the village.

Like all housing in this area of the world, each house was a natural fortress built around a courtyard. Animals were housed in the courtyard while people lived upstairs, or up ladders in these parts.

No opening was presented to the outside save a large wooden door on the main street. All other windows and doors opened on the courtyard. It was a familiar design to the ancient Romans and other defense-minded peoples.

The route Francine and Dewey were now following had been the route of invaders from the north. The Mongols had traveled this route on their way to conquering India. And to Dewey's delight, Marpha hadn't changed in the ensuing years.

"Too bad it isn't fall. They have apple orchards surrounding the town that are a wonderful treat." A German aid group had planted apple trees and shown the locals how to maintain them. The only other local fruit were small tangerines and bananas carried up from the lower elevations near India.

"I'm just glad we still have some canned dried fruit. It helps the oatmeal," she responded.

Dewey knew from experience that the food would get monotonous. At least they were carrying supplemental food with them. He recalled the food dreams he used to have when he lived off the native diet staying in guest houses. Every night he would have incredible dreams of wonderful meals only to wake up to pounding hunger pangs. Those never seemed to be satisfied with the local fare.

The rest of the week was much of the same. The trail followed the river south to Tatopani where it swung east and began climbing toward Ghorepani. It was during the long climb up Poon Hill that Dewey encountered five Tibetan women heading home with their laden baskets.

Stepping aside to take a break from the long ascent, he leaned over on one knee to relax. Francine stepped off the trail behind him as the Tibetans descended the hill. The young women were giggling as they approached. The giggles turned into subdued laughter as they drew abreast of the waiting Westerners.

Wondering what was so funny, Dewey stood straight up and made an inquisitive gesture to the woman. Since his Tibetan was lacking and the guide was nowhere to be seen, he attempted to discover the source of these women's amusement. It definitely seemed aimed at him, so he was curious.

In answer, one of the Tibetans reached out to Dewey's thigh and squeezed it with both hands. She made a motion of encircling his leg with both hands. Then she took her hands and placed them around her waist. Then back around his legs, indicating that her waist was smaller than his thighs.

At barely five feet tall but carrying over fifty pounds in their baskets, these Tibetans were hardy women. Dewey smiled at the comparison and nodded his head in agreement. His thigh was significantly larger than any one of their waists.

Francine jumped in to tease her dad. "Mom better not find out about your little encounters on the trail here. You know that Italian blood boils quickly."

Dewey blushed with embarrassment as he bowed goodbye to his admirers. "Namaste' was exchanged by all involved as the climb of Poon Hill resumed.

"At least they didn't do that to me," Francine said. "I think my thighs are bigger than their waists. And I'm a whole lot closer to their height than you are."

"But such powerful thighs. And getting stronger with each climb too."

Saying goodbye to their Sherpa and porters, Dewey and Francine settled into the Tibetan Refugee Camp outside Pokhara. They would relax for a couple of days before traveling to Kathmandu.

In the late afternoon, the two sat and discussed their completed trek. They stared up at Annapurna and the famous 'fishtail' mountain, Machapuchare. Although not as tall as the surrounding peaks, Machapuchare had the 'Matterhorn' shape people attributed to their ideal mountain.

"Dad, it is truly beautiful here."

"Yes, it is. And I'm so glad we got to experience it together," Dewey offered. "I never thought back in the old days trekking here that I would experience this with my own daughter."

"Can we go get something to eat now?"

Dewey smiled as they stood up from their stone wall seating and climbed over it onto the adjoining road. Stepping through the accumulated animal waste that they had endured for the past two months, they headed to the local Tibetan restaurant. 'Chotses' were on the menu. They had had enough 'dal bat' to last a life time.

Chapter 7

Bangkok, Thailand

"Oh, it stinks! Bad!" Francine was holding her nose. "You first."

Dewey reached up and pinched his nostrils with one hand. The other reached down and took a piece of yellow fruit from the vendors table. He placed it in his mouth. He swallowed.

"Hmmmmm. Delicious. Your turn."

The vendor smiled at the challenge. He received this reaction many times a day from the tourists venturing by his location. The Thieves Market was a huge open air market near the center of Bangkok.

Dewey and Francine had flown in after their Nepal trip ended in Kathmandu. They were shopping for some new clothes since their old ones didn't seem to fit any longer. The 'Extreme Makeover - Himalayas' had done its job.

"Do I have to? It's totally disgusting. It smells like -"

Dewey cut her off. He certainly knew what it smelled like and needed no reminder of that fact. He had just swallowed it and his hand still stunk from the experience.

"Come on, cultural experience number eighty-nine. I sort of lost count. But anyway, time to experience Durian."

Francine lifted the fruit up again while she squeezed her nose. Her eyes were beginning to water, her grip was so tight. She hesitated, then relented as her dad encouraged her.

She grimaced as the fruit crossed her lips. Waiting for something terrible to happen, suddenly a smile broke out. Francine opened her eyes and displayed a relieved expression.

"Heh. It tastes good. Like strawberries, sort of." The relief was immediate. Until she realized the death grip on her nose. Then the smell returned and the smile faded. "How can something that stinks so bad taste so good?"

"Nature's mystery, honey. God works in mysterious ways," Dewey answered. Dewey placed some money in the vendor's hand as they moved into the market.

They spent their time visiting the temples of Bangkok while shopping for new clothes. A new swim suit was the order of the day as they were heading to parts of the world that were dominated by the sea.

Francine was impressed with her new look as she tried on swimsuits. "Man, I should have done this years ago. Look at that shape."

Dewey looked in the mirror and was impressed. Gone was the pudgy body they had left in the States, replaced with one that was now lean and tight. A few days in Southern Thailand on the beaches would get her upper body matching the color on her legs. As part African-American, Francine tanned easily and would quickly take on a dark ebony glow.

Dewey remembered when Francine was about six years old they had taken a friend of hers and gone to a mountain lake about an hour from home. Francine was on the swim team that summer, with the resultant tan.

Earlier that summer Francine had decided on her own that she wanted bangs in her hair. With her African-American curly hair, that had turned out disastrously. The fix required a trip to the stylist to even out the mess and she went the rest of the summer with a short hairdo.

While at the lake, Dewey had blown up two inflatable kayaks for the girls to paddle. When they switched to swimming, the kayaks sat on the sand next to where the adults were sitting in their beach chairs.

Watching the two girls run and dive into the water, a boy walked over from an adjacent party. He stood in front of Dewey and asked, "Is that little black boy done using that kayak?"

Dewey was confused. He looked up at two girls running across the beach with typical one piece tank suits on and wondered what this kid was talking about. The boy asked again.

It was all Dewey could do to not break out laughing. He finally controlled himself and told him that the kayaks were still being used. As the boy walked away, Dewey looked at his wife in amazement. Dewey had fun calling Francine 'his little black boy' the rest of the summer.

* * *

Bangkok was soon left behind as the two travelers took the local bus headed south. After a week on the South China Sea beaches, they resumed their bus journey. Reaching Singapore on the end of the Malaysian peninsula, they finally felt like they had returned to civilization.

"Just remember, we need to get out every day and get our walks in. Otherwise, all that hard work in Nepal will slowly fade," Dewey reminded his daughter. They had made it a priority to get a long walk in every morning wherever they had stopped.

Francine had added core workouts to walking in order to strengthen her upper body. The Himalayas had melted away her fat and added leg strength. Now her upper body needed work to put on muscle.

"I'm glad we're in a place we can eat fresh food again," Francine offered. The risk of disease in Nepal and Thailand had prevented them from eating any food that they couldn't sanitize. Dewey had picked up Hepatitis A on his visit to Bangkok years ago and was careful to keep them both healthy.

After another couple of days shopping, they boarded their flight to Broome in Western Australia. They were headed for the Ningaloo Reef, the longest inland reef in Australia.

Unlike Queensland's Great Barrier Reef which lay fifty miles offshore, the Ningaloo Reef was an inland reef. A snorkeler only had to walk off the beach and swim a short distance to be over the reef. The two planned to spend two weeks exploring the two-hundred-and-fifty-mile reef.

Arriving by bus in Exmouth, they found a hotel and arranged a tour of the reef with a local company. Each day they were taken to a different location and enjoyed the large display of coral. Snorkeling among the shallow coral heads, the area didn't require scuba gear to experience a wide assortment of tropical fish and coral.

The warm water of the tropics attracted all sorts of fish. The area was also famous for being a place one could swim with whale sharks in their calving season. Francine was disappointed that they were there too early, but Dewey was OK with the timing. He had listened to people describe the thrill of swimming with thirty-foot sharks. Although strictly herbivores, whale sharks were still large wild animals and a certain risk existed just being near them.

But as Francine had frequently expressed, Australia still held numerous dangers. On the flight from Singapore, she had requested a listing of the critical ones they could encounter on the Ningaloo. Dewey tried to downplay the risks and continued to kick himself at reading those book excerpts to her long ago. *She would never forget them*, he thought

* * *

After a week, they took the bus to Coral Bay, located about one hundred and fifty miles down the coast from Exmouth. The Ningaloo Reef took up the entire distance and the ride confirmed to Dewey that Western Australia was one of the most empty places on earth. Combined with the bus between Broome and Exmouth, the two trips hadn't passed through a single town.

Dewey paid attention when the bus turned off the main highway for Coral Bay. In the 90 km distance he counted one car. That had been added to the fact that in the entire journey the only signs of life had been a gas station-restaurant combination on the side of the road every 100 miles or so.

Otherwise, a passing road train, as long haul trucks were called, were the only sign of human existence. That and the occasional road juncture with a directional sign for some far off place broke the bleak landscape.

Francine had commented on the number of dead kangaroos along the road. An Australian seated next to them explained that the kangaroos came out at night only to be bulldozed aside by the armored trucks. The road trains certainly looked armored. The tractors had numerous metal bars for protection from flying kangaroos to protect the truck and driver. *I wouldn't want to be caught out here at night driving a car*, Dewey thought.

He had noticed the seeming war that was waged each night between the 'roos and the trucks. *The kangaroos were definitely losing,* Dewey thought.

But the warm Indian Ocean off Coral Bay soon pushed the carnage of the Outback from their minds. The first evening the two took a stroll along the beach. Anchored off the beach was the glass bottom boat that they would take out in the morning to start their snorkel exploration.

Coral Bay had little else to offer. A small community of maybe one hundred permanent residents, in the tourist season the population probably tripled. Travelers from around the world would fly into Perth and rent a camper van to explore the Outback. Since Coral Bay was part of the area officially called "Where the Outback Meets the Sea", most campers pulled in for a couple of days to see the reef.

With one hotel, one campground, one gas station and a small block of shops with tourist type goods, the setting was little disturbed by over-commercialization. Dewey liked the simple resort town.

Dewey had always wanted to see this part of Australia. He had visited Melbourne and Adelaide on a previous trip many years ago. But he had always heard stories about Western Australia. About how different it was from the rest of the country. And now he could agree with what he had heard.

Back on his previous trip, he had thought the drive between Melbourne and Adelaide was bleak. That had been lush and cosmopolitan compared to what they had seen so far of Western Australia. After Coral Bay, they would take the bus further down the Indian Ocean Coast to see Shark Bay.

Shark Bay was a designated United Nations World Heritage site and home of the world famous Hamelin Pool with its stromatolites. The oldest living lifeform on Earth, stromatolites were a simple lifeform that resembled a rock. Dominating the world three billion years ago, they were credited with creating the Earth's oxygen based atmosphere.

That they still existed intrigued Dewey. When he mentioned why they were coming to this part of the world, Francine's only comment had been, "We're going how far to see rocks bubble?"

At Coral Bay, they settled into a routine of snorkeling each day with a local guide. The first two days had been similar to the sights they'd seen near Exmouth.

The third day the guide showed up with a small boat to take them out to the outer edge of the reef. He described a shark 'hospital' where injured sharks came to rehabilitate. The sharks were typically docile and they would be able to swim in the area.

Francine wasn't convinced. "Are you sure about this? Is this the 'pretty' safe part of Australia we've talked about?"

"Oh no. It's a beaut. I take sheilas out there all the time. No worries," the Australian guide responded.

"Sheilas is Aussie for woman," Dewey interpreted.

"I know that, Dad. It's the 'no worries' part that I'm thinking about."

"We didn't have any troubles up in Exmouth. And they don't want their tourists succumbing to shark attacks, so I doubt they would take us to a place that was dangerous," Dewey said.

"You're right there, mate. Haven't had a problem yet. Bloody hell, I'd bet my 'ute' on that," the Aussie offered.

"Well, there you go, if something happens, you get a 'ute'. That's his sport utility vehicle, honey."

Francine gave her dad the stare. She bent over and by grabbing her gear announced she was willing to risk death to go see wounded sharks. Dewey climbed aboard after her as the guide started the outboard. Pulling anchor off the beach, the boat headed out toward the outlaying breakers where they hit the outer reef.

The small skiff bounced over the waves as it motored across Coral Bay. Spray flew off the bow as Francine sat silent in the front, staring at a spot where the waves announced the reef underneath. The boat slowed and the guide grabbed the permanent moorage line that was set on the ocean floor. He tied off their boat.

"Now, as we get ready, be aware that they'll be a wee bit more current here than the other places we've been. Just stay together and we'll be right."

The three pulled on their snorkeling gear and adjusted their masks. Maneuvering over to the edge of the boat, one by one, they slipped over the gunwale into the Indian Ocean. The warm water washed over them as they floated above the reef.

The three headed out toward the reef edge. Dewey could feel the current. It was stronger here with an incoming tide. They would have an easier time heading back to the boat when they were done.

Using their flippers to move them closer to the shark hospital, they spotted their first shark. It was lazily swimming in place right above the reef.

They could see the mouth slowly taking in water and nourishment that was being carried in on the tide that was moving into the bay. Then another shark startled them as it loomed up out of the depths outside the reef. It also took up a stationary position atop the reef and slowly swam in position against the ingoing tide.

Suddenly the Australian guide tapped Dewey on the arm. Looking to his left toward the guide, he saw through the face mask the wide-eyed guide motioning toward the boat. Dewey could tell in an instant that the guide conveyed warning.

Dewey looked for Francine and spotted her about twelve feet ahead. He raced to grab her flipper and warn her of whatever the guide was concerned about. The guide was right beside him racing to reach Francine.

That was when Dewey saw what had thrown the guide into a near panic. A large sea snake was moving up off the reef toward Francine. It was right below and slightly back from her, out of her vision. He kicked harder to reach her.

Sea snakes are one of the most deadly creatures on Earth. On the list of the top twenty most poisonous snakes in the world, they ranked number seven. In fact, Australia accounted for sixteen of the top twenty and held the top ten positions.

Common in the tropical waters of the South Pacific, a sea snake encounter this far south was unusual. He had discussed privately with the guide the chances of sea snakes and was assured that they were rare in Coral Bay.

But now one was swiftly rising up from the reef and was headed straight for his only daughter. Dewey threw everything into closing the distance to his unsuspecting daughter.

From the corner of his mask Dewey caught the sight of the guide speeding beside him. But the guide was pointing in the opposite direction. His garbled voice could be heard through the water as he screamed into his snorkel.

Moving in from the right was a box jellyfish, the most poisonous creature on earth. Dewey almost froze when he saw the slowly pulsating instant death floating along on the current headed straight for his daughter.

Dewey lunged at Francine and hit her flipper. She stopped swimming and began to turn to see what had hit her. That's when she saw the sea snake coming up at her. She squirmed to avoid the snake and Dewey watched in horror as she swung her right arm into the jellyfish.

The instant pain of the stingers from the jellyfish caused her to retreat, throwing her right leg into the sea snake. Its bite struck home and she instantly jerked from the attack.

The guide grabbed her by the legs and pulled her away from both tormentors. He grabbed Francine's spandex suit and pulled her back to the boat. Dewey reversed direction and quickly followed.

The blood curdling screams from Francine were already racing across Coral Bay. The two men struggled to get Francine into the boat as she writhed in pain. On her right arm the welts of the jellyfish stingers were already red and swollen. Her right leg was swelling from the sea snake bite.

Over it all, Dewey was dying inside from the tortured screams of his precious daughter . The guide took a sharp knife and carefully but quickly removed the remnants of the jellyfish stingers. He avoided touching them as he threw them overboard.

The motor started, the guide raced the boat at full speed toward the beach. The soul-killing screaming never stopped as Francine fought the venom and poison racing through her body. Dewey held his daughter tight, but the screaming never stopped. *How long for the two poisons to do their work?* he thought.

Both attacks were considered to be lethal within half an hour. While a snake anti-venom was available, it had to be administered within minutes of a bite. For a box jellyfish sting, there was no antidote. Death was typically quick and painful.

It was the screams of his daughter that tore Dewey's insides. Screams that would torment him the rest of his life.

Chapter 8

Rome, Italy

The phone rang at the home of Lorenzo d'Alessandro. It was early morning in Rome and as he rolled over to answer, he thought that no good news came at this time of the night. He picked up the receiver.

"Pronto."

"Lorenzo, this is Dewey. There's been a terrible accident."

Immediately the grandfather knew that something had happened to his granddaughter.

He switched to his fluent English. "What is it?"

"At our last Skype call from Broome, Anna Maria was supposed to be with you," Dewey inquired.

"Yes, she is here. Shall I wake her?" Lorenzo asked.

"You need to get her immediately on the next available flight to Perth, Australia. I can't explain right now, but she needs to be here as soon as possible," Dewey said.

"My son, I can't just tell Anna Maria to fly halfway around the world without telling her what she's flying to. She'll want a reason."

"All I can say is her daughter needs her right now. If I give any more details she'd . . ." Dewey stopped. "You just have to trust me. It will be hard but it's better this way."

"We will pray for you both. I'll get her there as soon as possible," Lorenzo said.

The phone went dead. He stared at the clock. It was early morning in Italy. Lorenzo's mind raced for a solution, weighing different options.

He settled on one. *It was the quickest way,* he thought. Picking up the phone once, he dialed. Once he had his manager on the phone, he issued his orders.

He finished with, "I'll be there in three hours. I want everything ready for immediate take off."

Getting out of bed, he steeled himself for the next task. His wife was wide awake waiting patiently for an answer. He told her that she needed to be strong, the family was in trouble. She followed her husband to the guest bedroom.

"Anna Maria," he said quietly. She stirred and rolled over to see her parents standing over her. She sat up.

"What's wrong? It's Francine, isn't it?" she said as the panic rose to overwhelm her.

Lorenzo did his best to explain that they would be leaving immediately for Dubai in the Persian Gulf. As CEO of Alitalia, he was familiar with the flights required for the quickest time to Perth. He had already determined that waiting till the morning flights at Fiumicino Airport would delay them by hours.

By taking the company corporate jet to Dubai, they could catch up with the Virgin Australia flight he knew would be landing there after its flight from London. They would join the commercial flight to Perth by way of Singapore.

He would join his daughter for support on her trip to Perth. After he gave a speech that everyone needed to be strong, Lorenzo left his wife to help Anna Maria pack. He quickly showered, dressed and threw a small travel bag together. Moving fast meant moving light. No checked baggage on this trip.

Within the hour the two of them had left downtown Rome headed to Fiumicino Airport and the waiting Gulfstream corporate jet. The pilot and crew were just finishing up flight plans and had submitted their route for approval. An hour later, they were airborne.

It was a quiet but stressful flight to the Persian Gulf. After clearing customs, the two made their way to the main terminal. Lorenzo had been in contact with headquarters and all the necessary connections were waiting for them.

They boarded the Boeing 777 and settled into the First Class cabin. Lorenzo performed the fatherly duties of protecting his daughter from the doting crew. She was drifting somewhere between shock and incomprehension. Not knowing what they were flying into, the two sat and endured the hours as the big plane flew east.

Landing in Singapore, they had to change planes to a Virgin Australia flight to Perth. The one-hour wait seemed interminable as they paced the lounge. Finally they boarded the Airbus 310 for the final leg of their journey.

As the plane circled Perth, the two Italians were about to confront the man that put their precious Francine at risk. The long hours of waiting were about to be unleashed.

Walking out of customs, Lorenzo noticed a man holding a sign with what looked like d'Alessandro written on it. Someone had obviously called for a ride and the company had struggled with the name over the phone.

"Are you looking for the d'Alessandro party?" Lorenzo asked. His English carried a noticeable Italian accent

"Oh, blimey, that's how you say it. Well, I was told to pick up two 'Itals' at the airport, so if you're them, we're right, mate," the driver said.

Lorenzo ignored the slur. He had been in foreign lands ofter enough to know the locals had their own way of speech.

"And where were you to take us?" Lorenzo asked.

"The party making the call told the company I was to deposit you at King's Hospital. Unless you needed a hotel first. Then I was to take you to the Perth Hilton."

"The hospital first," Lorenzo said. His daughter began to cry again. She had suffered fits of crying throughout their whole journey. Now heading to Perth's main hospital forced the reality upon her. Lorenzo held and comforted his daughter.

The driver wheeled his way through the suburbs and into downtown Perth. It was early morning and the traffic was heavy. The Italians grew impatient with the slowness of the local drivers. *If this was Italy, we'd already be there,* Lorenzo thought.

The hospital finally loomed into view on a hill to the west of downtown Perth. The taxi pulled up to the front door and Lorenzo realized that he hadn't taken the time to obtain any Australian dollars. When he started to reach for his wallet, the driver stopped him.

"You're right mate. The bloke that called took care of it. I hope things are OK. Terrible to fly all the way here to visit our hospital."

Lorenzo thanked the driver and gathered the two bags as he helped Anna Maria out of the car. As soon as she was fully cognizant of where she was, she was gone. Lorenzo struggled to keep up with his daughter as she attacked the staff to locate her daughter.

Luckily, the whole hospital knew of Francine. In fact, all of Australia knew of Francine by now. When word got out of an American woman being flown from the Outback to Perth for medical care, the press took notice. Bad things happening to tourists was always a concern. Rumors had been swirling in Perth as to what had happened to the young American woman.

The Chief Medical Officer of the hospital met them as they got off the elevator on the Intensive Care floor. A staff member that had helped them excused herself.

"Mrs d'Alesandro. I'm Dr. Coleman, Chief Medical Officer here at King's Hospital. Your daughter is alive and resting at the moment. We have placed her in a medically induced coma to ease her discomfort."

"Doctor, where is my daughter?" Anna Maria was almost frantic.

"Please, just a minute. You need to know the whole picture before I take you to her. Your daughter was flown down in an air ambulance from Coral Bay two days ago. Your husband has been with her the whole time. As much as we are concerned about her, we are also concerned about him. He refuses to leave her side and continues to grow despondent. We are concerned for his health right now."

"You should be! My daughter, now!"

"Right this way." The doctor turned and led the two down the corridor toward a room on the end. "We have never had a case like this so we can't be sure what the prognosis will be. We are keeping her on fluids and medicine for the swelling. And of course we'll continue the coma till we know more."

Lorenzo followed his daughter as she kept pace with the doctor. When they reached Francine's room, Dewey looked up as his wife crossed over to him. Lorenzo was afraid she was about to hurt him.

At the same time as the Italian mother was about to unload, Dewey said, "I'm sorry. I'm so, so sorry." He collapsed into her arms crying uncontrollably. It was all Anna Maria could do to support him in his grief. "If she doesn't make it, I can't go on."

Anna Maria sat Dewey back down in the chair next to Francine and Lorenzo moved a chair over for her. She took her daughters limp hand in hers and began to sob again. Both parents now bent over their prostrate daughter and put their heads next to her side.

Lorenzo decided to leave the two parents in their grief. He hooked the doctors arm and stepped outside in the hallway.

"Now Doctor, is there anything you're not dong? Any place we can fly my granddaughter to? Anything?" Lorenzo almost pleaded.

"Mr. d'Alessandro, Australian hospitals are the equal to any in the world. This country has more things that will kill than anywhere else in the world. We're capable of dealing with most of the nasty things we see in Australia. But we've never had a situation like this. Francine should have been dead before she reached shore in Coral Bay. She was bitten by two of the nastiest things on Earth. Separately, her two assailants are 100% fatal. Why she isn't dead by now is a miracle. We can only wait and watch. And pray," Dr. Coleman said.

Lorenzo stood outside the door and stared at his granddaughter lying there. As a good Italian, he knew how to pray. The next few days he would pray like he never had before.

* * *

On the fifth day of their vigil, Dr. Coleman announced that he was going to stop the medically induced coma to see Francine's reaction. She had been suffering from body convulsions when she arrived but had settled down once the coma had been induced.

The next day the medicine was out of her system and Francine lay quiet. After the breathing tube was removed, Francine continued breathing on her own. The doctor announced he was encouraged. She still had eye flutter when her pupils were checked so he was reassured that her brain was still functioning.

Dewey and Anna Maria had taken shifts sitting with Francine. At Lorenzo's request, the hospital had made an adjacent room available for them so they didn't have to go far to sleep. Lorenzo commuted back and forth from the Hilton to add his support.

On the seventh day, things changed. Dewey was sitting beside Francine while Anna Maria slept. Lorenzo sat on the opposite side of the bed reading a little but mostly watching Francine. It was difficult to concentrate on anything while sitting there. While he was turning a page and looking at the pictures, a low voice attempted to speak.

"Grandfather, what are you doing here?" the voice scratched out in a whisper.

Lorenzo was startled to see Francine's eyes open and looking around the room. She looked to her left.

"Daddy," she rasped out. A quiet voice asked, "My throat is killing me. Can I have a drink?"

Lorenzo reached over and hit the button to summon help. Then he went into the next room to awaken Anna Maria. She was by her daughter's side in a flash.

"Mom, you're suffocating me. Why are you here?" Her voice was harsh.

Dr. Coleman walked in to confront a wide awake patient. "Well, never in all my years have I seen anything like it. You're are a miracle woman."

Everyone made room so he could examine Francine closely. He checked her over, first using his flashlight. Francine's eyes were alert and responsive. He listened to her heart and lungs. He pronounced them fine. He checked the monitor for her heart and respiratory function. Fine again.

The doctor handed her a cup of ice chips that the nurse brought in. Francine dove into chewing on them until the doctor took the ice back and placed it on the rolling table over the bed. He warned Francine to take it slow at first.

As he turned to give his pronouncement to the parents, he hit the cup of ice on the table in front of Francine. The cup of ice tumbled off the edge and succumbed to gravity as it headed toward the floor. The doctor realized his blunder and tried to retrieve the situation.

As he attempted to reach the falling cup, a hand shot by him, grabbing the cup. And the hand snatched it in such a manner that the ice that should have spilled out of the overturned cup stayed in place. Francine placed the now upright cup back on the table.

"How'd you do that?" Dr. Coleman asked.

"Do what?" Francine said, her voice recovering slightly.

"Not only grab that cup so fast from where you're laying but then flip it around so no ice fell out. That's what."

"Doctor, Francine has had enough lately in her life. Does she need an inquiry about catching a cup?" Dewey asked.

"It's my job to notice things in my patient. We will observe Francine for a while to see if the bites have had any effects on her. We have to be very careful."

"Well, I just reached out and grabbed. That's all," Francine interjected to stop any argument.

"Get some rest. If you do well on the ice chips, we'll move you up to some soup," The doctor announced as he left, still mumbling about the cup as he walked past Lorenzo.

"I'm starving, Dad. Can I get some real food, and not soup?"

"Take your time, honey. Take your time," Dewey answered.

Chapter 9

Perth, Australia

The next couple days little things showed up that announced that Francine was not the same as before the bites. At first it was subtle things.

No adverse effects were evident as she lay in bed. It was when she was allowed to use the bathroom for the first time that something showed up.

As the nurse assisted Francine getting out of bed, Lorenzo noticed it first. "Why are you bouncing?"

"Am I bouncing?" Francine asked. "I don't feel like I'm bouncing."

"Ahh, honey. You have a definite bounce when you walk. I see it too," Dewey added.

"Watch. I can stand perfectly still." Francine preceded to stand perfectly still with the nurse standing beside her in case she fell. "And now I can walk like normal."

Resuming her walk, a definite bounce showed. No matter how hard she tried, if she was moving, there was a twitch to her body. If she stopped, things returned to normal.

When the doctor was summoned to witness this change, he paused. "Most unusual. I think when you're up to it, we need to have you do a few tests. I'll get things ready."

* * *

Two days later Francine and her parents were sitting in the Rehabilitation Center of King's Hospital. By then Francine had been eating whole foods and appeared recovered. Lorenzo had decided it was time for him to return home and everyone had said their goodbyes to grandfather. Francine saved an extra-large hug to send him on his trip back to Italy.

Dr. Coleman entered the Rehab room with the head of physical therapy as they set Francine up for a battery of tests. The first one was a simple one. The PT held a playing card between his fingers in a vertical position. Francine held out her hand with her index and thumb on opposite sides of the card, but not touching. The PT would let go and Francine would try to grip the card with her two fingers before it fell past her.

It was a common bar trick people used to get free drinks. The bet was the grabber couldn't catch the card. It appeared to be a simple task, just close ones fingers. But the reaction time needed typically was too long and the card invariably fell to the floor.

"Ready, I'll release the card and you grab it with your finger and thumb. Just don't touch the card before we start," the PT announced. They all waited for the PT to let go. Francine watched intently for the card to be released.

The PT released and immediately Francine stopped the card from falling. "Ummm, let's try again," Dr. Coleman said.

The test was done again with the same results. A third and fourth test revealed a similar finish. Each time the card barely fell before Francine clutched the card.

"That is very good," Dr. Coleman said, the look on his face telling Dewey more than his vocal comment.

Dewey had tried the trick over the years and had seen it done many times. The quickest reaction he had ever seen was someone catching the very top edge of the card. The reaction time needed by the brain to witness the card release and transmit that information to the fingers in order to react was a split second, but long enough that most people only caught air.

Francine had caught the card in the middle, which was where her fingers waited. Her brain was processing the information from her eyes to her fingers so quick Dewey barely saw the card move.

They moved on to the next test. The PT explained that he wanted Francine to do a standing long jump. Stand in place, bend down without moving her feet and jump forward as far as she could. An area with mats had been set up in front of her for protection in case she fell on landing.

"Remember Francine. Stay in control of your jump. We don't' want you flying face first or anything like that," the doctor instructed.

"I understand," Francine answered. She took a couple baby bunny hops in place to test out her new sneakers. She hadn't been out of bed much over the past two weeks except to go to the bathroom and slow strolls around the unit attached to a nurse. Francine commented on her rubbery feeling legs as she hopped. "Dad, I'm afraid my legs have lost all that conditioning we got in the Himalayas."

"That's OK, honey. We know you can get it back quick once you get the clearance from the Doc here. Just give us a small jump for practice," Dewey said.

Francine lowered her five-foot six-inch frame down into a squat and released forward. She cleared the mats and landed on the carpeted floor beyond.

"I said a practice jump. We don't need an Olympic qualifier from you this morning," Doctor Coleman barked. His nervousness showed the concern for his patient.

"That *was* a practice jump," Francine said. "I think if you want me to really put some effort into it we'd better take it outside."

Dewey watched as the doctor and the PT looked at each other, their eyebrows giving them away. They asked Francine to move over to the wall containing the height graph for vertical jump measurement and instructed her to jump vertically from a stationary position.

Francine looked up at the ruler running up the wall. She picked out a spot she knew from volleyball drills that she had reached before. Again squatting, she released. She flew up past her old spot and went another eighteen inches.

"Wow! Double mother of jumps, wow!" she yelled.

"Was that a practice jump or did you put more in it that time?" the doctor asked.

"I put more in it, but not everything I have," Francine answered. "It was a little unnerving being up that high. I'm not used to it."

The PT wrote down the number from the scale where Francine had touched. He and the doctor went to the corner and quietly whispered. They returned to announce that two more tests would wrap up the work today.

The next test was a simple lateral quickness test. Francine would sprint from one mark on the floor to another. They repeated the effort for two minutes straight. Francine had done line running for both volleyball and tennis so the test was simple to her.

Even though she had been bedridden for the past two weeks, the quickness in her legs astounded her. Dewey could see the improved speed in his daughter.

The final test involved a machine that measured arm strength and quickness. The PT demonstrated first and then adjusted it to fit Francine's arm length. Again, Dewey could see the quickness in his daughter's arm had multiplied since her ocean near-death encounter.

Back in the room, Francine nervously awaited her doctor's conclusion. Anna Maria sat beside the bed, holding Francine's hand. Dewey stood behind his wife with his hand on his daughter's head. He played with her hair to take some of the tension out of the room.

"Dad, stop. I look bad enough with these bandages still on my arms," Francine protested. The doctor wanted the areas that had been bitten covered to avoid infection. Each bite site was still red with inflammation.

"Francine, I want you to relax for the rest of the day. We'll try some more tests tomorrow. We'll go outside where we have a bit more room. I'll schedule a time at the University of Western Australia's track. That should give us sufficient room," the doctor announced.

The next day only confirmed what the initial tests had demonstrated. Francine's quickness and her muscular reaction times were off the chart. In addition, they began to notice that her eyesight had been enhanced.

They needed a test to determine conclusively in what manner her eyes were now different. A visit to an eye specialist helped to determine that her eyes were now extremely reactive. But they weren't sure what effect that would have on Francine's vision. Otherwise she had 20/20 sight.

"So no X-ray vision. That's kind of disappointing," Dewey joked. *I have to inject a little levity into my daughter's situation,* he thought. *The rest was too difficult to comprehend.*

"Oh great. Now my dad wants me to be Superwoman! Stop speeding trains and catch bullets with my teeth," Francine threw back at her dad. "Hey, I just remembered. That movie, the 'Matrix', those guys in suits could dodge bullets. Do I have to do that test today?"

"Very funny. But this is all a little overwhelming," Dewey said.

"No dodging bullets, Francine. You are very quick, but that trick had better be left to Hollywood special effects," Doctor Coleman admonished. "You're going to have to learn how to deal with the syndrome that you do have. I think that will be challenging enough."

"Syndrome? What syndrome do I have?"

"Since you're the first, I guess you can name it. No one has ever experienced what you have and lived to talk about it," the doctor said. "I might suggest we call it 'Hydrophiinae Syndrome.'"

"Sounds medical enough, I guess, but what does that mean?" Francine asked.

"Hydrophiinae is the genus name for sea snake. I believe that the sea snake venom is causing your increased muscle activity."

Doctor Coleman began to explain how he thought Francine had such increased reactions. Sea snake venom leads to Rhabdomyolysis, which he explained was the rapid breakdown of muscle tissue typically leading to paralysis.

A typical bite victim would experience tenderness, aching and stiffness all over their body while the venom continued its breakdown of muscle. Then the victim's urine would turn dark red or black from the myoglobins being expelled from the body.

Then after six to twelve hours the victim would suffer severe hyperkalemia which would cause cardiac arrest. The doctor had contacted Australia's foremost snake expert and she had determined that Francine had probably been bitten by the Aipysurus Laevis species of sea snake. Those were the most aggressive found in Western Australia.

"Pretty safe, huh Dad?"

Anna Maria and the doctor looked at each other, not knowing the inside joke. Dewey teared up remembering what he had risked and how close he had come to losing the most precious person in his life.

Francine turned to look at her dad. Seeing the tears in his eyes, she added, "Sorry Dad, I won't bring it up again."

"Doctor, does my daughter need to hear all these details?" Anna Maria asked.

"Mom, I want to know everything about this syndrome I have. I'm the one who has to deal with it."

"Exactly Francine. Mrs. d'Alesandro, your daughter is a medical miracle. How long this will last and what effects it will have on her body, I can't predict. She will have to monitor everything for the rest of her life to assure that no ill effects are manifesting themselves."

The doctor continued. "Now, how the box jellyfish figures in all of this, I haven't a clue. Untreated, a box jellyfish sting kills within three minutes. Again, calling our jelly fish specialist, we figure Francine was bit by the Chironex Fleckeri, or 'Sea Wasp', as it's commonly called. Those three minutes would have been the time it took to get you in the boat and moving toward help. They aren't called the 'World's Most Venomous Creature' for no reason."

He explained that the guide removing the tentacles had certainly helped. But how Francine had lasted the time it took to get to shore, get help and then transport Francine to the hospital, he could offer no explanation. Somehow, the snake venom and the jellyfish venom combined into a strange brew that offset the lethal aspects of both.

"If she had been bitten by just one, I don't think she'd still be with us. But the two bites reacted differently inside you and that combination seems to have saved your life," the doctor said. "And not only saved your life, it seems to have enhanced your body beyond measure."

"So, what now, Doc?" Dewey asked.

"I would like to keep her close and just monitor her continued recovery. We have the expertise on these kinds of bites that you wouldn't have in the United Sates. I can set you up in an apartment nearby so you can get out of the hospital."

"Sounds great to me. I'm about done with hospitals for the rest of my life, thank you very much," Francine said. "Not that this isn't a great hospital, because it is."

"I understand totally," Doctor Coleman offered. "And I've had numerous requests for a press conference. We have had reporters checking daily on our miracle patient. They have not been told anything due to medical confidentiality here in Australia. But they will be hounding you on the streets if you don't provide them with something, I'm afraid."

Chapter 10

Perth, Australia

The next day, Dewey and Anna Maria packed up the few things they had and headed over to the apartment provided by Dr. Coleman. He explained the hospital maintained several flats nearby for such occasions.

Before Francine could leave and head across the street to a more normal life, a press conference had been scheduled by the hospital. Dewey advised his daughter how press conferences worked and some of the questions she might receive. They didn't fully comprehend yet what it all meant, so Dewey and his wife had decided that Francine's syndrome would remain unmentioned. As the three prepared to leave the hospital room for the press conference, two men in suits walked in.

"Mr. and Mrs McDowell, let me introduce myself. I'm David Knight, Counsel in the Attorney General's Ministry for the government of Australia. This is Dr. Keith Mountain from the Ministry of Health. We need to meet with you and Francine before you speak to the press."

"Ms. McDowell, let me express the government's genuine relief for what appears to be a full recovery," Dr. Mountain said. "Dr. Coleman has called us with his concern about ... what did he call it? Hydrophiinae Syndrome."

"Are we in trouble with the law here?" Francine asked.

"Certainly not. At least not yet. As our Health Minister for Australia has expressed to me, he has talked extensively with your doctor," Dr. Mountain continued.

"Can he discuss my case like that?"

"Of course. The Australian Government is concerned about this whole syndrome thing becoming public. Until we know more, we are here to advise you to keep the events of your attack private," Mr. Knight said.

"If you're worried about us suing you, that's not our style," Dewey offered.

The man from the Attorney General's Ministry gave him a long cold stare. "Mr. McDowell, this is not America. We don't have the litigious society you have. We are concerned about what Dr. Coleman describes as Francine's suddenly enhanced athletic skills."

David Knight continued, "We have talked to your guide at Coral Bay as well as all the people who have been involved in Francine's case. They have all signed non-disclosure forms."

"Are you asking us to sign a non-disclosure form also? Maybe I should contact the Italian Consulate?" Anna Maria said.

"Anna Maria," Dewey stopped his wife before her Italian blood become more agitated. Turning to the two Australian government officials he offered, "You should know that as a family we've already decided not to discuss Francine's syndrome."

"Right. Then we're good here. We'll escort you to the news conference," Mr. Knight said.

As the five reached the conference room door, Dr. Coleman and the hospital's public relations coordinator met them. The two Australian government officials quietly slipped into the back of the conference room.

Expecting a few reporters, the McDowells were shocked by the television cameras and the crowd that had gathered to hear Francine's survival tale. Dewey put his arm around his daughter as she stopped in the doorway .

"It will be fine, we'll be right beside you," he whispered in her ear.

Doctor Coleman and the hospital information officer escorted Francine to a seat at the front. Dewey and Anna Maria took spots near the front but off to the side.

The Public Relations Officer started the event. "Ladies and gentleman, Ms. McDowell has consented to answer a few questions from the press concerning her miraculous survival. I will advise the press that some medical information will be off-limits as her treatment continues. Accompanying her today are her mother and father who ask that you take into consideration their daughter's fragile health at this critical time. Ms. McDowell."

Francine sat next to Dr. Coleman. The doctor reached over and clasped her hand as it rested on the table top.

"Ms. McDowell, James Cameron of the Western Australian. As the local Perth paper, I want to express our readers' genuine concern and relief at your recovery. Could you tell us in your own words what happened in Coral Bay?"

Francine started to tell her story as she remembered it. Unfortunately her memory stopped about when she and her dad hit the water heading toward the 'shark hospital'.

The reporter followed up to Dewey for an explanation. Dewey gave a brief account of Francine's rescue and transport by air ambulance to Perth. Left unsaid were any specifics of what had happened on the reef that day.

The next reporter zeroed in more than the first. "There is a rumor that a box jellyfish attack was involved. Can you confirm that information?"

Dr. Coleman answered. "Yes, we can confirm a Sea Wasp attack." The doctor left unsaid any mention of the sea snake attack. The McDowells knew that the press wouldn't stop until some sort of answer was provided.

The reporter from ABC, the Australian Broadcasting Company television network, asked about any lingering effects. Francine hesitated since this was a subject they had decided to hold back on.

Again Dr. Coleman jumped in. "Ms. McDowell appears to have had no ill effects so far. Her bandages on her arms are to keep any infection from developing since the attack site is still inflamed."

Good answer, Dewey thought. *'No ill effects' covered things without mentioning the other symptoms.* They needed time to see what the enhanced quickness meant and if it was permanent.

After some routine questions the press got around as to how long the McDowells were staying in Perth and if they intended to see the sights. When Francine mentioned that she was anxious to get out for some exercise one reporter responded, "Well, if you're staying for a while, you could take in the Perth Open Tennis Tournament next week."

When the CNN reporter raised his hand, the assembled group rolled their eyeballs. Dewey noticed the decidedly icy reception the reporter was getting from his fellow reporters. Francine indicated to the man to ask his question.

"Thank you, Ms. McDowell. With your apparent luck at surviving your ordeal, do you hold any feeling that your father is somehow responsible for placing you in such a dangerous situation?"

The mood in the room went from icy to frozen. Anna Maria stared at the reptilian reporter as her Italian blood took over. She started to move to close the distance between her and the questioner when Dewey grabbed her arm. Francine started to cry at the viciousness of the question when Doctor Coleman leaned over the microphone and said, "The press conference is over."

Helping Francine stand, Dewey placed a protective arm around her. Anna Maria strained her restraint to get to the reporter. Doctor Coleman led all three out the side door into the corridor.

With just the four of them present, he offered, "I'm sorry about that. That reporter has a reputation here in Australia and I should have cut it off before Francine recognized him. If he bothers you again, let me know. We can arrange security for you while you are our guests."

"Doc, it will be the reporter that needs security if my wife ever sees him again," Dewey offered. He continued to hold back the angry, protective Italian mother. Doctor Coleman nodded that he understood.

Luckily, CNN didn't make any follow-up encounters while Francine continued her recovery. Growing tired of the daily morning visits to the hospital for Dr. Coleman's quick exams, Francine relished touring around the Perth area for the rest of the day.

She especially enjoyed heading out to the beach near Fremantle and getting in long walks. But she did notice her reluctance to go near the ocean. Each day she gave it a wide berth as she worked her body.

After a week, Anna Maria reluctantly announced that she needed to head home. Work was piling up and Doctor Coleman had said that everyone could head home in a couple of weeks. Things appeared stable from his daily exams and he was confident that Francine was past the point for any new complications.

At one of her morning exams, Francine purposely brought her dad to the office, announcing that she wanted to broach something. "Dr. Coleman, I would imagine that you might want to see me in a stress situation before you let me head home. My walks on the beach each day have pushed things some, but I was thinking a more strenuous test might offer more answers."

The doc looked at her and asked, "What did you have in mind?"

"The reporter mentioned that the Perth Open was this weekend. I've played tennis before and did fairly well in high school. Perhaps I could try my hand here?"

The doc looked at Dewey as Dewey offered, "The competition would stress her body. I'd rather find out here than back home."

"I agree. A three-day tournament will push you, and I can monitor the results. We'll be close to the hospital if anything comes up," the doctor said. "But it's late for getting a seeding. Let me call the Perth Tennis Club. I have friends there. I'll see what I can do."

Francine didn't have long to wait. That night she had a visit from the Doc with good news. "At first they said no, that all the slots were full two weeks ago. Then I mentioned that it was the Miracle Woman of Coral Bay and things quickly became available. You'll have to play a 'pig tail' tomorrow night and earn your way into the main draw."

"No problem. I can handle a pig tail," Francine announced. A pig tail was a pre-tournament match the night before with the winner advancing to the main event.

Dewey wondered how well his daughter would do. "Don't be too confident. You haven't picked up a tennis racket in six months, at least."

"You know me, Dad. I do better when I don't practice. I'll have to borrow a racket, though."

The doctor promised a selection to pick from for her the next day and had arranged some court time for Francine in order to warm up before her first match. One of his young interns had volunteered to be her hitting partner. "I understand he could have gone pro if he hadn't pursued his medical career. He'll give you a good bash."

Dewey and Francine spent the next morning locating a white tennis outfit for her play as the Perth Tennis Club required white only. This British tradition conflicted with the American standard of most anything goes. They also located some tennis shoes in Francine's size.

By the time they arrived for her warm-up sessions, her partner was already outside on the court hitting serves. The boom of each ball hitting the cloth curtains stopped

Dewey. *I'm not sure Francine is ready for that kind of power,* he thought.

The medical intern introduced himself as they walked onto the court. Dr. Coleman soon joined them and he and Dewey moved to the gallery located above the court to watch.

During warm-ups, Dewey grew more anxious when the intern hit his practice serves. The booming hits were bullets as they hit the curtain with a resounding thud. Dewey leaned over to the doctor.

The doctor recognized the concern from Francine's father and offered, "Don't worry. I told him we didn't need any injuries from any big hits today."

Dewey sat back, relieved. Warm-ups completed, Francine and the intern met at the net and spun a racket. Picking sides and first serve, they retreated to the base lines to begin the game.

Having first serve, Francine bounced the ball a few times and shuffled her feet. The new tennis shoes squeaked on the hard court as she bounced a little to get settled. Her opponent stood still, bent over with his racket held out in front of him. He was ready.

At least he thought he was ready. Francine pulled her racket back and threw the ball up over her head. Coordinating racket and ball perfectly, she drove the yellow ball toward the forecourt of her opponent. He didn't move a muscle. The ball went by him so fast he didn't even react.

Looking at Francine with a blank stare, he turned and walked over to pick up the loose ball. Shoving it in his pocket, he walked back to the opposite position on the base line.

He again readied himself for the serve. This time his feet were moving. *Better to react to the ball,* Dewey thought.

Francine threw the ball up and again swung perfectly, sending the ball speeding toward the intern. This time he caught a piece of it. Just enough to send it straight up into the air, landing finally on the adjoining court.

"30 Love," Francine announced as she slid over on the base line and took up her serving stance again. Now the intern was hopping and dancing as the serve came. He again caught enough of it to get it back over the net. But with too much speed, the ball went long.

The fourth serve resulted in the ball sailing over the curtain behind Francine. Francine matter-of-factly walked over to the score card by the edge of the net and flipped over the first number. "One game to nil. Your serve," she said as she handed the intern the balls.

Dewey noticed the frustration on the intern's face as he walked back to the baseline. *I think the doc's warning is about to be thrown out,* he thought.

The intern took his spot and bounced a ball in preparation. He went up on his toes as he threw the ball skyward, swinging and leaning as he contacted the ball. A bullet flew out from his racket toward Francine.

Wham. The ball came back just as fast but placed perfectly down the line past the outstretched racket of her opponent. The ball caught the corner by six inches before it slammed into the curtain. The intern walked over to retrieve the ball.

The next serve had even more heat on it. And the results were the same. But this time Francine hit a bullet cross-court shot.

"Love 30," he mumbled. The third serve flew toward Francine as his grunt echoed around the adjoining courts. He scrambled for a position on the baseline to receive a bullet but Francine didn't cooperate.

She lunged quickly to her right to take the ball on her forehand. But instead of a baseline power hit, Francine swung her racket downward at an angle with just the right speed. The ball hit the sideways moving strings and took on a spin that totally absorbed any forward momentum that the ball still retained.

The ball visibly warbled as it slowly lifted up and over the net, then died. The ball dropped slowly onto the court just feet behind the net. The intern attempted to rush to the forecourt to hit a return. Instead he almost tripped over a ball that hit the hard surface and died, almost rolling back toward the net from its remaining backward spin.

The intern ran up and kicked the ball in frustration. Dewey looked around and noticed a crowd had gathered. A light applause rose up from the people watching in appreciation of the fine shot Francine had just made.

A man dressed in a white tennis outfit and carrying a racket slid in to sit next to where Dewey and the doc were sitting. He said, "G'Day. May I ask the young woman's name out there?"

Dewey introduced himself and offered that it was his daughter they were watching.

A light went on in the man's face. "The Miracle Woman from Coral Bay? Well bloody hell. No one ever said she could play tennis. Mate, you are mean. Turning her loose on poor old Blake. He doesn't like losing. In fact he never loses around here. Serves the wanker good. Good on you."

"Thank you, I think. We just wanted to get her warmed up for the tournament. She has to play a pig tail tonight," Dewey said.

"Not bloody likely mate. Any woman entered in our tournament will take one look at what your daughter is doing to Blake here and quickly discover she has a bloody sprained ankle," the man offered. "She'll be lucky to have any competition until the finals, if then."

Francine continued to blank Blake. As Francine marched through her pro set, word quickly spread that Francine was the opponent for the night's match and the man's prediction bore out. After Francine beat the intern in straight sets, they walked over to check the board. The Tournament Board had a 'withdrawn due to injury' posted next to her opponents name.

"And I don't think my intern is coming back either. I just saw him heading out the front door," Dr. Coleman announced. Turning to Francine, he said, "That was some display of tennis my dear. Did you play like that before Coral Bay?"

"Yeah, right," Francine flippantly answered until Dewey scowled at her. "Sorry. No, that was definitely the best tennis I've ever played. I hope I didn't hurt your intern's feelings."

"He'll survive. One day he'll be able to tell his pub mates while they watch you on tele that he played you once. I'm sure he won't offer the score though," the doc said. "You, my dear, are one athlete to be reckoned with."

Dewey knew it too. His daughter suddenly had gifts of extraordinary abilities. *Life was about to get very complicated,* he thought.

The Perth Open was anticlimactic for Francine. Word spread and her other opponents dropped out of the draw. Only the finalist from the opposite half of the bracket chanced to step on the court against her. The results were predictable after the drubbing Blake had endured.

Holding her Championship Trophy, Francine smiled. Whether it was a smile to acknowledge her win or a smile in recognition that she was alive, Dewey wasn't sure. But in either case, she was totally enjoying the experience.

Chapter 11

Moscow, Idaho

"Well, Mr. McDowell. It is highly unusual to even consider a walk-on at this late date," the University of Idaho Volleyball Head Coach said. "We enter the summer with our team members set. To add a new member at this stage would be upsetting."

"Coach, before you blow us off, I think you might want to at least see what you'd be sending down the road." Dewey knew that getting Francine onto a Division I team would be difficult without a tryout.

At 5' 6", Francine would be the shortest woman on the team. Volleyball had progressed over the years to be a tall woman's game. Especially for any competitive NCAA Division I team. Short women could play for a Division II or III school, or a non-contender Division I school back East. But to play in the big leagues, one had to be at least 5' 10" and very athletic.

Dewey was betting on the very athletic option. He and Francine had talked on the way home from Australia on how she wanted to use her new athletic skills. The talk had gone back and forth until a plan was developed. It would depend on her syndrome continuing, but while it did, Francine would use it.

Volleyball had been first on her mind. It had always been her favorite sport. And after the bad experience of her college freshman year, Francine was determined to make up for that mistake.

The University of Idaho had been chosen by Francine because she had had a cousin who attended. Francine had watched her cousin play basketball for the Vandals whenever they were in the Denver area. The experience had developed a loyalty to the school early in her life.

"Tryouts are typically done early in the summer. We are three weeks from daily doubles and the official beginning of our season. By NCAA rules, I'm not even here," the coach said.

"Then as I understand it, by NCAA rules, this is an open gym. You're not allowed to coach. So if the players wanted to scrimmage with Francine, that would be allowed?" Dewey asked

"Again, highly unusual. You're right in that this is technically open gym time. But only Idaho students are even allowed in here."

"Well, we're OK. Francine has been accepted for the fall and will be attending if things go right. So, we just have one more Idaho student looking for a little pick-up volleyball."

The team was starting to grumble at the delay the discussion caused. They had been working out in the weight room before they took to the court. Now they wanted to keep moving before they cooled down. One of the players finally offered, "Look Coach, if it means we can get things moving, I'll put her in as a DS."

The coach stepped back as she couldn't interfere under NCAA rules in the player's scrimmage. Her face had a certain look of frustration as the women all lined up on both sides of the court. A ball feeder was selected to throw the ball in, alternating sides. Individual serving would come latter. Now was reserved for ball control during play.

Francine was already suited up in her volleyball gear; her old shoes from the year before along with her ankle braces, knee pads and spandex. Since arriving back in Colorado from Australia, Francine had spent the last month getting applications out to colleges and working on conditioning.

Feeling that her syndrome and its effects on her body wouldn't be enough for her athletic goals, she worked hard each day on weights and the elliptical machine. The added advantage of training at altitude that Evergreen, Colorado offered helped Francine obtain the best conditioning of her life.

She and her dad joked about not only 'Extreme Makeover - Himalaya' but had added 'Extreme Makeover - Australia' to their TV wish list. They knew if they could find the answer to Francine's changed abilities, they could become very rich.

Lining up in the back row center position, Francine crouched low to be ready to receive the ball. The player tossing balls into play complied by tossing the first 'free ball' toward her. Francine easily passed it to the setter who set the ball to a front row player for a hit.

But the hit wasn't strong enough and the ball came back much harder this time. As the kill flew toward the back court, Francine bumped into the woman beside her as they both went for the dig. The ball ricocheted off both of them into the arena seating. The other player scowled at Francine for getting in her way.

This won't be easy at this rate, Dewey thought. The next few plays were similar. For players to learn to play together takes practice. Francine was experiencing the opposite effect. These women weren't happy to be playing with an outsider, and were not going to be nice about it.

Finally, Dewey walked down to the court in frustration. He had to change this up or they would be thrown out of the open gym. He reached for his wallet. He opened it and pulled out four new hundred-dollar bills that he had gotten for this circumstance.

"OK, here's the deal. We can settle things faster. Who's the starting setter?" A woman raised her hand. "Good. You pick your best five players. Now, who's the backup setter?"

A woman standing on the opposite court raised her hand. She looked as though she wasn't sure she liked where this was going. Dewey motioned her onto his side of the court. He told the rest of the team players on his side to vacate the court.

"I have four hundred dollars here. Francine and your setter against your starting six. Winner gets the money to go have a nice dinner this weekend. Francine gets first serve. One game to 25."

The Vandal Coach had a look of frustration. "This is very irregular."

"Humor me for a minute Coach," Dewey said. "OK. Francine serves."

Francine grabbed a Baden volleyball and checked the pressure. She threw that one back into the cart full of balls and grabbed a different one. Checking the pressure, she bounced it on the floor a few times. She looked at her dad and nodded. She was ready.

Francine walked over to her dad. "Do you want me to serve it out on them?" she whispered. Dewey knew she was asking if she should 'bagel' the Vandal Varsity Team. A 'bagel' or 'donut', was a game in which the server hits twenty-five straight points and never lets the other side score.

Dewey leaned into Francine's ear so the others couldn't hear. "No. Give them a chance. Just mix up your serves. But blow a few by them so they can see your potential."

Francine nodded that she understood and walked back to the baseline. Stepping back from the court about thirty feet, she focused on the opposing six team members on the far side. She switched her gaze to the lone player on her side of the net. She smiled at her setter. The smile wasn't returned.

Francine switched her gaze to the Baden brand on the side of the ball. She took a step, tossed the ball high in the air while adding a rapid spin to it. Francine flashed forward as the spinning ball flew toward the baseline. At the exact spot where the ball starting descending, Francine leaped into the air and smashed her open palm into the ball.

Like a bullet, the ball flew across the court, just clearing the net. As soon as it was over the net, the air currents flowing over the spinning ball took hold. The ball suddenly changed angles and dropped toward the floor.

The opposing team scrambled to adjust to the ball's changing trajectory. They couldn't react fast enough and the ball fell in bounds for an 'ace'. One of the Vandal reserves on the sidelines retrieved the ball and rolled it back to Francine.

Dewey had been watching the coach the whole time. He thought he saw an eyebrow move on Francine's first serve.

Francine wound up for her second serve. Again, a high toss and leap sent the ball rocketing into the opposition. Again the varsity team scrambled to dig the ball. Although one player did get an arm out in time, the result was a volleyball that ricocheted into the stands.

A reserve player grabbed a new ball out of the cart and tossed it to Francine. Checking the air pressure, Francine was satisfied. This time, she threw the ball skyward, but left the spin off the ball. When she leaped she opened her palm up as wide as possible as she struck the ball.

Unlike the spinning bullet of the last two, this ball left Francine with no spin. The wind effect on the ball was totally different then on a spinning ball. The air current caused the ball to oscillate back and forth as it headed toward the Vandals.

Dewey knew from experience that the opposing players would be waiting for a 'jump serve' when a 'jump float' was now coming their way. A float serve was typically the most difficult to handle, and this one was no exception.

With the ball moving literally side to side about six inches, a defensive player on 'serve receive' had to adjust to a ball wobbling straight at her. The player misjudged the movement and only caught an edge of the ball. Again the ball glanced off the player and headed out of bounds.

Three straight aces, Dewey thought. He waited for Francine's choice for her fourth serve. This time she stood on the base line flat footed and tossed the ball. Without any foot movement, she hit the ball high. *A short serve*, Dewey thought.

The purpose of a 'short serve' was to catch the defense napping. Although slow, the ball had a high arc that just barely cleared the net. As the ball dropped onto the court for another ace, two Vandal players slid on their stomachs in an attempt to get under the ball. Called a 'pancake', diving onto the hardwood for a volleyball was common.

The coach's eyebrows were moving as Francine continued her demonstration. The setter that was supposed to be working on Francine's side of the net looked bored. She hadn't been called on in the game and score was already five to nothing.

Dewey caught Francine's gaze and gave her a quick nod. She got the message. She lined up the next serve and put it just out on the opposing baseline. Sideout and the ball moved to the Vandal Varsity Team. A reserve player on the sidelines flipped the score to 5-1.

The opposing team rotated and the server walked back with the ball. Dewey knew what she was thinking; with only two people on the opposite side, she could run up the score. She tossed the ball and ran to catch up. Jumping into the air, she smashed the volleyball.

Francine was down and ready as the ball was struck. She instantly adjusted as soon as she saw where the ball was hit and was waiting in a perfect 'platform' to receive the ball. A platform constitutes the correct stance a volleyball player takes to receive and properly pass a ball.

The ball sped toward Francine. She took the hit on her arms and easily let the energy of the hit be absorbed into her body. With a slight movement of her arms, the ball harmlessly bounced up into the air with no spin. Aimed perfectly at the traditional spot that the setter occupies, the ball floated up and then down toward the setter.

Francine instantly changed from defense to offense. She sprinted to her left side of the net to line up for her approach. She looked up to where the ball was supposed to be only to realize the setter had set the middle. The ball dropped onto their court. 5-2.

Dewey looked at the setter and raised his arms in a question. *Who were you setting?* he thought. With only one other player on the court, there wasn't any other option.

The next play had similar results. Francine went to the middle and the setter pushed the ball to the outside. Dewey watched as Francine had a quiet conversation with her setter. She went back to her position at serve receive.

Again a miscue had Francine going to the right side while the setter did a quick set to the middle. The score was 5 to 4 now. Dewey looked on in frustration but held his tongue. The score was tied up on another miscue. Certainly, this setter was determined to see Francine walk down the road.

"OK. I give up," Francine said in exasperation. She walked over to her bag and retrieved her sports warm up jacket. Turning to the coach she said. "I just wanted to come here and show you I had the skills to help your team. Maybe it would be enough to win a National Championship. That's right, a National Championship. Obviously, this team has much lower expectations."

The entire Vandal team had gathered on the opposite side of the net. A few of the women were talking amongst themselves.

"So you're confident that you can win the NCAA," the coach said.

"Yes. And if this team isn't interested in going there, there are other D-1 schools that will be. Thanks for your time," Francine challenged. "Come on, Dad, let's go see if Boise State thinks big."

Dewey wasn't sure if it was the Boise State comment or something else, but he saw a light click in the coach's eyes.

"Hold on," she said. The Vandal team froze in anticipation. "Just bear with me. We can settle this easily. Get the 'touch pole'."

The touch pole was the device used to measure leaping ability. Designed as a tall pole with light weight plastic fingers extended out along the top, a player would run and jump with the objective to knock the fingers aside as high up the pole as possible.

"Sara, Anna, Courtney, Meghan, you're up," the coach ordered. Sara and Anna were both over six feet tall and were the starting Middle Blockers for the Vandals. Courtney and Meghan we also over six feet, slightly shorter than the Middles. They were the starting Outside Hitters.

These four would be the girls to out jump, Dewey thought. Francine walked over to her dad and asked quietly, "By how much should I beat them?"

Dewey leaned down and whispered, "Whatever high-mark they put up, knock one more stick. Don't show them everything yet." Each finger on the pole denoted an inch.

Courtney was up first. She ran up to the pole, jumping while she reached up with one hand. The bottom nine sticks all pivoted around the pole. Two more attempts and she knocked one more stick aside.

"Ten feet even," the coach noted on her clipboard.

The assistant coach reached with a long stick and moved the fingers back into position. Meghan took her turn. After her three attempts, she had moved the mark up one more inch.

Again the fingers were placed back in position. The first Middle Blocker stepped up. She ran at the pole and leaped. Knocking the sticks aside, she landed satisfied. Her next two attempts added no additional height.

"Good job Sara. You beat your old mark. I'll put your new mark of ten foot five inches in the book."

Sara walked back to the gathered group of team members with a satisfied look on her face. Her teammates gave her high fives and fist pumps as she joined them.

Finally, Anna, the other Middle Blocker stepped up. She ran in and jumped. The sticks flew around the pole. Two more tries yielded two more markers.

"I'm afraid Sara still holds the team record. But you did improve your personal best. I'll mark it down as ten feet three inches. OK, we have our team marks. Francine, anytime," the coach said.

As the assistant coach went to adjust the markers back into position, Francine asked, "Could you leave them where they are?"

There were giggles from the team as they looked on the five-foot six-inch tall Francine. She was about to attempt to out-jump one of their middles. Anna had at least nine inches of height over Francine. The assistant coach backed off.

"Are you sure? We won't know how high you can jump if he doesn't move the fingers back," the head coach asked.

Without waiting to reply to the coach, Francine sprinted the short distance to the pole. Leaping straight up, she threw her arm up toward the remaining markers. The bottom one moved and spun around.

Ten feet six inches, Dewey thought. Then he noticed the look on the coach's face. There was a certain incredulous look that was mimicked by the entire Vandal Team. Francine landed and turned to see her mark.

"How did you do that?" the coach asked. "Nobody of your height touches 10' 6"."

"Do I get my three attempts like the others?" Francine asked.

Speechless that this demure woman wanted to improve on an already amazing score, the coach nodded for Francine to continue.

Dewey gave his daughter the 'don't overdo it' look. He received a wink in return.

Francine again lined up and ran for the pole. Leaping again, she knock one more marker out of the way. Ten feet seven inches.

The look on the coach and the team changed to one of awe. But Francine wasn't done. Her third attempt resulted in two more sticks pivoting away from the rest.

"Ten nine," the coach said. "Mr. McDowell, Francine, we need to talk."

The three walked away from the court and headed up into the stands. The coach yelled at her players to get back to work. The assistant coach tried to corral them into a workout, but to no avail. The team just stared at the touch pole and the mark that Francine had just set.

"Francine, forget everything that transpired before. The girls on this team are a good group, and they are going to love playing with you. We would be glad to have you join us if you still want to be a Vandal."

Francine hesitated. She had experienced bad coaching the previous year and Dewey knew she'd be leery of a team that truly didn't want her.

"I don't have any scholarships left for this year. But I'll work hard to find help for you if you decide to come here," the coach added.

"Money isn't the issue, although I would appreciate it if her tuition could be deferred to the new year," Dewey said.

"I know we can work with the Administration to make that happen," the coach said. "So Francine, ready to play Vandal volleyball?"

"I am if you're ready to shoot for a NCAA Championship. I know the PAC 12 is the dominant conference in the country. The University of Idaho is an also-run in an also-run conference," Francine said.

Dewey winced at his daughter's lack of tack in negotiating with the coach. No coach wanted to hear that her program or her conference were second rate.

"I know the Pac 12 is the standard that every volleyball program looks up to. We play our cross-town rivals at Washington State every year and have a difficult time of it. And the Cougars usually bring up the bottom of the Pac 12," the coach admitted.

"But that's why I want to play here. I want an underdog to rise up and challenge the big dogs. There are players in the Pac 12 jumping ten ten. I want that challenge," Francine said.

"Well, we don't play any other Pac 12 team except Washington State this year, but Kansas and Nebraska are on our schedule. They should be a good test for us. And of course, you'll see the Pac 12 teams at the playoffs. They typically take three out of the final four slots in the Championship," the coach said.

"Then lets get to work," Francine announced.

"Then call me Coach Brown. I'm very happy to have you aboard. Let me introduce you to your teammates. And we'll get you some workout clothes."

Dewey sat back as Coach Brown and Francine walked over to the team. The past was quickly forgotten as the coach announced the newest member of the Idaho Vandal Volleyball Team. Everyone gathered around and welcomed Francine.

We'll see how the team politics goes once the real practices begin, Dewey thought. *They might all seem happy for Francine to be part of the team now. But soon, players will find out that their roles and playing time will be affected by this new addition. Every team had adjustment periods.* Dewey would wait to see how this one transpired.

Chapter 12

London, England

"Good afternoon, ladies and gentlemen. We are here at Wembley Stadium for the final International Association of Athletics International meet of the year. This is Hugh Godley announcing. And beside me is my old friend, Jack Hawkins. How say you, Jack?"

"Well Hugh, we have a glorious day for our competition. The Duchess of Cambridge is in attendance for this opening day. But, unfortunately we are missing our world record holder in the one hundred meter sprint. He was knocked out just last month by allegations of illegal use of performance-enhancing drugs."

"Right you are Jack. The World Anti-Doping Commission has been busy this summer in Track and Field. It's President, Cubo Zoan, has personally taken it upon himself to clean out two of our world record holders for today's meet. I'm not sure where this sport will end up with the likes of Zoan patrolling the side lines," Hugh added.

The World Anti-Doping Commission had banned eight athletes in the past year for illegal drug use. Four had tested positive on a drug screen after competition. The other four had been banned based solely on questionable eye-witness testimony.

WADC was entering the very controversial area of removing athletes based on hear-say evidence. Neil Aldrin, multiple winner of the Tour de France, had only been the most visible victim of the WADC witch hunt.

Others were now being banished even though they had never tested positive for any banned substance. The attitude was swinging around to one of implied cheating. Athletes that performed too well were suspect.

And Cubo Zoan was leading the charge. His controversial reign at WADC continued at the behest of the sports federations that allowed the WADC to patrol its athletes. And so far, WADC was the dominant force in international track and field.

But there were rumblings of discontent brewing concerning Mr. Zoan. Oftentimes, the athletes being banned represented some of the biggest sports manufacturing companies in the world. After investing millions promoting young athletes, these same companies were getting frustrated at the less-than-objective investigation of the doping charges.

At the front of the list was Zeus Sports, the largest shoe and apparel company in the world. Headed by billionaire Stanley Day, Zeus Sports had seen too many of its top endorsements knocked out of competition. The company's bottom line was being affected.

Neil Aldrin had been the biggest of Zeus Sports' celebrities that had been thrown under the bus by WADC. Stanley Day had publicly challenged Cubo Zoan by continuing to support Neil even after his ban from cycling. The gauntlet had been thrown.

"Rumor has it, that, even as we speak, forces are meeting in America to address the Zoan problem," Hugh offered his listeners.

"They will need to be careful there, Hugh," Jack threw in. "The public seems to be very supportive of Mr. Zoan's campaign to clean up sports. It might not be the most up-and-up method he is using, but the public is frustrated by cheating athletes taking advantage of the system."

"But when blood tests don't reveal any evidence, is there really cheating?" Hugh queried.

"Everyone seems to feel that with the sophistication of today's performance drugs, the cheaters know how to stay one step ahead of the testers. Whether that is true or not is Mr. Zoan's problem at the moment," Jack said.

"You're right there, Jack. We can anticipate a major battle if Stanley Day of Zeus Sports can convince his counterparts that their money would be better spent fighting WADC," Hugh offered. "It could get very interesting indeed."

"Well, Hugh, we can put that aside for now, because here come the shot putters onto the field. It's amazing we have anyone left to compete considering their history of drug use."

* * *

In New York City, Stanley Day was calling a meeting together. The USAT&F was the governing body for track and field in the United States. Zeus Sports was one of the largest contributors to USAT&F and consequently had the director's ear any time it wanted.

"I want to discuss this whole Zoan thing. It's killing us. We pour millions into promoting our top athletes only to have them banned from competition by WADC. I know the other companies are feeling the same way," Stanley stated.

"Stan, I've been hearing from all the companies. We can't all meet together because, as you know, that would be collusion in the eyes of Washington. But they've all come to me individually with their concerns," the USAT&F director said.

"Then we can dump Zoan?" Day said.

"Not so fast Stan, Zoan has the public behind him in a big way. We had some dirty laundry that he cleaned up over the past couple of years and he's riding that support. I know how you feel, but you and the other companies need to be patient."

"Patient, my ass. He's killing us. Our sales are off twenty percent since he banned Aldrin. And on nothing more than a supposed witness! A damn competitor of Neil's no less. No blood test. Just innuendo. It's not American. Whatever happened to the rule of law?" Stanley demanded.

"Slow down, Stan. Zoan is riding high right now. Maybe we can sit together and work out a strategy to take him down a few notches."

"Now you're talking. The bastard needs to be chopped off at the knees," Stanley said. "What did you have in mind?"

Chapter 13

Omaha, Nebraska

The Vandal Volleyball Team had experienced unexpected success. At least unexpected by most of the volleyball sports world in America. Dewey had a good idea how it would progress once Francine had worked her way into the team.

She had already made her mark in the Western Athletic Conference where the Vandals were leading in the standings. The team had only one non-conference loss. That had been the early matchup against the Washington State Cougars.

The team was still adjusting to Francine's level of play. Against the Cougars, the setter had made the decision to play 'democratic' volleyball. While the setter had tried to involve all her hitters, Francine had gone underutilized. Unfortunately, the other players hadn't got the job done. Idaho had ended up losing in Pullman in a five set tie-breaker.

Coach Brown had sat a long time with her team after that loss and explained that everyone on the team wasn't created equal. 'Democratic ball', where each player got an equal opportunity to hit the ball, didn't work.

At least it didn't work against the top teams. Every top team had two or maybe three 'go to' players that could get the job done. The other players were there in support.

After their only loss, the Vandals began thinking like the top teams. But unlike those teams, the Vandals had only one 'go to' player. But Francine made up for any deficiency in numbers by her level of play.

She was currently leading the conference in aces, kills and blocks. Her passing percentage, when playing defense, was also tops in the WAC. Although picked to finish in the middle of the standings in the WAC, by midway through the season, the other conference teams had certainly taken notice. The Vandal level of play was above the norm for the Western Athletic Conference.

Now the Vandals were competing at the Cornhusker Tournament in Nebraska. The NCAA was getting its first real look at Francine's play. And it was impressed.

Idaho had proceeded to march through the four-team competition. The first day had seen the Vandals win in three against an overmatched Brigham Young University team. It was when the Vandals had proceeded to hammer Kansas that the eyes of the nation took notice. The eleventh-ranked Jayhawks hadn't lost a game at that point in the season and went down in three convincing losses.

On the last day of the tournament, Idaho would line up against the host school, the University of Nebraska. The Cornhuskers were currently ranked fourth in the nation and had a win against powerhouse Texas on its record. Besides the Pac 12, Nebraska was a perennial top ten finisher in the NCAA standings and had on its roster players with extensive post-season experience.

Dewey knew Francine was ready for the test tonight. He and Anna Maria had traveled with the team and hadn't missed a game. In fact, Dewey hadn't missed much of Francine's college sports career. Dewey had ended up renting an apartment in Moscow for him and Francine. Dads didn't typically go to college with their twenty-year-old daughters but Francine had asked Dewey to manage her athletic endeavor.

Her syndrome was setting the stage for her athletic goals and Francine had decided on some lofty aspirations. What she was attempting required a full time manager close at hand. Although their living arrangements raised a few eyebrows, Dewey knew his daughter was right. Someone had to keep the wheels turning behind the scene.

"Alright. This is our test tonight. Number four in the country. We take them out and maybe we finally break into the top twenty. This one is about respect for Vandal volleyball. Let's go out there and show them we're here to play with the big dogs."

"Woof! Woof! Woof! Woof!" the team all yelled in unison. It had become their signature yell for each game. It was their way of announcing they were running with the big dogs.

The Idaho fans that had all gathered joined in the chorus. "Woof! Woof! Woof!" The Vandal fans might be drowned out by the huge Nebraska contingent but they made up in enthusiasm for their under-dog team. Dewey and Anna Maria joined in the raucous yelling.

* * *

Courtside, ZBC Sports switched on the cameras of the game to their worldwide audience. Although tape delayed in most markets to early in the morning, American college volleyball made its way out to an international sports audience.

"Hello sports fans everywhere. We have a special treat for our volleyball fans. On one side we have the storied Nebraska Cornhusker volleyball team with three National Championships who advanced to the Sweet Sixteen in nineteen of the last twenty seasons. On the other side of the net we have the unknown Idaho Vandals. To help sort this all out, we have Frank Buck, member of the 1972 US Men's Olympic Volleyball Team. Frank, describe what we have for our fans tonight," Hugh Godley asked.

"Hugh, we have David versus Goliath. Nebraska comes into tonight's matchup ranked fourth in the nation. Their offensive hitting percentage is second in the NCAA. And of course, they are led by a coach with three National Championships. I'm afraid that little Idaho, out of the WAC, will have to play the game of its life if it expects to take down the Cornhuskers."

"But these same Vandals have marched through the competition this weekend, even knocking off nationally ranked Kansas. We could have an upset in the making, don't you think?" Hugh asked

"If Nebraska loses this match, I'll eat this microphone, base an all. The Vandals are totally over-matched. Their leading scorer stands five-six. I have pants longer than that. You can't expect to win at this level with that kind of player."

"Well, we're about to find out. We've finished with the prelims. The refs have tossed out the ball. The Vandals are serving. In fact, your five-six player is set to start play."

Francine stood waiting patiently for the whistle from the Up Ref to start. A whistle followed by an arm swipe started play. Francine took a step, tossed a spinning ball and pounded a bullet of a serve off her jump.

The Nebraska defensive players snapped to move under the dropping ball, but it skimmed off the Libero, into the crowd.

"That was an ace. Frank, ready to munch that microphone?" Hugh teased his partner.

"One ace. Let the game get warmed up," Frank retorted.

Francine took the volleyball and lined up her second serve. The Nebraska players moved to adjust their defense. They had obviously scouted the Vandals over the tournament and had seen Francine's complement of serves.

This time Francine aimed lower. The jump serve hit the top of the net, stopped for a second and then fell harmlessly down onto the Nebraska side. Two Cornhuskers dove to the hardwood in a vain attempt to dig the ball.

"Pure luck on that one, Hugh. But if you could perfect it, that serve could take you to Olympic gold," Frank said.

Francine proceeded to show that she had more than pure luck. The next four serves hit the tape on the top of the net and rolled onto the opposite side each time for an ace.

"We see how number six is leading her conference in aces," Hugh said, referring to Francine's uniform number. "In fact, our statistician just gave us a note that Ms. McDowell is third in the nation in aces."

"Luckiest server I've ever seen," Frank grumbled.

The next serve sailed out of bounds. No one but Dewey would have noticed the small smirk on Francine's face. It was sideout, Nebraska's turn to serve.

The Cornhusker player retreated to behind the baseline. The Up Ref whistled for play to resume. Nebraska threw the ball up and caught it on the way down. Francine readied for serve receive. The Idaho team had worked out that with Francine's quick reaction she would receive the ball every time if it was anywhere on her share of the court. Everyone else knew to move aside.

The ball streaked in and Francine adjusted her position lightning fast. She froze into her platform. The ball hit hard but Francine instantly reacted and absorbed most of the kinetic energy in her arms. The ball popped up and flew into perfect position for the setter.

Francine ran to her spot and waited. The setter set the ball right in front of the ten foot line. Francine burst into a sprint and leaped into the air. She was careful to leave the floor from behind the ten foot line. She met the ball six feet off the net and pounded a hit into the middle of Nebraska's court.

The speed and intensity of the back row attack caught the Cornhuskers by surprise. The Nebraska coach jumped out of her seat, demanding a call on Francine's jump. Attacks on the ball by the back row players have to be initialized from behind the ten foot line. The Up Ref waved her arm sideways, indicating no call was coming.

"Woof! Woof! Woof!" the small Idaho crowd yelled. The players all gathered at center court to check on the next offensive set. The next Vandal server stepped up. Her serve was a floater that Nebraska handled easily. The Cornhuskers set up their offense and easily smashed a winner.

The play went back and forth as each side gained a couple of points. Finally, Francine rotated onto the front row.

"This appears to be where the Vandals want their big hitter. We'll see if they make a run now," Hugh offered.

"And look at the Cornhuskers. They've got six foot five and six foot four on that side as defense. We're about to see why five-six Outside Hitters are rare in Division I volleyball. The big girls are about to build a roof over the Vandals."

Francine stood ready for her teammate to serve up the volleyball. Across from her stood two towering Cornhuskers. They began talking trash through the net loud enough that the courtside announcers could hear.

"Hey shorty. You might get hits off those WAC players, but you're in the big leagues now. Watch out. We're going to stuff your hits right down your throat," the Middle Blocker taunted.

Francine had heard plenty of such talk in her short college volleyball career. She could never understand such attitudes. She'd learned that it didn't help engaging such talk, it was far better just to show them.

When she didn't answer their taunts, they added, "What, too scared to talk? The last little scrimp like you we stuffed ended up back on the bench. Don't cry when your coach benches you. There's no crying in volleyball," the Outside Hitter threatened.

The Idaho player finally served the ball. Francine waited to see what play the Cornhuskers would run. Her tormentors scrambled into their offensive set, but the setter went to the opposite side. The hit came across right at Francine. She dug a great pass to the Vandal setter who also set the ball behind her, but put the ball wide.

Returning to her outside position, the trash talk began again.

"Oh, too bad. Your setter forgot you. It's better that way. If you don't mess up, you'll be out here longer. But that bench is calling you," the middle said.

The next play went away from Francine. Passing the ball, the Vandals did a quick set to their middle, but was stuffed. The trash-talking pair returned to taunt Francine. The next three points went Nebraska way. Francine had not touched the ball yet from her Outside Hitter position.

The Vandal Coach called timeout. "We're down by five points. We haven't gone outside yet. Why?" The ZBC Sports camera man was there to record the action.

"Nebraska has those two big girls over there. I thought we could get a better hitting opportunity if we stayed away from them," Haley said. As setter, Haley was responsible to run the offense. Like a quarterback in football, the setter made the decisions from where a team's attack would come.

"Well, I want to see the next five sets going to the outside or I'll find another setter who can get the job done. This isn't a team we can play around with. We play strength on strength. It's that simple. Now, get it done," Coach Brown yelled.

"Woof! Woof! Woof!" the team yelled. "Come on, let's go!" They all yelled at each other in their huddle at center court.

"There you have it, Frank. The coach knew right away. You go with the playcr that got you here," Hugh announced.

"I'm just not convinced that player will get the job done tonight. The setter may be right about getting her other hitters involved. Not that the outcome is going to change."

"Well, my friend. I'd be saying the same thing if I was staring at that microphone sitting in front of you." Hugh pushed his friend on the promise he had made at the beginning of the game.

Francine walked back to her outside position. Her tormentors were ready. "Oh, you're back. We thought we'd have someone across the net that we could actually look in the eye. Won't be long now. The bench is calling."

Francine dug down in anticipation. Nebraska served the ball and the Vandal Libero dug a good pass to the setter. Francine raced back from the net and got in position for her approach to the ball. A high arcing volleyball floated over the center of the net.

The Vandal hitter sprung off her mark and timed it perfectly to be at the top of the net when the ball arrived. The two Cornhusker players jumped in unison to thwart the hit. They extended their long arms up and over the net, creating a roof-like block.

But Francine had the muscle control and the quick eye reaction to see the defensive play unfold. She held back, hanging midair, until the defense was committed. Then she hit with all her strength and speed.

The ball hit the right arm of the Outside Hitter. The ball slammed her arm with such force that it rebounded straight into the floor. Francine landed and turned to the corner ref. The red flag was raised with her hand on top. Out of bounds on Nebraska.

The two tall Cornhuskers took up their talk, but with a little less enthusiasm. In between plays, Francine noticed the Outside Hitter massage her right arm where the ball had hit her.

After Idaho served the ball, Nebraska's Outside Hitter hit a shot cross court. Francine, playing right back handled the ball easily. The setter moved under her pass.

This offensive play was a copy of the last. The ball careened out of bounds straight down off the block. Again the two trash talkers tried to pick up the taunts while the Outside Hitter continued to rub her right arm.

After five straight plays, the Outside Hitter raised her arm to be replaced. She went over to the sidelines and checked out of the game. Francine noticed her pulling an ice pack out of the cooler by the bench and placing it on her arm. All five shots had hit her in the same exact spot with similar force. The Nebraska trainer was soon working on the player.

Her replacement stood in front of Francine but didn't say anything. The Nebraska Middle Blocker finally stood silent. Francine decided it was her turn.

The next set went to other Vandal hitters. Francine worked hard on defense, but to no avail. Nebraska got the ball back. After two aces, Coach Brown motioned for Francine to slide into the back court for serve receive.

Taking a jump serve and passing a nice ball to the setter, Francine was rewarded with a number two set. A numbered set denoted where on the net the ball would be placed. The number two spot was just in front of the tormenting Nebraska Middle Blocker.

Again, Francine judged the ball perfectly. Leaping up she powered her hit into the Middle Blocker's out-stretched arms. The hit had to be in the right spot and that's where Francine smashed the ball.

Deflecting off the middle's right arm, the ball flew out of bounds into the stands. Again the corner ref raised the red flag with a hand on it, indicating out of bounds on Nebraska.

In the huddle, Francine asked for more just like that one. Haley agreed and one after another, three more sets came Francine's way. The Middle Blocker raised her arm to be substituted and walked to the side lines.

The second player pulled an ice pack out and placed it on her arm. The trainer examined both players and reported to the coach.

"Looks like Nebraska may run out of players out there. They may have to bring in their football team. They're not used to the hitting display that Idaho is putting on," Hugh said.

He waited for his color to jump in, but Frank was noticeably quiet. Finally, Hugh prompted his color assistant. "Frank, have you noticed the hitting power that McDowell is displaying?"

"I'll admit I'm impressed. I can see why these Vandals are doing so well. But we'll see how they finish today. And then we can see how it all shakes out come play-off time. Those girls in the Pac 12 are known for their big hits. And the only loss for this young Vandal team has come from the Pac 12," Frank added.

The first game closed with a serving display put on by Francine. She served up either outright aces or balls that were so hard to handle that Nebraska couldn't get their offense going. And of the balls that came back over the net, there was Francine with her defense and back row attack.

After three straight sets, the match was over. Both teams lined up for their traditional handshake along the net. As the players passed each other, the two trash-talkers came to Francine. They reached under the net and dug their fingernails into Francine's arm.

"Looks like we have some bad blood out there. We have Nebraska players definitely showing poor sportsmanship in their loss," Hugh said. "And now Frank, did you want ketchup with that microphone."

But Frank Buck wasn't even present to add any color. He had grabbed a cameraman and microphone and was headed out onto the floor. He wanted to interview this phenom of a volleyball player from Idaho.

Francine was sitting on the court stretching with the entire team. The TV cameraman waited while Frank talked to the Idaho Coach. "Might I have an interview with Ms. McDowell?"

"In a few minutes," Coach Brown answered.

The team finished their after-game stretching and the Idaho trainer handed Francine an ice pack. He grabbed some Saran Wrap and wrapped the ice pack onto her arm.

"Are you injured Ms. McDowell?" Frank started.

"Just some scratches. I'll have to treat them later so I don't get an infection. But ice will keep the swelling down."

"I just want to start and state that your display of raw hitting power was impressive. To be honest, I don't think I've seen that kind of power since the Brazilian great Fernando. We went up against him in the Olympics and I want to tell you, that was a load. The man was the first volleyball player to touch twelve feet. Just a monster player," Frank reminisced.

"Thank you, Mr. Buck. Coming from you, I will accept that as a high compliment. I just try to leave it all out on the floor when I play."

"You certainly do that. What do you attribute your skill level to? You didn't come out of high school as a Fab 50. I see you played club volleyball in Colorado. But again, nothing of note in that. Where did this phenomenal skill come from?" Frank inquired.

"A gift of God. That's the only thing I can attribute it to. You are right. Before this year, I was a good volleyball player. But this last year, I've just felt my body's muscles and nerves take over me. It was as if I was struck by lightning and I woke up with this incredible athletic gift," Francine answered.

Francine and her dad had worked out early how she would answer the obvious question. Where did such talents come from? That had been every reporter's first question.

Only one player of similar stature had carried their team like Francine was doing. Angie Pressey was a five-foot-eight outside hitter that took her University of California volleyball team to the NCCA Final Four. Crowds had been similarly impressed with her leaping ability.

"Well, good luck in the rest of your season. I look forward to watching you in Sacramento in a month," Frank referenced the site of the NCAA Volleyball Finals.

After the camera was lowered and switched off, other reporters that had been waiting to interview the Tournament MVP jumped in with their questions. The reporter from the Omaha World-Herald yelled out over the others, "Will you be ready for the blood test the NCAA administers in the playoffs?"

Coach Brown, who had been lingering nearby, stepped quickly to the challenge. Francine slid sideways to make room for her coach.

"We will comply with all NCAA rules on performance-enhancing-drugs. The University of Idaho has a compliance officer monitoring all its student athletes. We are confident that we are in total compliance with all regulations," Coach Brown said.

"Does that mean your athletes have school help in making sure all their blood tests will pass? The NCAA frowns on collusion on campus. I think the WADC would be interested in how amazing your athletes performed here tonight," The Omaha Beacon reporter pressed.

"What the World Anti-Doping Committee thinks is no concern to me. The NCAA sets its own standards and runs its own tests. We will pass any one they choose to administer."

The coach turned and gathered up her star player. Her action announced she was done with any interviews. Dewey and Anna Maria hugged their daughter as she headed to the locker room.

* * *

"Anna Maria, we need to head this potential problem off." Dewey said as they walked to their rental car.

"And that problem is?"

"Francine is going to be dogged by this accusation of performance-enhancing drugs. We need to be proactive. If she decides to compete in track and field, she'll run into WADC. From what I've been reading, their Director, Cubo Zoan, is after anyone out of the ordinary. And we know Francine is not ordinary," Dewey said.

"Then you need to do whatever it takes to protect our daughter," Anna Maria said.

They decided that tomorrow Dewey would be on a plane out of Omaha heading west. And Francine would have to leave the team for a couple of days in order to accompany him.

Chapter 14

Portland, Oregon

Like most college sports teams, the Idaho Vandal volleyball team was sponsored by a sports company. Zeus Sports supplied the Vandals with their uniforms, shoes, workout outfits and travel bags. As such, Coach Brown was in contact with the area rep for community relations.

Dewey asked the coach to make the phone call that would set up a meeting at Zeus Sports Headquarters. The coach made the call and excused Francine from practice for two days. Dewey and Francine were on the next available flight while Anna Maria headed back to Denver.

They were met at the Portland Airport by a company limo and whisked out to the corporate campus of Zeus Sports. Now they were standing in front of the owner and president of the company, Mr. Stanley Day.

"Mr. McDowell, I'm happy to meet you. And Francine, I've heard so much about your volleyball skills. I'm glad you're part of Zeus Sports." Stanley Day said.

"Mr. Day. We weren't expecting a meeting with you. We just wanted to meet one of your assistants to see if we could arrange a meeting with Neil Aldrin?" Dewey asked.

"He's over in the next building. Let's walk over there while my secretary calls and lets him know we're coming. What is it that you want to see Neil about?" Stanley asked.

"You mentioned that you've heard about Francine's exceptional skills at volleyball. Well, her skills cross over to just about any sport she chooses. Track and field is one of the sports she hopes to pursue, and I know Mr. Aldrin has firsthand experience dealing with WADC," Dewey said.

"Don't start up with me on those people. They're the bane of my existence right now. Every time we get a world-class athlete sponsored, they run afoul of Cubo Zoan and his cronies. You've come to the right place for help in dealing with his sort," the Zeus Sports owner aid.

"Thank you. We're already getting the accusations and we need to know how to proceed," Dewey said.

They reached Neil Aldrin's office at Zeus Sports. After his Tour de France wins, he was one of the world's most recognizable sports celebrities. With his fame and money, he had started a foundation to help disadvantage children around the world to obtain a bicycle. In most parts of the world, a bicycle was a great advantage to improving one's life.

Zeus Sports had added its prestige and money to Neil's efforts. After Neil's banishment from cycling on innuendo charges, Zeus Sports had continued its full support.

Stanley introduced the McDowells. "Mr. McDowell, I'd be glad to offer advice. But I'm not sure I'm an expert on staying on the good side of WADC. After all, I'm banished for life from cycling," Neil offered.

"But if you can give us any pointers, we'd be deeply grateful."

"I guess I can offer two. Have your own doctor ready whenever any blood is drawn. You need to take your own sample at the same time. It will keep the WADC labs honest when they know a twin sample is being tested independently," Neil said.

"And second?" Dewey asked.

"Avoid doing or saying anything near teammates or opponents that might be misconstrued as admitting to anything in a performance-enhancing way. I'll assume you're not doping, but that's not enough. Passing all the blood tests doesn't clear you anymore. I'm afraid it's come down to 'he said' statements that can get you. If someone makes an accusation and your talents are above the norm, you'll be suspect," Neil offered.

"So Francine, we haven't heard from you," Stanley said. "What sport goals do you have?"

"Mr. Day, besides playing college volleyball, my big goal is winning a Golden Slam," Francine said.

"Whew! You set your goals very high," Stanley said. "I like that. So you plan on winning all four tennis majors plus taking home an Olympic Gold Medal in tennis. And since this is an Olympic year coming up, do you plan on accomplishing that goal next year?"

"Yes," Francine answered. Dewey noticed the others in the room waiting for more. But a clear 'yes' was all they would receive.

"Spoken like a confident player. But can I ask, what tennis tournaments have you entered and what were the results?" Day asked "The reason I ask is Zeus Sports is always looking for the next player to sign. If you're as confident of accomplishing your goal as you appear, we need to sit down and discuss your future with Zeus Sports."

Dewey jumped in. "Thank you, Mr. Day. At present Francine wants to complete her college eligibility year playing a winter and spring sport. She'll need to maintain her amateur standing."

"Say no more," Stan said. "We never stand in the way of athletes attaining their dreams. But we would be glad to provide support in keeping with her amateur standing. Tennis gear, shoes and all the things allowed under NCAA rules. When you want to turn pro, I hope you'll remember us."

"Thank you, Mr. Day. I'll work with the University Compliance Officer to make sure I stay on the good side of the NCAA," Francine said. "And thanks, Mr. Aldrin. I know my dad appreciates the advice on dealing with WADC."

"Well, if we're done here, then I have a surprise for you Francine," Stanley said. "You probably know that Selena Roberts is one of our cherished athletes. She just so happens to be here on campus recuperating from her injury last season. Would you like to meet her?"

Would she? You won't have to ask twice, Dewey thought. Francine jumped at the chance to meet the number one tennis player in the world.

The president of Zeus Sports took them over to another building on the company campus. The building held four indoor tennis court, one being used when they walked in. Selena Roberts was hitting with her coach. Dewey and Francine sat down with Stanley and waited for the session to be over.

Soon, Selena wrapped up her workout and looked over. She waved at her visitors as she talked to her coach. Stanley explained that she was slowly returning to the level that had seen her win seven major tennis titles. Selena and her coach finally walked over to the seated visitors.

"Selena, you need to know that you have a competitor here. Francine has some very lofty goals where tennis is concerned," Stanley said.

Dewey looked over at his daughter and thought she was going to die from embarrassment on the spot. He knew that announcing Francine's goal of a Golden Slam in front of someone like Selena would be seen as pure bravado.

Francine had yet to play in a major tennis tournament, never mind win one. And here she was announcing that she would accomplish what only one player in tennis history had ever completed.

"Selena, you've won all the majors and an Olympic gold haven't you?" Stanley asked.

"Yes. But not in the same year. Only Steffi Graf accomplished a true Golden Slam, in 1988," Selena said.

Dewey noticed Selena staring at Francine, sizing her up. Selena seemed as though she was used to encountering braggadocios individuals. Tennis was one sport noted for the type. From her looks, she was giving Francine a close examination. "Francine, would you like to hit with my coach? I'd like to see what my competition has."

Francine begged off, but the owner of Zeus Sports would have none of it. Dewey decided to stay out of his daughter's dilemma. She would have to handle a lot more pressure than this to reach her goals.

"Here. You can use my racket. And I'm sure we could find some shoes around here that might fit you," Selena offered. She handed Francine her racket and took the vacated seat. Dewey sat frozen. He also needed to get used to these situations if Francine continued on her sports journey.

Selena's coach lobbed an easy ball toward Francine as they settled into their warmup routine. Finishing their warm-up, and approaching the net, Francine started to spin the racket when the coach told her to serve first.

They proceeded to play a pro set to eight points. Dewey noticed that his daughter was so nervous that her tennis game was less than spectacular. She choked on too many serves and hit too many balls out of bounds. He felt her frustration grow as Selena's coach looked less than impressed.

But Selena was polite the entire time. She finally offered Dewey some advice. "Mr. McDowell, if I might suggest? You live in Idaho, correct? I have an old friend that lives here in Oregon. She was on the WTP when I turned pro. We played tournaments for a couple of years at the same time before she retired. I'll call her and see if she is willing to take a look at Francine. If she sees something to work with, she could help immensely in seeing that Francine has the best chance at success."

"Thank you Ms. Roberts. I know Francine was very nervous today. Her game is usually much better."

"And my friend can work out all those nerves and see what Francine needs to work on," Selena said.

As the match wrapped up, the coach, Stanley and Selena took their leave and headed out. The limo was made available to take them back to the airport.

In the limo, Francine was beside herself. "I blew it Dad. I'm sorry. I don't know what came over me. I couldn't make a shot to save me."

"It's OK. That was a pretty big audience you had there. You need to work your way up to that level of scrutiny. All in due time, honey," Dewey said. The flight back to Moscow, Idaho was quiet as both McDowells contemplated the future. Dewey decided to keep Selena's offer to himself in case he never got a call.

* * *

Settled back in Moscow, Francine was soon back with her volleyball team preparing for their next conference matchup. Dewey didn't have long to wonder if he would receive a call.

Dewey's cell phone vibrated while he was sitting having coffee at a cafe in downtown Moscow. He picked up his cup and headed out onto the sidewalk to take the call.

"Morning, Dewey here."

"Good morning Mr. McDowell. Selena Roberts asked me to give you call. She mentioned that you have a daughter that has set her sights very high. My name is Camille Benjamin. How can I be of assistance?" the voice on the other end asked.

The name didn't ring any bells in Dewey's memory bank. *But if Selena Roberts thought this woman could help, who was he to second guess her?* Dewey thought.

"Thank you for calling, Ms. Benjamin. My daughter, Francine, has set her goals on playing tennis at the highest level. She needs help in reaching that dream," Dewey offered.

"I'd be happy to have a look. Are you going to be in the Portland area anytime soon? I could come and watch her play. I understand it's her volleyball season right now. We could set up a tennis hitting session with a local pro so Francine could show me her stuff," Camille said.

"Francine's volleyball team plays at Portland State next week. I'm sure she would love to meet you. And she can bring her tennis gear."

"Till next week then. I'll check the schedule and meet you at PSU," Camille said.

Francine was excited by the news that her dad had found someone to work with her on her tennis game. She had been hitting with the members of the University of Idaho Tennis Team. After the Women's Team, Francine had worked her way through the Men's Team. Both had offered only limited challenge for her. But the Women's Tennis Coach had become very interested in Francine joining the team after volleyball.

The two did their homework and searched the internet for information on Camille Benjamin. Francine emitted a low whistle as they read about her tennis career.

Camille had played in the World Tennis Association for thirteen years. She had compiled an overall record of 262 wins against 298 losses. Camille had been ranked number 27th in the world in 1984 and had advanced to the quarter finals of the French Open before losing to Chris Evert.

She even had a winning percentage at both Wimbledon and the French Open. If she was willing to work with Francine, Dewey knew she could get his daughter ready for the challenge ahead.

* * *

The Vandal Volleyball Team arrived at the Portland State University campus for their weekend matchup. As promised, Camille was waiting to meet the McDowells. After introductions, she took her seat with Dewey in the stands. She explained that she would be able to tell a lot by watching Francine's athletic ability during the match.

Camille had seen enough by the end of Idaho's victory. "Mr. McDowell, Francine has the most impressive athletic skills I've ever seen in an athlete. Has her reaction time ever been measured?"

"No. We've been so busy with college volleyball that everything else has been put aside. She has been hitting with the Idaho tennis team though," Dewey said.

"And what were the results? Let me guess. She's beat all the members of both the Women's and the Men's Teams. Correct?" Camille asked.

"In straight sets," Dewey added. "The tennis coach has talked to me numerous times."

"I'm quite sure he has. If she brings her quickness to her game like I've seen today, she is very formidable. And her hand-eye coordination is like no one I've ever seen. Has she always had this level of skill?" Camille asked. "I'm surprised that she hasn't been recognized before this. She should have been on the radar of every coach in the country. They don't miss talent like this very often."

What do I tell her? Dewey thought. He realized that Camille, like many people, had deduced that Francine was an instant phenomena. *Was she suspecting drug-induced cheating?* he thought.

"She can pass any drug test they want to administer, if that's what you're implying?" Dewey said. His defensive tone was a little too obvious.

"Mr. McDowell, I wasn't implying anything. If you say she is clean, than she is clean in my mind. But her sudden talents are sure to raise eyebrows in certain circles. If I take on Francine, we need to be ready to deal with the accusations. It can be very distracting."

"I'm sorry. I apologize," Dewey offered. "Yes, it's been brought up already. I try to steer Francine clear of the inquiries the press continues to pursue."

"Well, let's get her hitting tomorrow. But from what I've seen, I'd like to work with her, if she is interested?" Camille asked.

Francine didn't need to be asked twice. She and Camille worked out a schedule for when volleyball season finished. They had a lot of work to do in a short time to be ready.

The Vandals were almost through the regular season. They still carried only the one loss to Washington State. More importantly, they stood at the top of the standings in the WAC with a perfect season. The NCAA playoff committee would take note of that when the seedings were set.

Meanwhile, Francine had moved up to become the top offensive player in the country. She led all players in Division I in aces, hitting percentage and total number of kills. The inquiries into where and how Francine had developed such amazing skills only increased.

As the Vandals flew back to Moscow, Dewey and Francine stayed behind in Portland. They met up with Camille at the PSU indoor tennis courts. Camille had imposed on the tennis coach to use his facilities to evaluate Francine's skills. The coach had heard the buzz created by Francine on the volleyball court and was anxious to see her playing tennis.

Francine did not disappoint. Camille had made a call and had come up with the top men's player in the Pacific Northwest. While tennis in the region certainly did not match up with California or Florida, it would be sufficient for Camille to determine if Francine had what it would take to play the majors.

The first set had been close for a while. Francine was tired from her weekend of volleyball. But once she got warmed up, the match was quickly over. Her quickness overwhelmed her opponent

Francine's incredible hand-eye control worked her racket like a surgeon's knife as she devastated her opponent's return game. And her booming serves drove him back as one after another were never returned.

Standing on the sidelines, Dewey and Camille looked on.

"Have you ever checked the speed on her serve?" Camille asked. "I'm guessing she puts Andy Roddick in the slow lane."

"Again, just too busy to get to all those little things," Dewey replied.

Francine shook her opponent's hand at the net in the traditional end to their match. She joined Camille and her dad at the sidelines. The Portland State tennis coach walked over from where he and some of his players had been watching.

"That was one impressive showing I just witnessed. I was just wondering if you're planning on playing for Idaho this spring?" the coach asked.

"Thank you. I'm not sure yet. My Dad and I have yet to work out my schedule. Once volleyball finishes up, we have some decisions to make," Francine answered.

"Well, I'll look for you wherever your skills take you. And thank you for the chance to see you in person," the coach said. "I think the next time I see you will be on television."

They all thanked the coach for the use of the court. The three then headed to a quiet corner to discuss Francine's future.

"I would like to work with Francine. If your goal is to win one of the majors, we'll have a lot of work to do. When does volleyball end?" Camille asked. "And I guess more importantly, do you plan on staying in college? We really need to head to Florida or Texas to get your game polished. The Australian Open comes up in just two months."

"Volleyball ends the middle part of December if all goes well in the playoffs. And I plan on staying in school for the year. My dreams don't just include volleyball and tennis," Francine said,

"Oh. I see. That makes things very difficult then," Camille said.

Chapter 15

Chapel Hill, North Carolina

The Idaho Vandals had made their statement in the first two games of the NCAA East Regional. The NCAA volleyball selection committee had once again snubbed the lesser conferences when they set the seeding. Even though Idaho had climbed into the top ten in the Coaches Poll by the end of the season, the perennial strong teams from the PAC 12 had dominated the bracket.

Seven of the twelve teams in the PAC 12 had been selected to the NCAA playoffs. Idaho had been seeded rather low and had been forced to travel to the East Coast to play. But as Coach Brown had explained to the team, it really didn't matter. They would have to beat everyone to get to the Finals in Sacramento anyway.

And the team had responded. They handily beat, in straight sets, the number two seed, UCLA. That had raised some eyebrows around the NCAA. One PAC 12 team went home.

Reaching the Sweet Sixteen for the first time in school history, the Vandals then took out the host school, North Carolina. Even the home town crowd couldn't help their team overcome a Francine hitting clinic as the Vandals again dominated in straight sets.

But now Nebraska loomed as Idaho got ready for an Elite Eight showing. The Idaho team was certainly not used to such rarified air in the volleyball world. With the

PAC 12 still seeing four of its teams surviving, the little team form Moscow, Idaho was certainly being labeled the 'Cinderella' team of the playoffs.

But first Nebraska had to be dealt with. Francine was excited about a rematch with the team that had been so nasty to her. She still had the faint red marks from her scratches inflicted after their last encounter.

The first set went Idaho's way as the Vandals clicked into their strong play. Francine was the 'go to' player as she hit away at the Cornhusker defense. While the score was close a few times, Francine made sure that it didn't stay that way.

In the second set, Nebraska came out fired up. They had been to the playoffs numerous times and were confident that they could turn things around. With a nobody team like the Vandals across the net, Nebraska used as much intimidation as possible.

"So the midget player thinks she's up to carrying her sad sack team past us," the Middle Blocker said, the same one that had trash talked so much in Francine's first meeting.

"Yeah, remember pip squeak. Lose now and you go home. I hope you have a plane waiting to take you back to whatever hick town you guys come from," the Outside Hitter added.

Francine just stood across the net from the two mouthy players and stared straight ahead. She reached over and rubbed the red marks on her arm. They seemed to be on fire suddenly. The thoughts of these two players digging their finger nails into her flesh raced through her brain. Anger began to overwhelm Francine as the two players picked up their bad behavior where they had left off the last meeting.

"Look, our little friend is getting all red. Working too hard, munchkin?" the Middle taunted.

"Yeah, watch out for the Wicked Witch of the East. She eats munchkins for lunch," the Outside laughed.

Francine wondered why it was taking so long to get the serve going. She looked to her right and saw the Down Ref motion to his opposite that play could resume. *Good, time to shut these two up,* she thought.

It was Idaho's serve with the score tied at six apiece. The Idaho team had missed some serves to let Nebraska back into the game but had just got a sideout. Francine would soon correct the close score.

The whistle blew and Francine turned to wait for the serve to cross the net. Nebraska dug the floater serve and the setter put both hands up to set the ball. Francine fell back into her defensive position to receive the ball. But Nebraska went to the opposite side and hit down the line. Point Nebraska.

Coach Brown motioned Francine to back up from her front row position for serve receive. The Cornhusker player jumped and pounded a hard ball right to her. She absorbed the energy in her arms and passed a perfect ball toward the setter. Then she ran to get into position. *Set me please,* she thought.

Haley set a high wide ball just right for a big Francine hit. Francine readied herself for her approach so she could time it perfectly. Her arm was fully warm now at this point in the game. She wanted it at full power for what was coming.

The ball reached the top of its arc and settled into its downward drop. It was lined up to clear just inside the upright wand that marked the outside of play on the net. *Perfect,* Francine thought.

She ran her approach and leaped at the right time. In the corner of her eye she saw both opposing players react with her. As Francine climbed into the air, she kept her eye on the dropping ball. In her peripheral vision she watched as the two Cornhuskers rose up to challenge her, arms extended.

As the defensive players reached over the net in an attempt to block Francine's hit, Francine adjusted her body so she was now lined up perfectly on the two tall opposing players. The ball arrived and Francine whipped her arm forward from its position behind her head.

The blur of her arm as her flat hand smashed into the ball indicated the force transferred. The ball shot ahead toward the Outside Hitter. But instead of aiming for her outside arm in the last meeting, Francine directed this shot right toward the woman's face.

With her arms extended up and out, the players face was exposed right at the top of the net. The ball struck squarely on her nose with a sickening, crushing noise. The ball fell back onto Idaho's side of the net for a Nebraska point.

The Outside Hitter came down onto the hardwood holding her nose. Blood ran down through her fingers as she collapsed onto the court, screaming in pain. The Nebraska coach and trainer ran out onto the court as the ref stopped play.

An injury timeout was called and each team headed to the side lines as the Cornhusker was attended to. The Vandals huddled together.

"Jesus. What was that, Francine?" Whitney asked. As Libero, she had a clear view of the whole play. "Did you mishit that one?"

"Hey. You don't play middle. It's part of the game. I get head shots all the time," exclaimed Sara.

"Sorry. But you don't get them like that one, I bet," Whitney continued.

"No. I'm glad Francine is on our side of the net. Teaches them for trash talking her. You wouldn't believe what they say up there. You back row players have it easy," Anna added.

"Are those the girls that scratched you last time?" Haley asked.

Francine confirmed that these two had been the culprits. The team looked on as they stood the injured player up and walked her over to the bench. An ice pack was grabbed and placed on her face. The tournament support staff showed up with latex gloves on to clean up and sanitize the blood on the court.

"Want another set like that one, Francine?" Haley asked quietly. As setter, she chose where the ball went.

"Please. But make this one a number two."

"I understand. One number two coming up," Haley said.

The ref pointed his arm to indicate Nebraska's serve. A jump serve flew toward the Vandals. Whitney dug a good ball and sent it towards Haley. The setter moved to square up under the ball. Francine moved quickly to her spot and lined up for a number two set.

The Nebraska Middle Blocker watched Francine warily and adjusted her position. The replacement Outside Hitter moved in unison with the middle. They knew who was going to get the ball before the ball was even set.

Francine took off just as the setter released the ball. But instead of a high looping ball, this one was a 'quick set'. The object of a quick set was to barely lift the ball above the net so that the hitter could hit the ball. Without the high arc of a regular set, a quick set left little time for the defense to react.

Francine caught the ball almost immediately after it left Haley's hands. She swung but the ball caught the Middle Blockers arm and drove straight down into the court. Francine landed in frustration. Point Nebraska.

"Too bad scrimp. Can't hit through me, can you? Remember the second rule of volleyball, 'remember where the big girl is'. And I'm here to tell you, I am the big girl!" the middle screamed. "And guess what, you're not!"

At the group huddle between points, Francine looked at Haley. The noise from the screaming fans drowned out all verbal communications. Francine gave a thumbs up and then held up two fingers. She was calling for the same set position but a high ball this time.

Nebraska let go a floater that Whitney struggled to handle. The ball popped straight up and Haley ran to track down the wayward pass. As she ran through the ball, she passed it with her arms extended in front of her. The ball lifted up, but would fall way off the net.

Francine went up for a hit from the ten foot line, but the Cornhuskers read the play all the way. Three players jumped up in defense and Francine's hit was stuff block. Point Nebraska.

Coach Brown called a time out. Nebraska was purposely serving away from Francine. As one of the leaders on the NCAA in passing, Francine was certainly the one to avoid by opposing teams. The coach drew out a play and the Vandals all nodded in agreement.

Returning to the court, the Vandals all shifted position so that Francine was now back row center. In order to have an Outside Hitter move to back row center meant the entire lineup was severely skewed out of a traditional alignment. The Nebraska coach looked to her assistant to determine if the Vandals were about to be called for an 'out of rotation' violation.

Volleyball requires that each player maintain her original position in relation to her teammates until the ball was served. The same position relative to each other was locked in for the entire game as the team rotated on each team side-out. In order to not be called for an out of rotation violation, the Vandals had to make sure each player was set properly on serve receive.

Looking over at the Down Ref, the Nebraska coach started to complain. The Up Ref motioned to the Down Ref to check his card. The Down Ref studied the lineup card carefully and then compared the position of all the Vandal players. He nodded that Idaho was in compliance and pointed his arm at his counterpart.

The Nebraska coach went ballistic at the no call. The Up Ref waved her off and she sat down grumbling.

173

The Up Ref whistled for a serve and the Cornhusker looked at her coach for instructions. Holding up her clipboard, she made her choice known. The server walked up to the baseline and lofted a short serve, trying to keep it away from Francine.

But Francine's quickness easily compensated for the ball falling into the front court. Once she had passed the ball up to the setter, Francine raced back to the ten foot mark and readied herself. She watched as Haley easily stepped under the ball and jumped up to meet it.

The ball sprang high into the air with its trajectory aimed for a perfect number two. Francine waited and watched as the Cornhuskers brought all three front row players together to again stuff block her hit. *Not his time,* Francine thought.

As the ball floated down into hitting position, all four players left their feet. Francine didn't have to get much height for this one. *This ball will hit the back of the arena if no one is in the way,* Francine thought.

But there was a big Middle Blockers face in the way instead. Francine mustered the maximum speed out of her arm as she flattened the volleyball with her hand. The reaction sent a careening ball straight into the Middle's nose. Like the Outside before her, the breaking sound of cartilage was noticeable as the ball did its damage.

But unlike the last time, this ball bounced squarely back so hard that it cleared the Vandal baseline before hitting the court. And unlike the Outside Hitter's reaction, the Middle Blocker's head snapped straight back as her legs flew out forward.

Momentarily suspended in mid-air horizontally, the big six footer dropped like a sack of potatoes. The entire arena froze as the thud of an inert body hitting the floor echoed through the building. The quiet of the crowd was palpable as they all watched to see if the Middle would walk off the court after the hit.

Francine walked back to join the huddle as the refs called an injury timeout. The Nebraska coach was all over the Up Ref as her trainer worked on her injured player. Slowly, the Up Ref reached into his pocket and pulled out a yellow card. He held it aloft and aimed it at Francine.

Like soccer, a yellow card was an initial warning to a player. A second yellow card, or a red card, meant ejection from the game. In volleyball, a yellow card could be issued for unsportsmanlike conduct.

The Idaho coach leaped off the bench and immediately began to defend Francine. Asking what had been unsportsmanlike about Francine's hit, Coach Brown only received a slight glance of annoyance from the Up Ref. Idaho was finding out it didn't swing the kind of political weight that Nebraska did.

After her continued protest, the Up Ref again slowly retrieved the yellow card from his pocket and held it up. Aimed at Coach Brown, she now had her warning of ejection from the game if she continued.

The injured Middle Blocker was now moving her legs as she continued to lie on the court. A doctor had walked out on the court to offer aid, and with the trainer's help, stood the big Middle on her feet. But the Middle Blocker showed she had no idea where she was as the trainer escorted her to the bench.

175

After further examination, she was guided away toward the locker room. Again the support staff arrived to clean up the blood. Play was resumed after the court was sanitized.

"You're going to pay for that," the replacement Middle Blocker growled.

Francine stood in her outside position with her head down. She didn't have a quarrel with these other girls. They hadn't deliberately injured her.

The replacement Outside Hitter joined in. "That's right. Those are my friends you just hurt. Watch your backside."

"Look. I don't have any beef with you. Your teammates deserved what they just got. I just want to play volleyball now," Francine finally said.

"No way. It's payback time. What goes around, comes around, witch," the Middle extolled.

Francine lowered her head. *If that's the way you want it,* she thought. But she knew she had to be careful. One more card and she was done. And the Vandals chances of a National title would go with her.

She looked over at Coach Brown and received the message in her coach's expression. The Vandals needed to hold their emotions together and finish off the game. No room for any more vendettas today. Francine nodded her head to her coach in agreement.

Francine took over the game. She was first receive on all Nebraska serves and placed the ball perfectly each time for her setter. The set went back toward Francine.

Even knowing who and where the sets were going didn't allow Nebraska to get any stops. Francine hit from everywhere on the court. And with her ball-hitting power added to an extraordinary control, balls glanced off the blockers arms out of bounds each time.

As much trash talk as the front row players were throwing out, none of it affected the Vandals as they increased their lead. Coach Brown continued her protest, since the trash-talking Cornhuskers weren't even subtle about it anymore. The coach pointed out that she could easily hear it from the bench and that maybe someone on the Nebraska side should get carded for unsportsmanlike conduct.

The Up Ref ignored her protests. Even the TV announcers sitting at court side began making comments about the rude behavior of the Nebraska team. While the Cornhusker fans ignored their teams behavior, the Idaho fans joined in with most of the neutral fans in voicing their displeasure at the ref ignoring it all.

Finally, the Up Ref acted. But instead of carding one of the Nebraska players for unsportsmanlike conduct, a red card was pulled and aimed at Coach Brown. The Idaho coaching staff went off with the vast majority of the crowd watching. With only three points remaining to match point and Nebraska down by twelve, Coach Brown admonished her team to wrap it up as she walked off the court.

Francine took her coach's instructions and served three straight aces to win the game. Each one was a flat bullet that hit the tape perfectly and rolled down the net. When the Cornhuskers attempted to adjust, Francine just picked a different spot on the net to roll a ball down.

The traditional lineup to shake hands was broken. After their huddle, the Vandals decided to walk down the net but extended no hands. They even kept their distance from the net to avoid any retaliatory moves on Nebraska's part.

But the win put the Idaho team into the Final Four. They would be traveling to Sacramento for two more games. News soon reached them that the PAC 12 had placed three teams in the Final Four and that Idaho would be up against number two Washington.

Chapter 16

Sacramento, California

"Well, who would have believed it? Little no body Idaho up against mighty perennial number one Stanford. No one could have scripted a NCAA Final like this one if they'd wanted to," Hugh Godley informed his worldwide audience watching ZBC Sports Network.

"And if someone wrote a script like this, no one would believe it," Frank Buck added. "Stanford, six time NCAA Volleyball National Champions, is where it was expected to be. On its way to winning number seven. And who stands in their way?"

Hugh jumped right in. He was enjoying this. "A five-foot six-inch outside hitter from Idaho, thats who. Francine McDowell is the real deal. She crushed Idaho's opponents at Regionals in straight sets. Then she comes to Sacramento and hands number two Washington its head on a platter. No one has been able to even slow this woman down, never mind stop her."

He looked over to see his announcing partner fidget. Frank had discounted the ability of the star Vandal when they had first seen her. Now the proof of her abilities was plainly before them. And Hugh was going to remind his partner every chance he could. It certainly made good ratings even if Frank looked perturbed by the abuse.

"Maybe so, Hugh. But don't forget, this is Stanford. They don't have a player under six feet. They never drop below six foot four on their front line. That's a lot of height to hit over for anyone. For a five-footer, it just might be impossible," Frank rejoined.

"Washington brought as much height to their match and they didn't win a set. That little five-footer you disdain seems to have magic eyes connected to her big arm swing. It is nothing short of amazing her ability to hit balls off the blocks. They could put the USA Men's Team out there with their seven footers and I'd bet on number six hitting off the blocks," Hugh said.

"And we seem to have some bad blood between these two teams already. Or at least between one of the Stanford players and your vaulted number six. After the turmoil Idaho had with Nebraska at Regionals, the Middle Blocker that got her nose broken along with a concussion is a sister to Stanford's starting Middle Blocker. News reports have been very graphic in describing what revenge the Stanford player is ready to extract from Ms. McDowell," Frank said. Hugh noticed a certain glee in his expression. This was getting personal all around.

"My friend, we are about to find out. The introductions are complete, the national anthem sung and we are about to determine the best volleyball team in America. Hold on to your hats ladies and gentlemen," Hugh added.

* * *

On the court, Francine lined up on the baseline with her teammates. They had all been in awe at the opening ceremony leading up to the night's game. As each player was introduced, the crowd's response was typical, until Francine's introduction. Upon the announcement of Number Six, Francine McDowell, the Idaho crowd roared its approval. Equally loud was the Stanford crowd and their boos.

Even the neutral fans from across the country seemed to pick sides in the Francine opinion poll. Francine ignored it all, took a half step forward and waved to the crowd. She stepped back into line and waited. Her thoughts were elsewhere than the ad hoc popularity contest being conducted.

Coach Brown had worked hard to get her players to come to the game like any other. *Yeah right,* Francine thought. *This was for the national title. Number one baby. This was as big as it got.* The Vandals ignored the coach and came out with the whole 'National Championship on the line' mindset. They proceeded to lose badly in the first set. And Francine had the worst game of her short volleyball college career.

During the court change over, Coach Brown rallied her team.

"Ok, that was bad. Now just forget it. It never happened. This is the start of the game, right now."

But the second set was almost as bad as the first. Again, Francine was totally off on her timing and hit ball after ball out of bounds. Stanford took the second set and both teams headed for the locker room.

Francine tagged along behind her team, head down. The Stanford fans were unmerciful in their taunts as they passed into the tunnel. As they reached the concourse on the way to the locker room, Francine suddenly felt a hand grab her arm.

Fearing a hostile fan, she quickly withdrew and looked up. Security personnel were right there to protect the players, but Francine recognized this fan.

"Camille, what are you doing here?" Francine shouted. Coach Brown looked back at her star player and waited to make sure Francine was OK. Francine waved her coach off. Camille leaned over and whispered in Francine's ear. The two stood, embraced for a couple of minutes while Camille quietly spoke. Letting her catch up with her team, Camille headed back to her seat.

"Are you OK? Who was that?" Coach Brown asked.

"A friend," was all Francine offered. Then added, "I'm OK now. Let's go back out there and get the job done."

Coach Brown kept her halftime talk short. The team gathered themselves in a huddle in the locked room and started their chant. "Woof, Woof, Woof."

As the Vandal team readied themselves in the concourse tunnel to return to the court the chant spread. "Woof! Woof! Woof!" the Idaho fans yelled.

The fans were doing their utmost to inspire the team to recover. The noise grew. Many of the uncommitted fans from other schools joined in. Stanford was the certain favorite, but now down two games to none, Idaho was getting the underdog support that had carried it through so many tough matches.

The Vandal team all looked up from their spot in the tunnel. Haley, as team captain, motioned for the players to follow as they ran out of the tunnel onto the court. Gathering as a team in the center of the court, they joined in with their fans.

"Woof! Woof! Woof!" the team yelled.

The crowd was in a frenzy. "Woof! Woof! Woof!" blasted out. The Stanford players stood by the bench in bewilderment at the support being shown their opponents. The Stanford fans were overwhelmed as their cheers were drowned out.

The Arena had decidedly swung over to a partisan Idaho crowd. The building rocked as the refs lined up the teams for the initial rotation check. The game balls were tossed out and Idaho stepped back to serve.

Francine knew that this first one had better be good. She walked back from the baseline and turned to face the Up Ref. He whistled and swung his arm, indicating permission to serve. Francine took a deep breath. The crowd continued its chant. "Woof! Woof! Woof!"

Tossing the ball high, Francine put as much spin on it as humanly possible. With her enhanced reactions, the spin was impressive. She ran and timed the descent of the ball perfectly. The ball left her outstretched hand as if shot from a cannon.

Just clearing the net, the spin took over. The wind over the ball caught up with the forward motion just as it crossed mid-court. The laws of physics for friction, kinetic energy, and gravity all kicked in together. The ball dropped like a rock, landing at the feet of the Stanford defender.

The deafening noise got louder. "Woof! Woof! Woof!"

Again, Francine lined up her serve. Another jump serve with extreme top spin dropped harmlessly onto Stanford's side of the court. The noise grew.

The Stanford defense adjusted to her dropping balls as Francine did her jump float serve. She watched as the ball wobbled side to side toward the Cardinals. A glancing arm sent the ball into the stands. The crowd roared its approval. Francine continued to mix up her serves. Like a good Major League Baseball pitcher, Francine switched serves as she watched Stanford try to adjust its defensive sets. It was soon eight to nothing when the Stanford Coach finally called a time-out.

Timeouts typically stop a hot server. The break in play put more pressure on the server. The result was usually a missed serve at resumption of play. But Francine came out laser focused and drilled another ace.

Four more serves and finally Francine hit the top of the net. The ball fell onto the Vandal court. The crowd finally settled down into a routine roar for the rest of the game. The game went back and forth, but the lead that Francine had given the Vandals held throughout. Stanford could never close the gap. Idaho took game three.

Game four started the same way. Stanford's serve was broken on the first point and Francine went to work. She again gave her team an insurmountable lead. Stanford worked incredibly hard and closed the lead slightly. But they ran out of time.

The match was now tied, two games apiece. A fifth set tie-breaker would determine the National Champion. Stanford won the coin toss and chose to serve first. Idaho selected its side of the net.

The two teams faced off. The sister of the Nebraska Middle Blocker had been noticeably quiet up until now. But when the rotation worked Francine onto the front row, she was ready.

"You hurt my sister bad. Her concussion will keep her out of volleyball for an entire year. You don't deserve to wear a team uniform. And I'm the one that will knock you and your cheating ways out of the game for good," she spewed across the net.

Francine wasn't about to back down now. There was too much at stake. "Be careful what you wish for. Things have a habit of coming back to bite you in the ass," she threw back.

She received a glare in return. The Stanford player was noticeably hostile and added a few choice comments under her breath.

Stanford was serving. Francine backed up into the convoluted rotation that placed her on the back row center for serve receive. As the ball was served, the Down Ref whistled and indicted a point for Stanford. Out of rotation was called on Idaho

Coach Brown leapt at the Down Ref demanding to know who was out of rotation. The Down Ref indicated that Idaho should return to their previous set. He pulled his card to check the rotation. Coach Brown was pointing to each player and why this defensive set was legal.

The Down Ref finally walked over to the Up Ref. Bending down from his perch above the net, the two refs conferred on the last call. Finally, the Up Ref stood up and raised two thumbs. Stanford lost one point and the play would be replayed.

The Stanford coach jumped up and began his argument over the reversal of the previous call. He started pointing at the position of the Vandal players attempting to influence the ref's decision. The Up Ref waved him off. The Down Ref explained why Idaho wasn't out of rotation with an Outside Hitter playing middle back.

Play resumed. Being on the back row to receive the ball, Francine didn't have to hear the venom emitting from the Stanford player. But as soon as she made her pass and ran to the front court, she heard the voice. It was going constantly as she waited for the ball to be set her way.

Haley punched the ball toward the outside. Francine readied herself to start her approach. The big Stanford Middle and Outside moved in anticipation of the hit.

As Francine began her run, the Stanford players held their spot. They would wait to time their leap perfectly so they would reach their maximum height just as Francine hit the ball. With their big arms extended over the net, it was like trying to hit through a roof over the hitter.

But Francine had seen this all year. Her skill was in hitting a ball just right so it hit the outside arm of the Outside Hitter and have it bounce out of bounds. She jumped and wound up to provide her signature smash to the play.

As she hung in space waiting for the perfect spot to hit the descending ball, she noticed out of the corner of her eye that her antagonistic Middle Blocker hadn't fully jumped. In fact, it looked like she hadn't jumped at all. She was just sticking her hands straight up as she stood flat footed.

This would be an easy kill. Just hit off the up raised hands of the big middle and the ball would fly backwards over the Vandal baseline.

Francine wound up in that split second observation and then noticed movement below her out of her extreme peripheral vision. She glanced down to see a big right foot of the Middle Blocker extended over the center line. The slight look down caused her to miss a good connection on the ball as it sailed past the two women blocking and landed out of bounds. Point Stanford.

On the way down, Francine had to contend with an intrusion on her side of the court. She tried to move her feet to land on the court but was only partially successful. Her right foot caught the outside of the Stanford player's foot. Francine landed in a heap, clutching her ankle.

The Down Ref blew his whistle and called the Stanford player for encroachment. The point was taken from Stanford and awarded to Idaho. But the damage was done. Francine gripped her ankle as she rolled on the court in pain.

Coach Brown and the trainer raced to their star player. They checked her ankle as the refs called an injury time out. Helping Francine off the court, the Idaho coach had to substitute a player for her now hurt player. Play was resumed.

The trainer took off Francine's ankle brace and manipulated her joint. Tears flowed as the pain pounded through Francine.

"Tape me up," Francine barked.

The trainer looked at the coach. Coach Brown barked, "Tape her up."

Stanford was rolling now and the score steadily increased while Francine sat on the bench. The trainer feverishly but carefully applied tape to Francine's injured ankle. He made it as tight as possible without cutting off the blood flow. The ankle brace was retrieved and Francine strapped it up.

Sprinting for the side line, Coach Brown quickly called time out to get her star back into the match. Stanford had moved to within three points of clinching another National Championship.

The team stood on the sidelines while Francine walked back and forth getting her ankle to respond. The coach laid out the play she wanted to stop the Stanford run. The team all came together. The crowd sensed the dire position Idaho was in and began the chant. "Woof! Woof! Woof!"

The Vandals moved to their huddle and joined in. Francine was noticeably favoring her right ankle as they hopped and yelled, trying to get the fortitude to finish off Stanford.

Walking up to the net, Francine noticed that her attacker had rotated over to the opposite position from her. Standing beside Haley, Francine leaned over and whispered to her setter a quick instruction. Haley nodded in agreement.

Stanford served a floater that Whitney handled perfectly. Haley moved to get under the pass as Francine sprinted across the net to take up her position on the outside. She thought she heard some threats as she passed the Middle Blocker.

Each player was moving from their required position for the serve to their normal position for play. Francine looked up and saw the ball hurtling to the outside. She glanced and saw the Stanford Middle moving over to join the outside to form a double block in front of her.

Francine waited with one eye on her attacker. The ball began its downward flight and Francine started her approach. The two defensive players both crouched down in preparation of their jump.

The ball hit the perfect spot and Francine was there to meet it. But again, out of the corner of her eye, she saw the Middle standing flat-footed.

Smashing the ball off the Outside Hitter, the ball flew out of bounds. Francine now looked quickly down and saw the big foot of the Middle Blocker again crossing the center line. She was waiting to finish off the ankle that she had injured previously.

But she hadn't figured on Francine and her enhanced reaction skills. Francine adjusted in the air for the encroached foot plainly across the center line.

Landing on either side of the Stanford Middle's foot, Francine snapped her legs tight against her opponent's leg, locking it in place. With both her knees almost behind the Stanford players calves, the encroaching player struggled to remove her foot.

Francine looked over at the Down Ref and pointed to her opponent's large leg on her side of the court. The ref blew his whistle and swung his arm under the net, indicating encroachment on Stanford's part. Point to Idaho.

The Stanford Middle Blocker now struggled to retrieve her leg from a firmly held Francine. One large pull and her leg broke free, throwing Francine to the court. Using her best imitation of a fawning Italian soccer player attempting to draw a penalty, Francine rolled on the court and grabbed her injured ankle. She let out a scream of pain for affect and looked at the Up Ref.

Not receiving the desired result, she added to the drama by rolling around with added sound effects. Coach Brown leaped to Francine's cause and admonished the Up Ref on the repeat play that attempted to injure her star player.

A red card finally came out, aimed at the Stanford middle. She began to complain vehemently but the Stanford coach cut her off. The player quickly left the court, headed to the locker room. After a quick trip to the bench, Francine was back in the game on the next play

The Stanford coach did argue the encroachment call feeling that Francine's feet had landed on Stanford's side of the center line. This would require a 'do over' call with no point awarded. He continued to plead his case as the Down Ref stared straight ahead.

Finally, the ref had had enough. He turned very slowly and said, "Teach your players to keep their body parts on their side of the net. You know the risk when players cross the line. Now sit down."

The Stanford Coach looked to the Up Ref for relief but saw his hand heading to his pocket. A move that threatened a yellow card. Or a red card.

The rotation that brought Francine back into the game put her on the baseline to serve. She tested her ankle and decided that jump serving would be difficult. She walked up and stood on the base line.

Idaho was still behind by six points. She needed nine points to finish the game. With her jumping ability now limited, half her serving options had just been eliminated. She would have to rely on her old standby.

The Up Ref indicated for her to serve. She focused like she had never done before. The arena disappeared along with the crowd noise. The world went very small as her eyes focused. Only the ball, her hand and the net stood out.

She gently tossed the ball straight up and reached back with her arm. Snapping forward, her hand struck the ball flat handed. A float serve of incredible oscillation flew forward. The Stanford Libero quickly shifted to take the ball only to misjudge the play. The ball flew off her arm and out of bounds. Eight points to go.

Again Francine checked Stanford's defense. They had shifted slightly. The ball went up, but this time Francine aimed the ball at the tape on top of the net. The ball hit the tape, hung there motionless for a second and then rolled down on Stanford side. Seven points to go.

Francine went back to the floater for the next three. All were mishandled for three more aces. Four points to go.

The net shot was next. With the rule change in volleyball that allowed the ball to hit the net on a serve, everyone commented that to perfect such a serve would make someone unstoppable. Francine had come the closest to mastering the net shot. Although risky in the extreme, Francine had the hand-eye coordination to consistently pull it off. One more net shot tied the game up.

With three points to go to win the game, Francine pushed the pain in her ankle aside. Everything was on the line.

Stanford was now positioning their front row players strategically along the net. It was the best option to try and handle a net shot. The back row players were reaching down and pounding the court trying to energize themselves for serve receive. The Stanford Coach continued to spew invective at the officials.

The ball went up. This time Francine stood flat-footed but spun the ball for a drop serve. The ball flew toward the defenders and dropped as it crossed the net. But without the jump adding the additional height, the back row easily handled the serve.

Francine and the Vandals moved to their defense, Stanford to offense to finish the point. Finally getting a serve they could handle, the setter pitched the ball to the outside. The Outside Hitter flew through the air and smashed the ball down the line.

The Idaho blockers missed the ball completely. Stanford knew that their best Outside Hitter would crush the ball into the floor. A ball hit down the line offered very little reaction time to the defender. Unlike a cross-court hit that allowed a split second more time to react, a down-the-line kill was like money in the bank.

But the teller at this bank was above average in her reaction. There would be no withdrawal from any account as long as Francine had one good ankle. She popped up a high ball that was going to be out of bounds. But not so far out that the setter couldn't move under it.

Haley ran past the out of bounds line toward the bench. The reserve players and coaches all scattered backwards taking their chairs with them. With the space clear, Haley set the ball over her head toward the ten foot line.

Francine saw her opportunity and she ran for her spot. The pain in her right ankle screamed as she moved. Leaping, she saw the three Stanford players all jump at once to defend the back row attack they saw coming.

Hanging and waiting for the ball. Francine swung her arm and stopped just as the ball touched her hand. She gently touched the ball and dinked the ball over the extended defender's arms and watched the ball slowly float into the open space behind the blockers.

As Francine landed on her good foot, she witnessed the futile slide of the back row players as they dove for the ball. Two points to go and Stanford called time out.

"Sorry, Coach. I won't do that serve again." Francine said in the huddle.

"You're doing fine, Francine, just remember," Coach Brown held her hands up beside her eyes and extended her two index figures. Her symbol for 'focus'. "And team, back up your server. Great job on that last play. We're in it to win it."

"Woof! Woof! Woof!" the team all yelled. The team forwent the traditional hop and spin move. They hopped in place so Francine could sort of stand in one spot and bounce on one leg.

The crowd all joined in the "Woof! Woof! Woof!"

Taking the ball from the Corner Ref, Francine lined up for her serve. Again, standing still on the baseline, she tossed the ball up. She hit the ball with a hand that actually hurt from being straightened so much. The straighter a hand is, the less movement the ball receives.

A ball leaving a flat-hand hit with no movement generates its own movement from the air currents fighting to control its flight. And this floater was at the top of the movement scale. Seen from the baseline, it would appear to move on two broken wheels as it flopped back and forth.

The Stanford Libero was ready. She waited and watched as the wobbling ball came right at her. She shifted her platform slightly and reached out with her arms. Just as the ball was about to make solid contact, it shifted three inches. The ball ricocheted off her left arm and went out of bounds. Game point.

One point, Francine thought. The Idaho fans were yelling. The Stanford fans were yelling. Francine again blanked out all of it. One more good serve and it would be over.

Focusing on the ball in her hands, she decided what serve she would do. She checked the Stanford defense. *Should work,* she thought. If it didn't, the ball would definitely sail out of bounds.

She took the ball and tossed it high into the air. She studied the ball as it went up. No spin was good. As she jumped she hit the ball flat-handed and at the angle she figured would work.

The ball flew forward and just clipped the top of the net. But instead of stalling and falling straight down, this serve slowed slightly, but carried on toward the back court. But the slight bounce off the tape of the net had added spin to the ball. The defense readied for an easy ball. But this ball suddenly took on a downward spin as air currents mixed with the air dynamics induced a now top-spinning ball to succumb to gravity.

Again, the ball beat the diving Stanford players to the floor. Game over. The Vandals all piled onto Francine in celebration of winning the National Championship.

Once they had all extracted themselves, the Idaho and Stanford teams both lined up to do the traditional hand-shake. Two of Francine's big players, Anna and Sara, lined up on either side of Francine as support if there was trouble. But the Stanford players all went through the line congratulating the Idaho players in a show of sportsmanship. Both teams lined up as they received their trophies and individual awards.

As the crowd all gathered around, many of the Stanford players came over to offer congratulations to Francine for being named MVP of the playoffs. Some even commented that their Middle Blocker was wrong in what she had attempted to do to Francine.

While Francine was getting hugs from Dewey and Anna Maria, the Stanford coach approached the trio.

"Excuse me, I just wanted to offer my congratulations. That was one heck of a display of volleyball skills out there. And I want you to know, if I'd have had any inkling of what my player was up to, she would have been benched for the duration. That's not volleyball," he said. "And since you're a Freshman, I'll be looking forward to seeing you again."

"Thank you," Francine said. She knew it had taken a lot for him to come over.

A now familiar voice behind her asked, "How's the ankle feeling?"

"Camille, I'm afraid to unwrap it," Francine responded.

"Well, the Australian Open is a little over a month off. We need to get you checked out and hopefully into physical therapy right now. We don't have much time to get a major injury healed up, I'm afraid," Camille said.

The concerned look on her parents faces confirmed the threat that was looming over Francine completing her dream. *Will I be ready?* Francine wondered.

Chapter 17

Evergreen, Colorado

The two weeks following the University of Idaho's winning the NCAA Volleyball National Championship was hectic for Francine. Arriving back in Moscow, Idaho, the team experienced a campus-wide celebration for the unlikely celebrities.

Francine had begun physical therapy immediately on her injured ankle. Her sudden fame in the small community of Moscow overwhelmed her and her dad. Camille Benjamin, now committed to helping Francine get ready to accomplish her next dream, arrived soon after. Coach Brown offered Camille a room in her house for the short time before Christmas break.

Camille would join Francine and Dewey on their daily trip to the PT. That was followed by daily medical treatment to hasten the healing in her right ankle. Francine worked on conditioning doing water aerobics and keeping weight off her ankle.

After two weeks of therapy, the physical therapist announced, "I've never seen anything like this. Your ankle has regained almost a full range of motion from where you were when you first started. I've never seen anyone heal this fast."

Dewey and Francine didn't offer any comment. After they finished up, Camille suggested they all go for coffee before starting their prescribed stretching session.

Over coffee, Camille finally asked. "I need to know what's going on here."

"What do you mean?" Dewey shot back.

"We can't ignore the performance-enhancing drug controversy that has swirled ever since Idaho won its Championship. I've taken your word on that since we first met," Camille inquired. "But now this miracle cure. What should have taken at least six weeks is now healing in half the time."

"Francine passed the NCAA blood test. Just like we promised," Dewey answered.

"But you had your own doctor at the blood draw. I'm sure Dr. Turpin just happened to be in Sacramento from his practice in Denver to observe Francine's blood draw," Camille said. "And I'm sure he just happened to have his own syringe and shipping container for an independent blood sample."

"You're right. We need to explain," Dewey offered. "The doctor was there as a check against any bad sample or false positive that the NCAA's lab might generate. That was all at the suggestion of Neil Aldrin after his run-in with the WADC."

"Alright, I buy that," Camille said. "It's a good idea to protect yourself from political sabotaging by double sampling. But this healing thing, it's related to the performance thing, isn't it?"

"We don't know, but it appears so," Francine finally answered. Then she started to cry. The crying became uncontrollable sobbing.

With the coffee shop full of customers, the three left and found a more private setting. Francine finally gained some composure and admitted, "My body is out of control sometimes. And it affects my thoughts. I should be dead, and I can't get that out of my mind." Francine again broke down.

"What, how should you be dead?" Camille asked.

Dewey waited for his daughter to answer, but her crying overwhelmed her. He finally offered, "We can't tell you the whole story. The Australian doctor who treated Francine has explained to us the danger in her story ever getting out. He and the Australian government demanded signed non-disclosure letters from everyone involved in Francine's case. Even the diving guide had to sign off."

"Diving guide? Non-disclosure? What are you talking about?" Camille demanded.

"And I hurt those two girls so bad. That's not me. I love volleyball. I don't play like that. What's wrong with me?" Francine blurted out. It was the first that Dewey had heard that Francine's psychological make-up might be being affected by her Australian event.

"Slow down, honey," Dewey said. "We've reviewed the tape over and over. The whole world has reviewed the tape. Those hits on the Nebraska blockers were totally legit. It's just you hit so hard."

"But I could have hit it anywhere I chose," Francine said. "But I chose to smash their faces. What's wrong with me?"

Both Dewey and Camille sat silent. Neither had an immediate answer. Finally Camille offered, "Francine. Before you came to see me, I was working in Sports Psychology. I helped athletes work out things in their head that might affect their performance. Maybe I could help you understand these things better."

"Yes, I'd like that."

"But we need to go back to our original question. And I guess it starts in Australia?" Camille asked.

Dewey began to tell her about the accident at Coral Bay. He continued with the story of Francine's rescue and transport to Perth along with her treatment in the hospital. But he left out what had originally caused the emergency.

"You can't tell me what happened?" Camille inquired.

"Not the specific details. We refer to it as the 'stite'. That would be a combination for sting and bite, hence 'stite'," Dewey finally admitted.

"And you can't say the kind of sting or bite?" Camille asked.

"No. When Francine luckily survived what should have been a 100% fatal event and when her enhanced muscular response, nerve synapses, and eye control became evident, the Australian government stepped in. They did not want the actual events broadcast, knowing that others would try to replicate the 'stite' in order to gain the physical skills Francine has."

"Wow. That certainly would be the case. People would risk their lives in order to have such dominant athletic abilities. And, you're right, I don't want to know the details. Its much too dangerous," Camille said. "And you're absolutely sure your secret is safe?"

"The Australians were so nervous about it that Francine's doctor lobbied the government. The Prime Minister put a rider on a bill that now makes it a Federal crime in Australia to even talk about Francine's case. Sort of 'Hippa' on steroids," Dewey offered, mentioning the United States law protecting patient confidentiality.

"And did they offer how long the effect would last and what the side effects would be?"

"No idea. No one has ever survived either the bite or the sting. And certainly no one has ever gotten both at the same time. We are in uncharted territory," Dewey answered. As Francine recovered from her crying, Dewey continued to hold her tight.

Camille dropped her bad news, "We have a problem on top of everything else. I was anticipating getting Francine into a qualifying tournament before the Australian Open since I assumed she hasn't been in any qualifiers before her incident. Your ankle injury killed that idea."

"Are you saying we won't be able to qualify for Melbourne?" Francine asked.

"They only have so many slots, so you have to prove yourself beforehand to be invited. Unless we can come up with some way to get you qualified in the next couple of weeks, we won't get one of the slots," Camille said.

"I was in the Perth Open right after my accident. That's where we sort of discovered what gifts I'd suddenly been blessed with," Francine said.

"Perth Open? I don't recall that tournament as a qualifier? But I can check," Camille said.

"Let me make a phone call, too. I made friends with the Director of the Perth Tennis Club when Francine won there. Maybe he has a suggestion," Dewey said.

* * *

Two days later they had their answer. Camille had discovered that the Perth Open did not qualify Francine for the Australian Open. But Dewey had better news.

Informed that under a very obscure rule in the Australian Open governing by-laws, each Australian State could enter one participant. The rule had been included right after the Open's founding in 1905 to try and involve the entire country.

The rule had been used less than ten times since its inception. Considering Francine's local fame, the Tennis Club Director stated that he would see what he could do, but warned that the ten times previous the rule had been used were for Australian players. The rule had never been used before for a foreign player.

Waiting on news about the Australian Open, they had a stop to make. Francine's sports dream had another component.

Arriving home to Colorado for Christmas Break, Francine and Dewey had an appointment to keep. Loading up the car, the two headed to Colorado Springs, Colorado, home of the USA Olympic Training Center and an appointment to meet with the Head Coach of the US Women's Volleyball Team.

The Women's Olympic Development Team was working out under the watchful eye of the coaching staff as Dewey and Francine entered the gym. The team had won a Silver Medal at the last Olympics, and a new coach was determined to improve America's chances at winning

Gold. Dewey and Francine stood and watched from the sidelines as drill after drill were completed.

The Head Coach blew his whistle and called his players over. "Alright, I want to finish this session with some three-on-three play. Coach will toss the ball in. Loser steps out. I've got a meeting but I'll be right over here watching. I want aggressive play."

He left the team with the assistant coach and greeted Francine. He shook Dewey's hand and offered them a seat in the stands.

"I want to say up front that this is unusual. And I only met you out of respect for what Francine accomplished at the NCAA. What can I do for you?"

"I came here to see if I can be part of USA Volleyball," Francine said. "I know that with the Olympics just eight months off, you are working hard with your players to have them ready. I was hoping that you could give me an opportunity to play for my country. It's a dream I've had since I was little."

"I can understand your dream of playing for the United States," the coach said. "Every woman that's here has expressed that same dream. If they don't, they're history around here. But out of a country of over three hundred million, I have to select twelve to represent the rest. All these women have worked years to be here."

"I'll work just as hard, Coach. And I think my skill set can contribute to this team competing with anyone in the world," Francine offered.

"I won't take anything away from you. You proved you have the skills to get it done. But our process is a methodical one. We select players to be on our development team. No one knows ahead of time who'll be selected to make the Olympic Team. We have women that will work hard and not get to go. And they've been here, some for years. This will be the third Olympics for some. That's at least twelve years they've been with us."

"If you'd like a tryout, Francine would be glad to workout with any of them," Dewey tried to help.

"That's just not how we do things. We have a system. You were successful at the college level this year, but like I said, some of these women have been successful for years. Maybe the next Olympics we can give you a look. You'll be just finishing up your college play then. That might be the best time," the coach said. He stood up and yelled at his players to work harder. Dewey knew the meeting was over.

"Coach, thank you for your time," Dewey said. "Francine has a fire that is driving her. I guess we'll just have to see what other options there are."

The head coach looked at him quizzically. Then he took his leave and returned to his team. Dewey looked down at a dejected daughter who was watching part of her dream evaporate. *Yes, I will have to see about other options*, he thought.

Chapter 18

Melbourne, Australia

Francine, Dewey and Camille boarded the Virgin Australia flight from Los Angeles to Melbourne without certain knowledge if they would compete in the Australian Open They would arrive in Australia not knowing Francine's disposition.

The flight had been smooth but long. For seventeen long hours, the packed Boeing 787 droned southwest. Luckily, Anna Maria had used her Alitalia connections to secure three first class 'seats' for her travelers.

In recognition of Francine's athletic abilities and also to keep their star athlete happy, the University of Idaho had accommodated Francine's trip during classes. Now officially part of the University Indoor Track Team, the Track Coach had arranged classes for Francine and she had been given her school work. Francine worked hard during the long flight on her studies.

The reclining lounge chairs in individual cubicles made the flight luxurious compared to the cramped cattle car seats in the back of the plane. All three passengers were refreshed as they stepped off the plane.

Emerging from Customs, they were met by Edward Bourton, Director of the Royal Perth Tennis Club. After introductions, the four climbed into the shuttle van for the trip to the tournament hotel.

"I don't have good news for you. But I don't have bad news either. The Open Committee is still reviewing our request," Mr. Bourton said.

"I can't thank you enough for your effort on Francine's behalf, Mr. Bourton," Dewey offered.

"Edward please. Since we're all in this together, we can drop the formalities," Edward said. "And I think Francine's case has merit. She is still quite a celebrity here in Australia. It should help her request."

"Is the nature of her accident discussed here?" Camille asked.

"On no," Edward said. "The lid has been clamped down tight on that. Luckily, Dr. Coleman of Perth's King's Hospital put the word out as soon as he knew what had happened and the effect it had on Francine. Don't need any stunned mullet types attempting their own experiments in athletic enhancement. Bad for tourism if too many blokes drop over crook."

Two days later, the McDowell party was called before the Open Committee. They learned that the committee had accepted the Perth Tennis Club request on condition that Francine would have to play a 'pig tail' match the night before the official tournament opened. Her opponent would be another young player who had just qualified. The winner would have to meet the number one player in the world, Svetlana Trenschenko.

Svetlana had taken over the number one spot at the end of last season when Selena Roberts had missed the US Open due to injuries. If Francine won her qualifying match, the competition level would immediately increase.

* * *

"Ladies and gentlemen, Hugh Godley, here at the Australian Open. With me is my old friend, Jack Hawkins, who will be offering his unique observations today. Also joining us is our resident tennis expert Karl Mahr. Well Karl, we certainly have a final like no other in history."

"Who would have believed it?" Karl said. "Even Hollywood couldn't make this stuff up. We might have expected Dominique Richard of France to be here. She took out a still-recovering Selena Roberts in a grueling three-set classic. Although Selena didn't look like she was fully recovered, Dominique certainly raised her play."

Jack Hawkins couldn't resist and jumped in on Karl. "But what an opponent we have for Dominique. A total unknown. It took an obscure hundred-year-old rule filed by the Perth Tennis Club to even get her into the Open. After drumming her opponent in the qualifier, she took the number one player in the world and gave her a lesson. Beating her in straight sets, Francine McDowell preceded to hammer her side of the bracket, never dropping a set. Simply amazing. And on top of that, now we understand that Ms. McDowell will be representing Italy here at this tournament. "

"I agree. This is the same Francine McDowell that we witnessed a little over a month ago win an American national collegiate title in volleyball. I was lucky enough to see her dominance in that event, and now we'll see how she handles the rarified air of one of tennis's biggest events," Hugh said. "Karl, does she have the experience and skill to complete what will be one of the most amazing sports stories of all time?"

"We're about to find out. They've completed their warm-ups. We're set to play," Karl said.

"We'll take a commercial break and when we come back, it will be the world's number four player up against the world's first unranked rookie player to ever reach a major final," Hugh said.

* * *

Camille was sitting in the court-side box provided by the Open Committee. Joining her were Francine's parents and grandparents who had flown in after she had made the tournament. Also in the box was Francine's personal doctor, Mike Turpin.

Camille quickly discovered that the doctor was a rabid tennis fan. The doctor repeatedly kept mentioning that he wouldn't have missed this opportunity for anything. And to have his patient in the finals of one of tennis's majors was a dream come true.

Camille waited impatiently for the match to begin. *Francine had done everything right through the tournament,* Camille thought. The short matches reduced the wear on Francine's injured ankle and so far it hadn't caused any problems.

Dominique lined up for her first serve. Camille crossed her fingers and settled in. She looked over at the family members. Each was in their own little world as Francine smashed a return down the line. The ball skipped past Dominique for Francine's first point.

"Good start," Dewey said.

"Yes. Francine just needs to continue using her quickness and power," Camille offered.

The next point was fought over as the early volley tested each player. But Dominique continued to serve well and the first game went her way.

While the two players switched courts, the fans continued to buzz about the play. Francine had caused a major stir with her march through the competition. Stories in the press were emphasizing her near-death experience in Western Australia and reporters had been digging for details the entire two weeks.

When the Australian government came out and reminded the press of the special Federal law concerning the whole incident, their curiosity only increased. When each of Francine's wins had meant the obligatory press conference, the Australian government had provided David Knight from the Attorney General's Ministry to sit beside Francine.

Now, with the finals taking place, the pressure had reached an extreme. Camille was worried that the whole thing would affect Francine's play. As she tried to stay relaxed, the players resumed play.

Francine wound up her serve and hit the ball. The ball exploded off her racket and just caught the corner of the opposite service box. Dominique ran to return the ball and caught just enough to get it back over the net. Francine raced up to the net and pounded her return to the opposite side line. Dominique started to run after it but soon realized it was useless.

The next serves were repeats as Francine served and volleyed. Her quickness kept all of Dominique's returns in play. Her enhanced hand-eye ability combined with her incredible quickness made play at the net a nightmare for Dominique.

Francine easily reacted to any shot. Dominique tried some lobs, but again, Francine's quickness allowed her to run them down and return them. There appeared to be no weaknesses in Francine's game.

The score for the first set showed Francine's dominance as she closed it out 6-1. The second match started out the same for Francine. She was cruising toward victory when it happened.

A hard cross-court return had Francine sprinting to the opposite sideline. As she slid to a stop to hit the ball, she felt it. Her right ankle tweaked on her as it came to a stop. The sideways stop had rolled her ankle slightly. But it was enough to send a stab of pain up her right leg.

She missed her opponent's return as Dominique scored a winner. Francine was busy trying to walk off her new challenge and Camille noticed the slight change in her walk.

"Did Francine just twist something?" Dewey asked.

Camille didn't answer. The next point would be the proof. Camille wondered if Dominique had noticed yet.

Dominique pounded a serve to the far side. *She knew,* Camille thought. *Make her opponent move and test that ankle. That's exactly what I would have done too.*

Francine sprinted left to meet the serve and hit a line shot. But she didn't follow the shot forward into the front court. Returning to center court on the baseline, she hung back. Francine waited.

Dominique hit a shot to Francine's right, again testing the ankle. Francine raced after the ball and came up limping slightly after hitting it. Dominique earned one more point and continued to attack Francine's right side. Each time the ankle came out of the play a little weaker.

The game went to Dominique. Francine still led, four games to one, but her opponent now knew she was wounded. There would be no relief.

Calling an injury timeout between sets, Francine motioned for Dr. Turpin. Camille joined him in the room off center court where they had a short time to determine if Francine could finish the match.

Dr. Turpin removed Francine's tennis shoe and manipulated her ankle. Francine grimaced in pain as her joint stretched and contracted. The doctor made his diagnosis. It was a bad sprain on the same ankle that had been injured before.

"Tape it up." Francine demanded. The doctor reminded her of the risks of finishing the match. "Tape it."

The trainer went to work under the watchful eyes of both Dr. Turpin and Camille. Putting her shoe back on, Francine tested her movement.

"Any words of advice, Coach?" Francine asked.

"Serve it out. If you hold serve, you win."

Back in the stands, Camille quietly informed Dewey and Anna Maria of Francine's condition. Then she sat on the edge of her seat and waited.

Francine stepped up to the baseline. She tossed a high ball, rose up on her toes to meet it and smashed a hard shot toward Dominique. The ball blew by her, just clipping the center service line.

Dominique called for a review. The crowd waited for the instant replay of the shot on the big screen. As the camera zoomed in, the edge of the line was just evident under the ball. Very close, but in.

The next shot went to the outside. Again the ball just caught the line and Dominique missed completely as she lunged for the ball. Thirty to love. Two more for the set.

Francine stood and focused on the far court. She took a breath as Dominique danced in anticipation. With her feet already moving, Dominique was ready to move sideways for the serve.

But Francine hit this one right at her. Dominique tried to move slightly to the side to take the ball with her forehand, but only managed to clip the ball with the handle of her racket. The ball flew into the stands.

The crowd exploded in applause when the speed indicator came up at 142 mph. They had just witnessed the fastest women's serve in tennis history. Andy Roddick, noted big server, hit balls at that speed. With the women's record standing at 129.9 mph, no woman had ever gotten close to his kind of speed.

As the chair umpire called for quiet, Francine wound up again. This serve only slightly slower, the ball flew past Dominique. Francine had won her fifth set. Now she had to endure Dominique's serve.

The serves all went to the outside as Dominique pushed Francine's ankle. Camille realized that Francine had listened to her advice. Francine just stood still and let each serve go. The set went quickly to Dominique. The crowd murmured at the turn of events, feeling that Francine wasn't attempting to play out the set.

Just keep it up. Serve out this game and you win. Ignore the crowd, Camille thought. For Dominique to win, she would have to break Francine's serve. And she would have to break it more than once.

Francine checked the balls tossed to her and selected two that suited her. Placing one under her shorts, she rolled the other around in her hand.

Adjusting her grip on her racket for the next serve, Francine tossed the ball. She threw her racket back and twisted it with her arm. Bringing the racket forward, she turned the racket so it struck with a severe slicing motion.

The ball spun forward, catching the wind as it progressed. As in volleyball, the wind over a ball affects its flight. But with tennis, the racket strings add significantly more spin to a ball than a hand can provide. As the strings grip the ball and bite into it, the sideways dragging motion of the racket adds to the ball's rotation.

And this ball was rotating. Francine watched as the ball made a decidedly sweeping motion toward the side line. From Dominique's perspective, Camille knew that she would see a serve coming at her that appeared to be heading out of bounds.

But the spin added to the balls resistance, causing the ball to drop quickly. A ball that at first looked headed out, now dropped just inside the service box. Dominique reacted, but was too late.

The next two serves were the same slice serve. Dominique began adjusting for the extreme movement of the ball but still missed both. Match point.

Camille could see Dominique favoring the outside, waiting for one more slice serve. *Now for the power,* she thought.

Holding the racket behind her legs, Francine changed her grip again but made sure it wasn't obvious to anyone, especially Dominique. She tossed the ball but decided she didn't like the result and let it fall. She refocused her concentration. Again, she tossed the ball and lifted her feet up onto her toes.

Swinging with all her strength, the racket caught the ball. The leverage gave the ball a huge burst of speed as the ball streaked toward the opposite court and just caught the inside line. The ricochet hit the backboard with a resounding boom. The sign came on, 130 mph. Dominique froze as the bullet whizzed by her.

It was over. Francine dropped to her knees in joy. The crowd exploded in applause at the new Australian Open Champion. Camille stood and joined the applause as tears ran down her face.

Francine gathered herself and walked gingerly over to the net to shake Dominique's hand. Then she walked over to shake the Chair Umpire's hand. Looking around for her family, she located them. She hobbled across the court and climbed up into their box to give them each a hug.

Taking the stairs back to center court, she lined up for the formal proceedings. Camille knew Francine's second part of her dream had been accomplished. But she didn't know then that Francine's nightmare was just beginning.

The press was about to go crazy. Francine's mystery was now the center of discussion in the sports world. The world wanted to know how a totally unknown twenty-year-old American, who might be Italian, could defeat the best women's tennis players in the world. And the Australian government sitting in on the press conference only added to the mystery.

Even the other players were suspect. They'd never seen a totally unknown person show up and win the top prize in tennis. Nor had they ever seen a player with their own governmental protector. Questions flew that would not stop until more answers were forthcoming.

* * *

"Hugh Godley of ZBC Sports Network. I'd like to ask Ms. McDowell if the rumors of something happening in Western Australia to you are true. It seems that powerful forces are at work in keeping the truth from the public here."

The Australian representative from the Attorney General's Ministry jumped right in before Francine could answer. "The events that may have transpired to Ms. McDowell in visiting Australia have been ruled by the Australian government as privileged information. No details may be divulged under penalty of Federal Law. Anyone flouting that law is subject to a maximum twenty-year prison sentence."

"OK. I understand the serious nature that Australia has placed on this subject, but there must be a few details that could be offered to explain Ms. McDowell's amazing abilities. If they aren't related to whatever we can't talk about, maybe Ms. McDowell could explain how she elevated her athletic abilities so quickly," Hugh persisted.

But every time any question as to Francine's abilities was raised, David Knight of the Australian government cut off all discussion. The reporters were visibly frustrated and the press conference ended quickly.

Back in their hotel room, Camille raised the obvious question. "When we head to the next tennis event, we won't have the Australian government there to run cover for us. We need to come up with a public relations campaign that offers enough information but doesn't get us in trouble with the Australians."

The French Open was at the end of May and Camille would concentrate on getting Francine's ankle healed. But of Francine's prowess, the world continued to clamor for an answer.

Chapter 19

Rome, Italy

Construction workers were busily finishing the new Olympic Stadium in the background as the press gathered a short distance away. Television cameras scanned across the entire Olympic venue as Italy made ready for the upcoming games.

With the approaching Olympic Games as a background, Cubo Zoan, Director of the World Anti-Doping Committee stepped to the microphone. He waited for the cameras to zoom in on his face before he spoke.

"Today I want to announce one more athlete that has flouted the rules of track and field and has been caught. The use of performance-enhancing drugs in our young athletes is a crisis of monumental standing, and as long as I hold my position of trust for all the honest athletes competing out there, I won't rest until the cheaters are discovered and summarily banished."

The press shuffled slightly at Zoan's pompous attitude. They had heard it before and wanted him to move on to who his latest victim was by announcing the name. Already over the last six months, four world-class athletes had been banned by WADC. The Rome Olympics were lining up to be a historical game, but more for who *didn't* compete.

Zoan continued, "Nigel Hook-Smithers of Great Britain, hammer thrower, has been listed as a user of illegal performance-enhancing drugs. His name has been sent to the IAAF, who will do the formal banishment proceedings."

"Lying bastard," a voice yelled from the crowd of reporters.

Looking who had shouted out, a print reporter from the London Daily News glared back defiantly. Zoan zeroed in on his antagonist.

The reporter hit first, "Hook-Smithers has never finished in the top ten in the hammer in his life. Seems that WADC is bottom-feeding to put scalps on their belt. What blood test did he fail?"

Zoan, Director of WADC, stood erect as he surveyed the faces that suddenly turned toward him for an answer.

"Mr. Hook-Smithers has been observed self-administrating drugs by numerous witnesses."

"You stupid bloody bastard, the poor sod is diabetic. You want him to die on the field to satisfy your daft rules?"

"His blood test at the European Championships came back with irregularities," Zoan said. "He refused a follow-up test saying he was only required to provide one sample."

"And why are you testing athletes that don't even place in the top positions?" a reporter from the Sydney Spectrum yelled. "Not bloody likely to be cheating and coming in tenth. And if they are cheating, they aren't doing a very good job are they, eh?"

That drew a loud round of laughter from the assembled reporters. Zoan's face grew red at the insult directed at him and his commission.

"WADC takes the stand that cheaters are cheaters, wherever they may be found. I will personally seek out and destroy all who dare to bring disgrace on their sport. If you find that humorous, then maybe you should all find another profession if you're not willing to fight for the integrity of your chosen endeavor."

Zoan was finished with this rabble and turned to leave. He had more important things to do than immerse himself with common reporters. A challenge stopped him in his tracks.

"So when are you going to take on this wonder woman, Francine McDowell? She seems to be the leading candidate for cheater of the century."

Cubo Zoan returned to the microphone and swept his long locks back off his forehead. He shifted his stare to the person who had just challenged him.

"Ms. McDowell is certainly on WADC's radar. Unfortunately, the ITF that governs professional tennis refuses to admit that it can't handle the job of policing their own sport. It is obvious that this McDowell is using some sort of illegal substance to gain her huge advantage over her competitors I don't understand the ITF's reluctance to act, but I do understand she will be competing in track and field at the Olympics. She will receive a much different reception when she does."

Zoan was gone before any follow-up questions could be hurled his way. The reporters were left talking amongst themselves over his latest victim and what sounded like his future promise.

* * *

"There you have it Hugh. Zoan is definitely gunning for your darling of tennis," Karl Mahr, ZBC Sports Network color man for tennis said.

"Well, he can try," Hugh said. "But until she competes in track and field on the international stage, he's out of the picture."

The two sat in the production studio of ZBC Sports just outside London. They had just watched the live feed from Rome of the WADC press conference. They were doing their preliminary work for the French Open that started in a week.

The two had watched tape of Francine's performance at the NCAA Women's Indoor Track and Field Championship that had been held the previous month. Francine had set an Indoor World Record in the Triple Jump, extending the previous record by just over a meter.

"Breaking the world record by a meter will put her in international competition in a real hurry. That performance turned some heads, not that winning the Australian Open hadn't already."

"Let's look at the tape of her NCAA Women's Tennis Final," Hugh said.

"I've already heard," Karl said. "She won in straight sets. No one took a game off her. What would you expect after she crushed the best in the world in Melbourne? College players were never a match for her."

"So that makes three NCAA Championships for her in one year. And now the announcement that she'll turn pro for the French Open," Hugh said.

"I guess her college career at Idaho is over," Karl said. "She certainly put them in the spotlight for once in the school's life."

"For sure, my friend," Hugh said.

Chapter 20

Paris, France

"We've got a big problem," Camille announced. "The WTA has just signed up with the World Anti-Doping Committee. It seems that the Francine question has gotten too big for the WTA to handle on their own."

"But we passed the WTA administered tests in Melbourne. Dr. Turpin supervised the blood draw and we took our independent sample. What more is there?" Francine asked.

They had arrived in Paris after wrapping up Francine's NCAA Women's Singles Tennis National Championship. Along with her NCAA Women's Indoor Triple Jump National Championship, Francine had completed her first year competing in college. It would be her only year.

After discussing things with her dad, Francine had decided to turn professional. With little knowledge about her future due to her syndrome, Francine wanted the opportunity to collect the prize money professional sports could offer.

With three major tennis tournaments left, those winnings could be substantial. Camille had agreed with Francine's decision. She thought that the McDowell's might need prize money if Francine started experiencing any bad side effects from her 'stite'.

Camille focused on getting Francine ready for battle at Roland Garros Stadium. It would be Francine's first experience with clay and the change in play it required. Camille knew of a small tennis court in a quiet part of town where Francine could conduct her workouts. Contacting a friend who would act as her hitting partner, they attempted to keep a low profile so as to avoid the press.

Cubo Zoan being named as chief adversary in the Francine mystery brought the reporters to full alert. Cubo lapped up the attention. Having the WTA choose the WADC to oversee their sport, Cubo was on his way to corralling all the major sports.

The world would finally be safe from cheaters. *At least that's what Cubo Zoan would thin*k, thought Camille. *The McDowell team had better be prepared.*

With her miraculous rise to the top of the tennis world, Francine didn't have any friends on the WTA. The questions about Francine and her overwhelming talent underscored the jealousy involved. Francine was on her own with no support from her fellow players.

Camille counseled Francine that it would be tougher as she moved ahead. With so many unanswered questions swirling around her, she could expect no one coming to her defense. The small team of family members that gathered to support her would be her only safe zone.

As the start of the French Open approached, the press finally located Francine. Suddenly, she could not leave her practice court or her hotel without the scrutiny of cameras. Questions came at her at every opportunity. The other great tennis players competing were forgotten as the reporters fed off each other in the hunt for a Francine scoop.

Camille was nervous her player would break under the pressure. She decided to try to relieve the pressure and made a phone call to an old friend.

Meeting the next day at her practice court, Camille greeted her friend, Selena Roberts.

"Selena, thanks for taking the time," Camille started.

"I'm glad to see you, but I'm not sure I can help in all this. Your player is in way over her head with this mystery story. And what's with the Aussies and their national state secret?" Selena asked.

"This kid needs one sign of support out there. I was hoping you could be that for her. You do remember that you offered my name to her in all this," Camille said.

"Sure I remember. But I sure didn't expect you to turn her into a Grand Slam winner overnight. How did that go now?" Selena asked.

"She's totally legal. I haven't heard the entire story because of that Aussie law sitting out there, but from what I do know, Francine is a victim in this too," Camille said.

"Well, old friend, I just might have to face that victim soon. I've watched the tapes from Melbourne. She is a complete nightmare. Speed that is over the top. Power that will knock you out of your socks. Ball control that no one has ever witnessed before. She would eat up the men's tour right now. The only weakness I can see is . . ." Selena stopped. She looked right at Camille. She added quickly, "I forgot who I was talking to."

"But, if I explain what I know, it might help. She just needs someone who will stand up for her. You wouldn't want to have someone persecuted because of something beyond their control?" Camille asked

"Like the color of their skin? You pushed those barriers for me when I first hit the tour. I've pushed them further. Your Francine certainly has the blood in her, besides whatever voodoo blood those Australians pumped in her," Selena responded. "Tell me what you can, I'll think about it."

Camille proceeded to lay out the facts as she knew them. The 'stite' was left at that, since Camille had no knowledge of what lethal creatures had mixed it up inside Francine. When she was done, Selena could only whistle.

"Wow. That poor kid. To go from gifted athlete to super woman overnight. And to pass mortality twice while you're doing the transformation. I feel for her."

"And not knowing what's going on in her body," Camille said. "Just imagine, two highly lethal substances working inside you. Not knowing if the gift goes away today. Or if death is standing at your shoulder. I've tried to talk through the whole thing with her. Let's just say Francine has issues to deal with the rest of us could never imagine."

"And now the WTA has tied our sport with that Cubo creep. That was a big mistake. Take care with him," Selena offered.

"That's why Francine and her Dad were at Zeus Sports that day you meet them. Francine wants to compete in track at the Olympics and knew they would be dealing with the WADC eventually."

"Track and field. Great sport. Tell Francine to go have a field day. Just leave Olympic tennis alone," Selena said.

"Afraid not, my friend. My player wants to complete a Golden Slam. Hasn't been done but once," Camille said.

"Steffi Graf. Win all four majors and an Olympic Gold Medal, all in one year. And she wants to compete in track and field in the mix. She is a dynamo."

"And don't forget volleyball. The United States turned her down but . . ." Camille offered.

"That's why she's competing as an Italian. She's planning on playing for the Italian Volleyball team in the Olympics. The press will be after you in Cubo Zoan's wake looking for cheating. No one has accomplished anything close to what your player is attempting."

"So, are you on board as a Francine supporter?" Camille asked.

"Up until she's across the net from me," Selena responded.

* * *

Camille didn't have long to wait as Francine marched through the competition. It wouldn't be Selena at the French Open. Selena was on the opposite side of the bracket from Francine and proceeded to lose to Svetlana in the semifinals.

Francine, meanwhile, didn't lose a set as she reached the finals. That left the Italian Francine

McDowell, versus the Russian, Svetlana Trenschenko for the Championship.

The opportunity wasn't lost on Cubo Zoan. With his natural distaste for Italians lingering from his grandfather and father, Cubo began his innuendo campaign against Francine.

By the time of the finals, the world was convinced that Francine was using performance-enhancing drugs and was just very good at hiding the results in her blood tests. The WADC would sort that all out in due time, its director promised.

The only place in the world where Cubo's accusations fell flat was in Italy. The country had taken Francine as one of their own, and now Italian honor was at stake.

* * *

Once again Hugh Godley and ZBC Sports Network was there for every exciting minute. With Karl Mahr adding color and Jack Hawkins providing the proverbial side kick role, the TV cameras would catch every minute of the battle, both on the court and off.

"The ITF has finally put its head in a noose. Signing with WADC has unleashed our friend Cubo Zoan on the unsuspecting tennis world. They don't know what they've done," Jack said.

"You're right there, my friend," Hugh said. "Zoan and his sycophants in the press will gladly march right over any and all before them. I pity poor Ms McDowell. She may have the sports world a-buzz with her play at

Roland Garros but I'd say she's in for a full press rectal exam whether she wins or not." The producer shook his head at his lead announcer to inform him he couldn't talk like that on TV.

Ignoring him, Hugh continued. "So Karl, these two have met before at the Australian Open. Do you see anything that says different results today?"

"No, Hugh. I'm afraid Svetlana is up against it in a big way. We can only assume that Francine's ankle has had sufficient time to heal since Melbourne. I expect a pounding for the big Russian is in order today," Karl added.

Jack jumped in. "I would say we can put any concern over the ankle to rest. Ms. McDowell just came off that American National Championship in college tennis without missing a beat. Certainly the competition there wasn't anything like we've seen this week, but her ankle caused no problems."

"And don't forget her world record-setting performance in the Women's Indoor Triple Jump," Karl added. "She was absent for most of the winter college season so we can assume her ankle was getting treated. But one meet at the end of the indoor track season got her qualified for Nationals. The ankle sure didn't slow her down there."

Hugh clinched the discussion. "You're both spot on. We haven't seen her favor that ankle over the two weeks of competition here. I believe we have two healthy players ready to battle for the clay court title in the majors."

"And much to the delight of the Italians," Jack said. "They've only had one winner in a major before, when Francesca Schiavone took this event in 2010. The Italians are ready to celebrate today, I can assure you."

"Yes, our producer has switched to our camera set up at the Spanish Steps," Hugh said. "The Rome officials have closed the street and set up a Jumbotron screen. As you can tell, it's a seething mass as the Italian fans await the start of play. They haven't shown this kind of enthusiasm since Sophia Loren came up for air in her wet shirt in 'Boy on a Dolphin'." The producer rolled his eyes, but Hugh couldn't care less. The ratings told the story.

"That's one of my favorite movies too," Jack joined in. "I don't even bother with the sound when I watch it."

The producer switched the camera view back to center court. The two players were finished with their warm-up and were taking their spots. Play was about to begin.

The match went as predicted. Svetlana struggled to keep up with her faster more powerful opponent. Except for a few miscues on Francine's part, the results showed complete dominance. Francine won in straight sets and continued her new tradition of finding her parents in the stands and climbing up to hug them.

The ceremonies took place at center court with the trophy being awarded. The trouble began in the after match press conference. ZBC Sports Network had Karl Mahr at the head of the crowd.

As Francine walked in, in an unusual move, she was joined by David Knight.

The first question asked, "Why is the French Open allowing the Australian government to attend this event?"

As David was about to answer, Francine held up her hand. David waited.

"Mr. Knight has been approved by the French Open Committee to be present today. Due to the sensitive nature of my standing in the sports world in regards to the Australian government, he is here to assist me in any questions related to my visit to Western Australia," Francine said.

Seeing a possible opening to get to the center of the controversy, Karl blurted out his question, "Ms. McDowell, congratulations on another stunning victory. Your mastery of the court is certainly unprecedented. To what do you attribute your success?"

"Mr. Mahr, thank you," Francine started. "I'm certain that everyone assumes that with the Australian government sitting here to block any and all inquires as to my sudden athletic gifts, I have something to hide. I can say with certainty that my skills were obtained naturally, with no drug enhancement, legal or illegal."

David Knight jumped in to add, "Prior to this news conference, Cubo Zoan and the WADC administered their blood and urine tests to Ms. McDowell. Also present was Dr. Michael Turpin, Ms. McDowell's personal physician. A second test was taken so that an independent lab might corroborate the WADC results."

"Are you accusing WADC of doctoring tests then?" a reporter yelled.

"If they aren't, then I am."

Everyone turned to see who the identity of the new accuser. Standing at the back of the room was Stanley Day, President of Zeus Sports. Standing beside Stan was Al Garbarino, President of Athena Athletics, the second largest shoe and sports apparel company in the world. Headquartered in Milan, Italy, Athena had suddenly taken an interest in this aspiring Italian tennis player.

Between Zeus and Athena, the two companies controlled three-fourths of the multi- billion dollar athletic wear business. Seeing the two owners standing together in support of Francine brought the focus of WADC into proper perspective.

Francine, learning the ways of power sports, knew a gift horse when she saw one. "Perhaps Mr. Day would come up her and offer a few words on the subject being discussed."

"Damn straight I'd like to offer some comments," Stanley Day said. "But this is the French Open Committee's little party it would be rude to interrupt. But I have scheduled a news conference the week before Wimbledon to make an announcement. We'll be able to talk then."

Stan Day and Al Garbarino both exited. There was a decided drop in the oxygen level after they'd left. The two companies had the majority of the top athletes on retainer as promotors of their products. What one or both of these titans had to say influenced the world of professional sports. The reporters all forgot why they were there and began chatting about the upcoming Zeus press conference.

Only Karl remained on task. "Ms. McDowell, will you be competing at Wimbledon?"

"Yes, I will. Thank you all for coming," Francine said. She quickly left the room, David Knight following her out the door.

Watching their personal Australian bureaucrat leave, Dewey waited for Francine in the corridor. "Mr. Day has invited us to his farm tonight. He would like to talk to us. After you shower, he will have a car waiting at the back door for all of us."

The 'farm' turned out to be a one hundred room chateau located near the Loire River. Nestled in with the other chateau that France was famous for, Stanley Day's 'farm' sat overlooking the river.

Rooms had been set aside for the entire McDowell party for an overnight stay. With Wimbledon a month off, Francine thought a little break was appropriate. Especially when it was on a two hundred acre estate far from the prying eyes of the press.

Chapter 21

Amboise, France

The Loire region of France was home to some of the most opulent houses that the French had ever built. Stretched along the Loire River, huge estates with massive chateaus scattered the area. In its heyday, this was the summer retreat for the ruling class from the heat of Paris.

Now, it was an oasis for Francine as she struggled with her notoriety. She sat on the wooden bench by the grass tennis court, lost in her thoughts. Her water bottle hung lifeless in her hand as the stress of the whole affair weighed on her.

"Come on Francine, we need to practice," Camille said as she attempted to get Francine playing on grass in preparation for Wimbledon. "You've never played on grass and the game is totally different. You need to get the timing down."

Francine's head sagged even lower as her coach implored her to get back to work. She couldn't understand why she was so tired. It had been four days since her win at the French Open. Plenty of time to recover from the physical exertion of the match.

Camille walked over and sat down beside her player. "You know Francine, part of the game is putting all the commotion in a box and locking it. You know tennis is a totally mental game. You've been relying on your physical gifts to muscle your way through the matches."

"I know. But why can't I just play sports? Why is everyone on me about what happened in Australia? I sometimes wish it never happened."

"And miss out on being on the world's stage and number one in the world in tennis?" Camille asked.

"No, I guess you're right. Things happened that were beyond my control. I guess I should just be happy to be alive. The alternative is sobering, for sure."

"So, are you ready to learn how to win on grass?"

Francine stood, took one more sip and placed her water bottle on the bench. Her hitting partner stood up and walked to the opposite end of the court. Camille threw a ball to Francine and started the hitting session.

A grass surfaced tennis court is very different from a typical hard court. Grass, cut very short, is softer. A tennis ball bounced less due to part of its energy being absorbed by the soft surface.

Less bounce makes the game slower. Francine had done well on the clay surface at Roland Garros Arena in the French Open. Clay is less responsive than a hard court, but not as soft as grass. The big difference for players on clay is the traction on their feet, clay being a lot more 'slippery' than a hard court.

When playing the baseline, or end of the court, players rely on a quick back and forth response to balls hit toward either corner. A clay surface makes a quick change in direction more of a problem and forces players to adjust their game.

Grass is similar to clay where the player's feet are concerned, but with the ball moving slower, the quick turns are more manageable. Francine, who had only played on hard courts, focused on learning the strategy of grass courts.

"OK, let's try some drop shots. You'll see they come off grass totally different. You need to watch your opponent's wrist as she strokes the ball and react quickly if they put a slice on it," Camille admonished her player.

The hitting partner began hitting drop shots, which is when a player puts an underspin on her return so the ball reacts more to the air resistance. This forces the ball to drop more quickly.

This would be in comparison to a normally hit ball in which the ball has an overspin. A top spin tends to lift the ball and carry it further.

A drop shot forces the player to charge the net to pick up the ball sooner than normal. On grass, the opposing player needs to close quickly on the net. The resistance offered by the grass when the ball hits takes energy out of the ball, offering less bounce.

Francine charged the ball each time and returned to the baseline for the next one. She moved side to side as her opponent drove balls into each corner and then mixed in a drop shot. She was sweating profusely when Camille called a stop.

"Both of you grab some water," Camille yelled. "I think we've done enough this morning. You look like you're getting a feel for grass."

"It is different. My ankle is enjoying the soft surface," Francine said. While it seemed healed, hard pounding often caused her ankle to swell and she was careful to ice after any activity.

"Well, you go ice anyway. For all you have planned, you need to maintain your regime religiously," Camille said. "We'll have another session this afternoon. Go see the trainer and get that ice on. Your shoulder too."

Francine walked toward the field house that was hidden in the trees behind the chateau. The owner had been careful to keep the historic nature of the 18th century home intact while he added more modern features.

An outdoor pool sat beside the field house and the other guests were stretched out taking in the French sun. Dewey stood up as his daughter approached.

"How did it go, kiddo?"

"Good, Dad. I think I can handle grass. Camille says I need to hit the trainer now. I'll join you when I'm done," Francine said after giving her dad a sweaty hug.

* * *

"Good afternoon, ladies and gentlemen. I'm Hugh Godley and we're here at the Women's Finals at Wimbledon. Beside me is my partner, Karl Mahr. I think we have a stunning matchup for our viewers today. Karl, what's your assessment of our two competitors today?"

"Well Hugh, first we have the former number one player in the world who has twice won here at Wimbledon. Svetlana Trenschenko is no stranger to the rarified air that a grand final brings to any court. She has done a splendid job taking out her side of the bracket to get here. Only Selena Roberts took her to a third set in that epic battle in the semi-finals."

"You're right there, Karl. That was a match for the ages. But did she leave it all in the semis? Does she have enough to challenge our upstart?" Hugh threw out.

Karl continued, "Francine McDowell is certainly an upstart. From total oblivion just a short six months ago to number one in the world. And she shows no sign of wilting under the tremendous pressure both on and off the court. As the accusations swirl around her, mostly emanating from WADC and its chief shill, Cubo Zoan, Ms. McDowell seems poised to add another grand slam title to her belt."

"The press has certainly joined in the Zoan witch hunt for answers to the McDowell mystery. But with Mr. Knight of the Australian government never far from her side, no one has made any in-roads into answering the question," Hugh said.

"And now we have the challenge laid down by the CEO of Zeus Sports last week as our competition opened, Karl offered.

"Yes, that has certainly upped the ante for Mr. Zoan," Hugh added. "As promised, Stanley Day, CEO and majority stock holder of the world's largest sporting goods retailer has set his sights right on WADC's Director. While short on details, it would appear that Zeus Sports, along with other unmentioned, sporting goods companies, are evaluating their relationship with the sports federations."

"That is huge," Karl said. "If the sports firms throw their money and athletes behind new governing boards, the sports world as we know it will be history."

"And who can blame them?" Hugh said. "They pour millions into promoting their athletes only to have

237

Cubo Zoan and the WADC ban them from competition. This news certainly has cast a shadow over the upcoming Olympics."

The ZBC television producer motioned it was time to go to a commercial. The monitor switched to an advertisement for Zeus athletic gear. On cue, it was an ad shot of Francine and her new line of tennis shoes. Then the ad switched to Francine playing volleyball in her line of volleyball shoes. That was finished by a shot of her in her track and field shoes competing in the triple jump.

With a flashy new logo to wrap up the pitch, Francine appeared in a close up with sweat running down her face. As the music built, her face slowly dissolved into the Zeus corporate logo on the screen. The fade led into the corporate moniker especially selected for Francine's television ad; 'Because you can'.

As the producer pointed, the monitor came back onto Hugh sitting next to Karl. The two were smiling as Hugh offered, "So Karl, we do have a lot riding on this final. Two grand slams down and two to go. And with an Olympic Games soon taking place, the opportunity is there for a Golden Slam. It's only happened once before. Steffi Graf completed the miracle in 1988. Does our young rookie have it in her?"

"A lot of people are rooting for her, that's for sure," Karl said. "She still carries her underdog status to a lot of fans. Whatever happened in Australia intrigues many people. And with her multiple sports, she's bringing a lot of new people to tennis to see how she does."

"You're right there. She has shown great class both on and off the court. A lot of people have been turned off over the years by the attitudes of many of the players, both men and women," Hugh added.

"Yes, and she doesn't grunt. Finally a woman that can win without grunting on every shot. That seems to be a big hit with the fans too."

"Well, the players have done their preliminaries to the match. We'll start play after this commercial break. Stay tuned everybody. And hold on to your hats, I think we're going to have quite a test today," Hugh said.

* * *

Hugh Godley was off on his estimate by a large margin. Francine's quick reactions ate up every ball that Svetlana attempted to hit at her. Drop shots were spotted as they came off her racket and Francine raced to cover them. Corner shots in a baseline game were chased down unmercifully by Francine and returned. The Russian woman's normally powerful serve was attacked with a vengeance by Francine as Svetlana was pushed back on her heels.

Winning the first set 6-1, Francine sat and waited for the second set to begin. She looked up into the crowd to where she knew her family was seated. Sitting with her mom and dad were her grandparents from both Italy and the United States.

She looked over to her coach and Camille gave her a big smile. Francine nodded back to her coach but kept her game face on for everyone else. The Up Ref called time and the two players stood to return to play.

As Francine walked by the net to take her place on the opposite side, Svetlana purposely bumped into her as she passed. The two stopped in mid-stride before Svetlana shoved slightly and kept moving. Francine shook off the attempt at intimidation. *Well, if that's how she wants to play,* Francine thought.

Francine was set to serve first in the new match. She threw the ball high and rocked forward on her toes. Her racket swung through with all her power and the ball shot toward the opposing player. Hitting the grass, the speed dropped and Svetlana moved to cover. Her stroke drove the ball toward the far corner.

Intercepting it near the net, Francine was there. Taking the kinetic energy out of the ball, Francine gently touched the ball and dropped the ball into the forecourt. The ball limply dribbled before it died.

Svetlana ran to the ball as it rolled by her feet. Her scowl registered as she swung at the ball as she walked back to the baseline. In her frustration, she hit the ball with such force that it flew and hit one of the ball persons in the face standing by the back wall.

The young man dropped over in pain as he clutched his face from the hit. Play was stopped as the officials checked his injuries. Refusing to leave the match, the ball retriever stood at his post with a large red mark just below his eye.

The crowd began booing at the bad sportsmanship displayed. It was all downhill from there for the Russian. Her play drew boos at every turn while Francine had the entire stadium behind her as she ran the score up.

During one sustained volley, Svetlana charged the net on one of Francine's drop shots. Reaching the ball in time, she snapped a cross-court shot hoping to catch Francine out of position.

Francine had gambled on such a return and had taken a position close but off center of the net. Svetlana's hit came right to her. Francine positioned her racket in front of her with both hands as she moved the racket slightly and caught the ball fully.

The ball flew back across the net and hit Svetlana in the face. The crowd roared its approval even as Francine was raising he hand to apologize for the errant hit. The Russian just scowled back in defiance.

The match continued but the results were obvious. With Svetlana's eye swelling from her hit, her game slowly collapsed. Francine finished the second match, winning 6-0.

In the split second that she realized she had won, she dropped her racket and sprinted up into the stands to find her family. With the crowd congratulating her, she climbed to her mom and dad. Giving everyone a hug, she then moved over to where Camille was standing and applauding.

Back at mid-court, a small international incident took place. While the two opponents had performed the ritual handshake at the end, things got decidedly icy during the trophy presentation.

Francine applauded politely as Svetlana received her second-place trophy. For the normally reserved English crowd, the abuse of the Russian continued. When Francine received her Wimbledon plate, she received a rousing applause as she walked around holding the plate above her head.

After the ceremonies wrapped up, Francine took her winning racket and walked over to the boy who had been hit by Svetlana's ball. She pulled out a marker and signed the racket and gave it to him as a memento. The crowd roared again in approval.

The press session after the match continued the frosty international relations between the two players. Svetlana's eye was noticeably swollen as she held an ice pack on the right side of her face. Francine walked in with ice wrapped on her ankle and shoulder and sat down at the microphone. The Wimbledon official invited questions from the press.

"Ms. McDowell, was that ball hit on Ms. Trenschenko's face a payback for the ball boy hit?"

"No, that was just part of tennis when players play close to the net. I apologized for it at the time if you might recall," Francine answered.

"It didn't look like it from my side. It was a shot purposely intended to hurt me. It's just another example of the cheating this player resorts to in order to win at any cost," Svetlana threw out.

"Is that true, Ms. McDowell? Are you willing to do anything to win?" a reporter demanded.

"It was an errant ball. Happens all the time. Players get hit and move on. There's nothing sinister here," Francine said. Her frustration quickly grew at the questions from the press.

"But are you saying that your Australian experience gave you an advantage and that you're willing to use that to win?" the reporter continued.

Before Francine could answer, her old friend, David Knight of the Australian government, stood up. He didn't say anything but just stood against the press room wall. The entire press corps groaned in unison at his presence. He had successfully headed off every opportunity to question Francine on her sudden surprising athlctic gifts.

"As you can see, any and all questions on my Australian experience are closely monitored. Next question?" Francine asked.

The reporters returned to the normal questions on the play and the two players answered from their perspective. Although things remained icy between the two, Wimbledon protocol required a certain decor be displayed between them. Francine knew she hadn't seen the last of Svetlana, and that today might come back to haunt her.

Chapter 22

Orvieto, Italy

Francine relaxed in the bed of her grandparent's summer home. Located in Orvieto, a small hill town about an hour's drive north of Rome, the city was famous for its cathedral. Orvieto had been built, like many Italian towns, on a hill for defense. What set Orvieto apart was the hill itself.

More than a hill, Orvieto had natural rock cliffs of over 300' in height. This natural wall was pierced in only one spot by a road that had been constructed in modern times. The medieval city itself was practically impregnable.

And that was what Francine was hoping for now as she relaxed in her soft bed. Her window looked out over the distant hills, many scattered with small towns.

After winning Wimbledon amid more controversy during her win, she was happy to be ensconced in the stone house on the very edge of the cliff. While scary to look straight down out her window, the isolation it offered suited her mood.

She could hear her Italian grandmother busy. Like all good Italians, life revolved around food and the kitchen. Smells of breakfast drifted up from the open windows and enticed her to leave her safe cocoon.

Pulling on her warm-up outfit especially designed for her by Zeus Sports, Francine headed down the stone steps. Her entire family was sitting in the living room chatting as she walked in.

Her American grandparents had accepted the invitation to join the Italian side and a neighbor's townhouse was made available to house the extra bodies. But now all gathered, they awaited the official call to breakfast.

Anna Maria walked in and announced that everyone should move into the dining room. Francine, as the honored guest, was allowed to go first. Francine loved Italian breakfasts. In fact, she loved every meal in Italy. *The Italians know how to eat*, she thought.

Francine especially loved the 'dolce', or sweet desserts. She just had to watch herself as she continued to train for her next challenge.

She would soon be joining the Italian Women's Volleyball Team in order to get ready for the upcoming Olympics. Already a mega-celebrity in Italy, she had yet to step on a court with her teammates.

As she ate quietly, the table buzzed around her in typical Italian banter. She loved the loud side of her family and noticed the more reserved American side was a little taken aback. But soon they joined in the boisterous crowd as the Italian way of life took over.

Today would be a break from training in order to spend a little time with the relatives. After breakfast and a quick cleanup in the kitchen, Grandpa Lorenzo led a personal tour of Orvieto. Walking from their house on the edge of the cliff, they headed into the center of the old town. While a new town had sprung up at the base of the cliff where the railroad station sat, the old town was the tourist part.

And today, like most days, the tourists were out in force. The group soon reached the 'domo', or cathedral. Famous for its stone carved relief on the outside, Francine studied the figures as Lorenzo gave a talk in English on their meaning. Soon, other tourists had gathered around to listen in on an obvious local talking about his town. It was then that someone recognized the woman trying to remain quiet in the back.

"It's Francine McDowell!" someone yelled. Everyone turned to look at the woman trying to appear invisible. Quickly other tourists from the center of town rushed to see the famous celebrity. As the crowd grew, Lorenzo gave up his art appreciation talk. He gathered up his flock and moved them off to a side street.

Luckily the crowd of well-wishers didn't follow and Francine could return to being just a tourist. Lorenzo suggested that they call a cab and head out to see Civita. A van soon arrived and the group loaded in for the short fifteen minute ride to Civita. Civita was an even older hill town just west of Orvieto. It had been settled by the Etruscans before Rome dominated the Italian peninsula.

A small village, the hill had eroded to the point that Civita looked seriously endangered. To help with the flow of tourists seeking to visit the unique site, the government had built a footbridge across the chasm that separated the new town from the old. Not wide enough for motor vehicles, Civita was a step back in time.

Entering the small village square as the group walked through the covered entrance gate, the few tourists didn't pay any mind to the Italians. Lorenzo again started his talk on the local history as the relatives followed him around.

Seeing the local Etruscan carvings and artifacts, Francine understood the long history she represented. Her Italian family had always been just like everyone else's family. On her previous visits to Rome she had been a tourist taking in the sights of the Eternal City.

Now Francine felt the strong ties of her Italian family. She had always considered herself American first and foremost. But now that she represented Italy in her sporting endeavors, while having the Italian flag next to her name whenever her picture came up, it drove home her heritage.

She still thought of herself as American, but now understood better her other side. And those feelings didn't bring in the African heritage her father had given her. Those genes were what had started her athletic dreams. The Australian experience only kicked those genes into overdrive. *Would I be the same if I didn't have African blood in me?* she thought.

She was yanked back to reality when a tourist noticed who was standing with them in the town piazza. "It's Francine McDowell, everyone!" a woman yelled. "Look! Hey Frank, get over here right now. I need a picture of me and Francine. You don't mind, do you honey?"

A large blonde woman with "I 'heart' New York" across her chest barged into Francine's small group. Frank rushed over with his camera ready.

Francine tried to be polite at the intrusion as she learned the price of fame came with a downside. "Certainly," she offered.

Soon a large gathering of people maneuvered for photo opportunities. Pen and paper soon appeared as autographs were requested. Francine was inundated by a throng as she attempted to please everyone.

Suddenly a man appeared and moved boldly into the crowd. In very broken English he said, "Scusi. scusi. I'a need madame McDowell."

He placed his arm under Francine's arm and practically lifted her up as he took her physically. As he passed Lorenzo, he scooped him up with his other arm. He pushed through the small crowd saying, "Scusi, scusi."

Closing a door behind him, Francine stopped in her tracks. Lorenzo smiled at his old friend.

"Giberto, thank you for the rescue," Lorenzo offered in Italian. Then switching to English, "Let me introduce my granddaughter Francine."

"Very pleased to meet you. You looked like you needed rescueing out there. Please, sit, I bring some refreshments. I'll go and get the rest of the family as soon as the crowd thins," Giberto said.

Returning with the rest of the family, Giberto announced, "As your grandpappa knows, I run a small ristorante here. I am closed today for the tourists, but I make a special meal for my special guests." Everyone gave Giberto a small round of applause for both the rescue and the offer of food.

When Giberto began bringing out the dishes of food, Francine knew no one was leaving hungry. What was lunch turned quickly into a full Ittalian meal. Francine knew enough to pace herself, but when Giberto brought out Baccone Dolce for dessert, she knew she was done.

Baccone Dolce was her favorite. Made with layers of baked meringue, each layer was filled with whipped cream and strawberries. Melted chocolate was dripped over each layer just to add to the heavenly treat. Measuring about eight inches high, each slice contained enough calories and fat to kill a horse.

Her dad referred to it as 'artcry putty', much to the disgust of her mom. But it didn't stop Dewey from indulging. Francine dove into her slice and resolved that tomorrow she would be back at her training. *Time enough to work it off*, she thought

* * *

The sweet life soon ended as Francine and her dad arrived at the practice facility used by the Italian Volleyball Team. Located on the outskirts of Rome, Grandfather Lorenzo had arranged a car and driver for the short trip.

Francine stopped and looked at the court. It had been a long four months since she had stepped on a volleyball court. Tennis had consumed most of her time since winning her NCAA National title. She walked over and dropped her bag on the floor by the bleachers. Dewey took a spot in the stands to watch.

The Italian team had just started warm-up drills as Francine joined in. After the warm-up run around the gym, the coach had everyone form a circle.

"I want to introduce Francine McDowell," he said in English. He knew all his players spoke English since most had played in college in the United States. He continued, "Since Francine's Italian is limited, we'll start off in English. As she improves, we can switch to Italian."

He went around the circle and introduced each player. Francine had done her homework on each player and already knew each one and where they had played college volleyball. She had studied their records and then watched videotape of the Italian team playing at the World Championships the year before.

While a couple of the players hadn't returned, the team was essentially the same as last year. Only Francine would be a new player.

The team had just started its first drills when a commotion by the main doors stopped everyone. A large group pushed their way into the gym holding tape recorders and video cameras.

One of the assistant coaches ran over and stopped their progress. Francine listened as Italian was rapidly spoken. She didn't catch any of it until the head coach yelled in English, "This is a closed practice. There is no press allowed in here."

With much commotion and arm waving, the press was escorted from the room. The players all looked at Francine.

"OK, let's get back to work. Enough of a distraction."

"Coach, we've never had reporters interrupting our work-outs before. What's with that?" one player asked.

"We've never had the number one tennis player in the world on our team before either," the coach said. "You women need to adjust your outlook. Francine brings a lot of media interest to this team. Suddenly we are considered contenders for a medal."

Francine stood as the other players stared at her. She had anticipated this from the beginning having been around team sports enough to understand the jealousies involved. Some players would soon find themselves in roles they hadn't anticipated. *How would they adjust?* she thought. *Would they be able to adjust?*

She knew how hard each had worked and now she showed up at the last minute to take someone's place on the team. Only twelve women got to go to the Olympics. Someone, probably a good friend to a number of the players, would be left home. *Not a good recipe for success*, she thought

Francine didn't have long to wait. In a warmup to the Olympics, a European-based tournament had been organized in the Rome facility that would house the Olympic venue. With four team pools, Italy was in a Pool C with the Germans, Dutch, and Serbians.

Italy lost all three matches badly as the team went through the motions as if Francine didn't exist. Out on the court on offense, the other players stiffed Francine constantly out of getting the ball. When on defense, one of the other players would step in front of her to take Francine's ball.

No matter what the coach tried, the other players wouldn't involve their new player. The partisan Italian crowd responded in vocal manner at the poor play of the home team. Bracket play would start the next day and Italy would be in the loser bracket.

The coach was beside himself as the Italian press crucified the coach and the team on its bad showing. Some even questioned whether Francine should even be on the team since it obviously wasn't working.

That evening after the team dinner, the coach took the entire team into a conference room. The assistant coach stood ready at a television monitor. As soon as the team was all settled in their chairs, the head coach walked to the front of them.

"I want you to watch what we have for you. If I see one cell phone out, you know my policy, you're off the team. Pay attention, there'll be a test at the end," the coach said.

The assistant coach turned on the DVD player and a men's volleyball game came on. Francine immediately recognized it as the 2012 London Olympic Men's Final with Brazil versus Russia. She remembered watching with her dad at the time. It was one of the most amazing volleyball games in history.

The other players all groaned at having to watch more video. They routinely watched game film of their opponents to learn what other teams liked to do. But watching a men's game which they knew they'd never have to play was work to them.

The first set finished to a small applause from the players. One down, who knew how many to go. The Brazilians had crushed the Russians in the first set. The second set also went the Brazilians way.

Francine marveled at the men's game. It was all about total power. Most men didn't even wear knee pads since if the ball wasn't blocked at the net there was no chance to dive for it in the back row. Francine loved the total power game. It was her style of play. She just wasn't over seven feet tall like some of these players.

Brazil put the Russians away and kept it rolling in the third set. It appeared the Russians were going to lose in three straight sets. The Russian coach scrambled to find an answer to the Brazilian hitting.

It was down to match point in the third set, when the Russian coach finally found an answer. It came in the shape of seven footer Dmitry Muserskiy. Suddenly, every Russian set was going to Muserskiy.

At over seven feet tall with a leaping ability to match, the Brazilians suddenly couldn't put a block up to stop him. They tried three blockers to no avail as Muserskiy just hit over them. He hit over them from the front row, rotated into the back row, and proceeded to hit over the Brazilians in back row attacks.

The Russians closed out with a win in the third set. They continued on their streak and won the fourth set, forcing a tie breaker. The Russian coach knew enough to not mess with success and Muserskiy continued to receive every ball. And he answered by hammering every hit over the frustrated Brazilians for a point. The game ended with the Russians pulling off a huge win.

The Italian Women's Volleyball Team sat in silence as the lights came back on. The coach took up his spot at the front of the team.

"OK, who can tell me what was the turning point in the game we just watched?" he asked.

All the girls looked at each other in stunned silence. It was painfully obvious to anyone with a brain what the turning point was, but each hesitated, not sure if there was a trick to the answer. When no one offered a suggestion, the coach turned to Francine.

"Everyone seems a little confused. Francine, could you offer an opinion as to what turned the game around for the Russians?"

In her best Italian, she said, "I think the tall guy hitting over everyone else."

The giggles from the other players made the coach frown and turn on them.

"She's right. The tall guy suddenly was allowed to carry his team when they needed it. There was no hesitation to climb on and ride him to an Olympic gold medal. Now, I want you to watch this tape."

He pulled out the Russian DVD and placed a new disc in the slot. The little drawer closed and the screen flicked to life. Francine instantly recognized the NCAA Finals from the previous fall. Francine was taken back to her triumph.

The room remained quiet as Francine noticed some of the girls looking her way after an especially hard hit. The screen continued to the final frames of Idaho standing holding their national championship trophy. The monitor went blue as the coach switched off the machine.

"OK, Carmen, you played for the University of Kansas two years ago. You ever heard of the University of Idaho as a national powerhouse in women's volleyball?"

Carmen quietly shook her head no.

"Anna, you spent four years at North Carolina State. Idaho ever cross your horizon while you were playing?"

"No coach," came the response.

"Sophia, you were in the area. Just down the street in Missoula, Montana. Idaho ever beat up your team?"

"No coach, we beat them every time while I was there."

The head coach let the information settle in. If they didn't get the message, he had only one other option.

"That's right. Idaho was never a volleyball powerhouse. And with Francine turning pro, I don't see Idaho rising again. But for one brief point in time, the right player with the right skills came along and led them up the golden ladder."

He focused back on Sophia for his next question. "Sophia, you've been on this team longest. How many World Championships has Italy won in Women's Volleyball?"

"None that I know of coach."

"And how many Olympic Gold Medals has Italy won in Women's Volleyball?" This time aimed at no one in particular. He waited for an answer. "Carmen, care to guess?"

"I'd guess Italy has never won."

"That's correct. No gold, no silver, not even bronze. Italy has been shut out of the medal stand in volleyball." The coach stopped and stared at his team. The quiet built as the tension grew.

255

"But like little Idaho that came out of obscurity, I intend for Italy to have its one chance in the sun. I intend to have a team standing on the podium receiving a gold medal. If you are not ready to accomplish that goal, I will go find the players who will at least try. Do I make myself very clear?"

The entire team sat up and focused. Gone was the certain Italian disdain for competition that tended to exist. A more American level of determination grew on their faces as each remembered their time playing in the United States.

The results the next day showed the changed attitude of the Italian women. While still stuck in the bottom bracket with the other losers, their play was a harbinger for a different outcome. Francine was included in the play as she began her quest for an Olympic Gold medal.

Chapter 23

Rome, Italy

"Mr. Zoan, with the start of the Olympics tomorrow, has the World Anti-Doping Council made any decisions on the status of Francine McDowell?" a reporter from the Herald Gazette asked.

Jack Hawkins from ZBC Sports Network looked around at the reporter who had asked the question. It was still early in the WADC news conference and already the McDowell woman was the hot topic. Jack waited patiently to get his licks in on Mr. Zoan.

"No, our organization is still under advisement as to the playing status of Ms. McDowell. As you know from our previous work, Ms. McDowell continues her claim that she has not used any performance-enhancing drugs of any kind. As her prowess on the court continues to demonstrate, this fiction flaunts the results," Cubo said.

The same reporter followed up with, "Could you elaborate on that phrase 'flaunts the results'. Are you calling her a liar?"

Jack winced at the bluntness of the question. Cubo certainly had a way of insinuating something without coming out and really saying it. *But it was a bit obtuse for some of these guys, I guess*, he thought.

"I wouldn't call Ms. McDowell a liar certainly. But the facts of her performance level speak volumes as to where she might have obtained such abilities. That's all I'm saying."

Jack raised his hand to be recognized. Cubo looked at the ZBC reporter and nodded to him.

"Jack Hawkins, ZBC Sports. My viewers want to know how WADC can determine if any performance enhancing activity has taken place without the blood tests to determine any doping?"

"These athletes are very good at what they do," Cubo said. "Time and again our tests are finally ready to fully register the level of cheating only to have them change their doping regime. These new drug cocktails are missed by our tests and we are forced to go back to our laboratory to develop new tests. But cheating is taking place, I can assure you."

Jack jumped in for his follow-up question, "And you know that because of informants reporting their observations to you?" Jack hung on the word 'observations' for emphasis. He continued, "Isn't that like the Hitler Youth technique on ratting out anyone they don't like? Seems a bit arbitrary and capricious to me, I'm thinking."

Cubo glared at him in response. He wasn't used to such pointed questions from the press. The entire sports press world had grown frustrated with the cheating going on and had assumed Zoan was the only answer.

"Mr. Hawkins, my organization has the highest intentions to make sports the respectable endeavor it has always tried to be. We have to find the truth any way we can. If our blood tests don't cover every situation, we have to use other methods. I want to announce to everyone concerning the McDowell investigation that we have made important strides in gathering the truth about her Australian activities, as they term it. I can assure you that WADC will have an answer soon," Zoan said.

The press conference returned to the usual sorting out of doping issues. Jack put his recorder away and sat politely. He knew this issue was far from over.

* * *

The news from Cubo Zoan didn't register at the McDowell family camp. Other crises were unfolding long before the WADC threw their gauntlet down over Francine's eligibility to compete. With the WADC now providing drug testing for the ITF that controlled tennis as well as IAAF that ran track and field, two out of her three sports were covered.

The IFVB that governed volleyball was still doing its own drug testing so Francine knew all of Zoan's insinuations stopped there. *But did they?* she wondered. If she was banned by tennis and track, could volleyball ignore that fact? As Camille had taught her, she placed such issues in a box and locked them in her brain.

Francine had more immediate concerns. When the final schedule of events came out, the Rome Olympic Committee had caused a mix-up for Francine. Her attempt at a gold medal in the triple jump was conflicted.

If her volleyball team won the games it needed to get into the medal round, she would not be able to compete in the triple jump. She had sat down with the Italian track coach to try to come up with an alternative plan. They had settled on her competing in the discus.

Francine had thrown the discus in high school and finished 4th at the state meet. She was familiar with the technique and with her heightened reaction she should be able to substantially increase her distance.

Italy had qualified two women in the discus event. Only if one backed out, could Francine step in as an alternate. In practice, Francine had out-distanced both women and came close to tying the European record. It had been an ongoing argument ever since.

"No, I won't take another person's spot on the team. She earned her chance to throw and I won't be a part of denying her her dream," Francine said.

The Italy track coach was just as adamant, "But Francine, she wants you to take her spot. You have a much better chance to medal than she does. She's thinking of the team."

Francine had heard it before. The pressure the Italian press and public was exerting to have an Italian accomplish what no other athlete had even attempted was only increasing. Winning a gold medal in three different sports was tantamount on Italian minds

Francine was the favorite to take a gold in women's tennis. Her chances had improved in volleyball with the Italian team finally coming together around their star player. But track was in the way of a three-peat. And the pressure was enormous.

"I've talked to Patritsia. I know she wants to make everyone happy and withdraw. But I won't allow it. So stop with the pressure. I've already told her I won't take her spot even if she quits," Francine said.

"Then your dream of a three-peat is gone," the track coach admitted.

"Then I'll work hard to earn two," Francine countered.

She had her first volleyball game that afternoon. She excused herself and headed home to her grandparent's apartment. Francine had opted to stay out of the Olympic Village to avoid the commotion. With what she was attempting, a quiet place to recover between events was essential.

Her grandfather had arranged an Alitalia van to transport her wherever she needed to be. Two security guards were added when the crowds became aware of her location. With tennis being competed at the Rome Tennis Club away from the Olympic Village, she traveled frequently through the Rome streets as she changed venues.

Track was scheduled for the second week so Francine could put her disappointments off for a time. Juggling volleyball and tennis matches consumed her first week.

Everything progressed as planned and the Italian volleyball team played out pool play. Matched up in Pool B with Spain, Argentina, and Canada, Italy struggled at times to find their rhythm. Francine was still new to the other players and miscues on assignments kept the team from hitting their best form.

Canada was the most difficult test. Francine recognized a couple of the women players on the Canadian team from her NCAA tournament. The United States was the breeding ground for the best volleyball players in the world and Canadian players headed south for the experience. All their players had attended American universities playing against the best.

Italy won in the fifth and deciding set and would advance to the medal round. They would have to match up against Brazil in the first round. The United States would take on Russia on the other side of the bracket.

But before she could focus on that, tennis called her away. Her first two opponents were from Bulgaria and Mexico. Francine won easily, which put her in a match against Dominique Richard of France. Dominique had moved up to number four in the world and Francine would finally be tested.

The match with Dominique ended up like the previous match-ups. Francine's quickness and power overwhelmed the French woman as Francine moved into the semi-finals where the medal rounds were determined. The top four players would go head to head and three would end up standing on the podium.

Francine would be playing a surprise of the competition. A Russian woman ranked 44th in the world was having the Olympics of a lifetime. Camille scrambled to watch tape of Francine's next opponent .

Tennis was put on hold as volleyball took back over. The test between Brazil and Italy finally saw the Italian team pull together. Francine dominated the game and set the court on fire with her aggressive play.

Brazil would play for the bronze medal against Russia. Italy would have to get through the United States Team to earn its gold medal.

Francine sat down with her personal support team. Sitting with the star athlete were her parents, Coach Camille and her personal physician, Mike Turpin

"We've accomplished our first goal. Francine is in the finals for both her sports," Camille offered.

Dewey added, "It looks tight for the schedule though. The tennis finals is right before the volleyball finals. If tennis goes long, we'll miss the first part of volleyball."

"I'm concerned about that also," Camille said. "And with the two venues in different places, that could be a huge problem."

"I've clocked the time from the Rome Tennis Club to the Olympic Village. On a good day it takes 15 minutes. On a bad day it takes over an hour. Rome traffic is less than predictable," Dewey said.

Francine turned to her mom as Anna Maria added, "I've talked to Lorenzo. He might be able to get Alitalia to help."

"Good, keep working on that. It may prove critical," Camille said. "And track and field is still a no go?"

Francine jumped right to the answer, "I told you I won't take another woman's spot that earned a chance to compete. It's just not right. I don't care how many Italian newspapers are calling for her to withdraw so I can compete."

"OK Francine, that's settled then. We don't have to worry about track. It would have been tight with the discus prelims scheduled right before the tennis finals anyway."

The meeting wrapped up and Francine went to her scheduled physical therapy session with her trainer. The pounding her body was taking while competing in the two sports was affecting her and Dr. Turpin closely monitored her health.

Chapter 24

Zurich, Switzerland

The Swissair flight from Dubai lowered its landing gear as the flaps of the Boeing 767 moved another notch. The whirring sound of both attracted the attention of the passenger sitting in the third row of the First Class section.

He took another sip of the Australian wine he had ordered and looked out the window. Off in the distance the afternoon clouds built up over the Swiss Alps. Directly below, cars and trucks moved along the Autobahn heading into Zurich.

The man had never been to Switzerland. In fact, he had never been to Europe. Asia was as far as he'd gotten, and then it hadn't been that far. From Australia, Asia is the closest place one can go to if one didn't count New Zealand.

He had spent some time in Bali on one trip. Another had taken him to Bangkok and the beaches of southern Thailand. Both times he had passed through Singapore.

In fact, like many Western Australians, he had been to Asia as many times as he'd been to the eastern portion of his own country. It was cheaper most days to fly from Perth to the resorts in Asia than to fly to Sydney or Melbourne.

And the people at the Asian resorts were a whole lot more fun than those New South Wales blokes who he had learned to avoid. Even if most of the other people in the Asian resorts were fellow Australians on holiday and in a party mode. And Asia was cheaper to stay in than Australia's big cities.

But he had been warned about the Swiss by his mates back in Coral Bay. It still amazed him how many Europeans flew out from their home countries, rented a 'ute' and toured around the wilds of Western Oz. He had met his share of them in his duties as tour guide and he could attest that the Swiss weren't the 'party till you drop' type. *The Italians, now there was a fun bunch to be around. But those northern Europeans --- especially the Germans --- watch out,* he thought.

When he got the offer to travel to Zurich on an all-expense paid trip, he jumped at the chance. Now he wondered if anyone would be here to meet him.

He didn't exactly compute that there might be strings attached at the time, but the long flight left plenty of time to think. Although too late to back out, his apprehension as to what he had gotten himself into lingered as the plane touched down on the runway.

Stepping out of Customs, he saw a man in a suit and hat holding a sign. It read 'Smythe Party'.

"I'm Tony Smythe."

"Please, a car is waiting. I'll take your bag," the man said.

Tony hesitated slightly. The man took his one soft travel bag out of his hand. As an Australian, Tony wasn't used to servants. Real Aussie men did everything themselves. Especially if you came from Western Oz.

Western Oz was a world into itself. Huge and empty, people who settled in the western part of Australia were different than the rest of the country. Although similar to the other residents in the outback of the Northern Territories or Queensland, Western Oz raised fiercely independent people.

And considering how independent all of Australia was, Western Australia spawned exceptional individuals. And Tony's hesitation at being served by others only grew.

Arriving at the fanciest hotel he had ever seen, the driver handed him off to the waiting hotel staff. Whisked through the lobby, he was taken straight away to a room on the top floor. As the door opened, Tony walked into a suite overlooking the park in downtown Zurich.

His small bag was placed on the luggage rack as the servant asked, "Is there anything else you need, sir?"

Tony was transfixed at the luxurious accommodations and hardly heard the question.

The servant cleared his throat. "Sir, will you be needing anything else?"

"Oh, no, I'm good, mate. Say, this is a bloody nice place."

"Yes sir, we pride ourselves on having the finest accommodations in all of Zurich. I hope they meet your standards." He lingered, waiting for the normal gratuity that was expected.

Tony, being from Western Australia, was a little slow on the traditional awarding of favors to servants. He continued to survey his room and the view of downtown it afforded.

The servant was growing a little antsy when the door to the bedroom swung open and a man walked into the sitting area. He was dressed in an Italian suit and had his long hair swept back but loose. The man pulled his hand out of his trousers, a five Euro note in it.

Walking over to the servant, he handed the man the money. The servant thanked the man, turned and left. As the door was quietly closed behind him, the man turned to a stunned Tony.

"Let me introduce myself. Cubo Zoan, at your service. Mr. Smythe, it is so good to meet you finally."

"Good on you. Tony Smythe of Coral Bay, Australia." Tony dragged out the pronouncement of Australia as most of his countrymen did. As he stepped across the room to take Cubo's hand, he added, "Are you the bloke I should be shouting the beers for then?"

Cubo's confused look belied his utter lack of understanding of what had just been said. "I'm not sure I caught that Mr. Smythe."

"You paying for all this," Tony offered. "Shouting a beer means I'm buying where I come from." He would have to watch himself with these foreigners. *They don't understand English well,"* he thought.

"Ah yes, I would be the one to shout beers for then. Or at least my organization would be the one," Cubo said in an attempt to use the local colloquiums. "The World Anti-Doping Council is really who you should be thanking."

Tony's stomach tightened at the mention of WADC. *So, that's who's being generous on my behalf,* he thought. Alarm bells were ringing in Tony's head as he sized up the man.

"I told your mate when they came to interview me. I can't say anything on account I'll be in prison soon after. Those bloody bastards at the Ministry of Health have been all over Coral Bay warning everyone that to talk about what happened was now against the law."

"Yes, yes. We understand all that. But we can wait to discuss all that. You're tired from your long flight. The hotel restaurant is excellent. Just charge it to your room. Enjoy yourself. We'll talk tomorrow."

Before Tony could get another word out, Zoan was out the door. Tony's mind raced as he went through what he had gotten himself into. *Yes, I know the truth of the whole McDowell transformation into international sports super star,* he thought. *I had been the one in the boat administering help to what was a lost cause.*

That the woman survived at all was a miracle. That she survived with superhuman traits was a double miracle. But now he was trapped by this Zoan creature who was paying for information about the whole thing. And the Australian Ministry of Health just waiting back home to have any excuse to throw someone in jail just for breathing a word about the McDowell case.

Tony had seen the reports of the foreigners who had insanely tried to repeat the McDowell experiment. Nine individuals had actually traveled to Australia and subjected themselves to what was rumored to have been the elixir for superhuman strength. And nine really stupid people had died horrible deaths in their attempt at fame.

The Australian government had ramped up the threats to the locals for anyone assisting the wannabe sports superstars in their fatal endeavors. Tony had one mate grilled by police for three days after he reported two Germans had asked about the whole thing.

The Germans never followed through with any of it, but just their asking got his mate in a bloody mess. Tony suddenly knew he was in over his head. Maybe dinner would give him time to think. *And a couple of bloody beers might help,* he thought.

The restaurant was a little over the top for Tony's taste. He settled on lamb chops since the place didn't even offer fish and chips. *What kind of place calls itself the best in town and doesn't offer fish and chips?* he thought.

And what was with the waiter? He thought he saw the man almost retch when he asked for chips with his lamb chops. *Back in Coral Bay, everything came with chips, so what was his problem?* he thought.

And the beer, what's with that? he thought. Fosters wasn't available so he tried the recommended Dortmunder. The first taste of the heavy dark German stout almost killed him. He waved the waiter down and asked for a lighter beer.

An American Budweiser was produced and though it was from the States, at least Tony could get it down. *Not bad piss for Americans*, he thought. By the fourth beer, it was tasting pretty good to him. He was contemplating a fifth one when his thoughts were interrupted.

"Excuse me, I couldn't help but notice, you're from Australia aren't you?" a voice spoke.

Tony looked up from his drink at one of the most striking Sheilas he had ever seen. And this one was talking to him.

"Yes mam', Tony Smythe of Coral Bay, Australia at your service."

"Oh, I just love the way you talk. May I sit down?"

Tony jumped to his feet and offered her the chair adjacent to his. As she sat down, he did his best gentleman act to slide the chair in for her. He would never have done it in Australia, but he realized he was in Europe now.

"Thank you. And a gentleman too," she offered as Tony quickly took a seat.

"Care for a drink? They don't have Fosters here, but this American piss is bonzer." He immediately kicked himself for talking like someone from the outback. He attempted to recover. "Excuse me, this American beer is acceptable."

He noticed a slight curl to her mouth at the suggestion of an American beer, but agreed that she would try one. Tony flashed the waiter down and ordered two more beers.

"Can I order you something to eat? The lamb chops weren't bad if you scrape all the cheese off the top. What's with that anyway? Can't they just throw something on the barbie and call it right?"

The woman laughed and said, "I just love how you talk. What brings you to Zurich?"

Tony looked over the woman sitting next to him. She was way above the level of women he ever saw in Coral Bay. Once in a while a European tourist would float through for a couple of days that would have all his mates talking.

But Tony had never meet anyone who looked like what was beside him. And to be having a beer and conversing was beyond his thought process. Sure, he had met some bonzer Sheila's having a good time at the resorts in Asia, but none like this one. She even smelled sophisticated. He sat transfixed as they talked.

After another round of beers, Tony was starting to feel the effects of his American beer. The woman listened intently as she let Tony ramble on about life in Australia. At one point, when the wait staff didn't respond fast enough, Tony took up drinking the German beer that had sat in front of him. *It doesn't taste so bad now,* he thought.

Tony awoke the next morning in his bed in the large suite. His head hurt from the night before as he blinked repeatedly at the sun streaming in through the open windows. He climbed out of bed and pulled the drapes closed.

With the room darkened, he crawled into bed and fell back asleep. A knock on his door awoke him finally. He rolled over and checked the clock. *How did it get to be noon already?* he thought. *What bloody time is it back home?*

Another knock took Tony back to reality. He tried to clear his groggy head as he pulled on some pants. Opening the door, he was greeted by Cubo Zoan.

"Good morning Mr. Smythe. I trust you had a restful sleep."

"Zoan, I don't know what time it is in Oz, but I'm still beat. Can I hold off on any fun for right now?"

"I'm afraid not. We have pressing business together, you and I. I'm afraid it can't wait."

"Well, if this is about that McDowell woman and her deal with death, I can't say anything. If I do, the Australian bastards will put me in chains and I won't see the light of day for a fortnight."

"I understand your reluctance to talk even though this McDowell woman is obviously cheating and should be stopped. I was hoping that you would want to do the right thing," Cubo said.

"I'd like to help you, I sure would. But the bloody government is really bollocks about the whole thing. I'd miss my girlfriend sitting in prison and I know she wouldn't wait for my release."

"I'm sorry you brought her up, Mr. Smythe," Cubo said. "We have something that might change your mind about talking about Ms. McDowell. Let me show you."

Chapter 25

Rome, Italy

It was still three days till Francine would compete for the two gold medals in her two sports. She was with her trainer in her grandparent's home getting her legs worked on. All the jumping was taking its toll and she had limited herself during the team practice.

She went through the drills but didn't put the leaping portion into them. When the ball was set her way, she would sprint to the spot where she would normally take off from and just stop and grab the ball as it fell.

The Italian coach was a little concerned about his star player and whether she would be ready for the main event. Francine assured him that she was just being conservative and saving her stamina for the match.

But her right ankle was bothering her. It was the one that had been broken in high school and the one that was reinjured playing college volleyball. As the trainer finished up manipulating her ankle, he announced he was done.

Francine sat up and reached for a water bottle by the table. As she grabbed it and lifted it to her mouth, the bottle dropped and bounced on the floor. The trainer turned around startled.

"What happened?"

"I just dropped my water bottle. That's all," Francine said.

Francine watched the trainer carefully. She could tell that he was computing something. She dreaded that he would figure it out. She reached down and lifted the water bottle more carefully this time.

"I saw you drop your tennis racket the other day in practice."

"Players drop their rackets all the time. My hands were sweaty and it slipped. That's all," Francine responded.

The trainer looked at her with a more critical eye. *Is he figuring it out?* she thought.

She sat holding her bottle on the massage table hoping he wouldn't put things together. Noticing the trainer's eyes drift down to her right hand holding the water bottle, she stared straight in his eyes and noticed his recognition.

She followed his stare down to her right hand. It was shaking. She tried to stop the shake but it continued.

"Your hand is shaking. Make it stop," the trainer demanded.

The hand continued to shake, very slightly, but noticeable. Francine's eyes began to tear up as she sat mute.

"You can't stop it, can you?"

Francine shook her head. The tears streaked down her face as she lowered her head.

"How long have you known?" the trainer asked.

Francine finally could croak out an answer. Very quietly she said, "Last month."

The trainer continued to watch her hand and the shaking subsided. Finally the hand was still.

"How often do you get the shakes?"

Francine thought for a minute before answering. She hadn't recorded the dates and times of each episode, but they certainly were coming more frequent. "Once a day now. When I first noticed them, they happened every few days. Usually when I was extra tired or under stress."

The trainer took her hand and manipulated it to see if the shakes returned. Nothing happened, so he asked, "Any other body part showing similar shakes?"

"No, just my right hand," Francine answered. "Please don't tell anyone. They'll make me stop. I can't stop now. I'm so close. You can't tell anyone." Her voice almost became panicky at the mere thought of her secret being revealed.

The trainer put his hand on Francine's shoulder to calm her. Then he asked, "Has Dr. Turpin given you a good physical lately?"

"I don't want anyone interfering in this," Francine said. "I can hold it together long enough. I haven't experienced it during a game. I relax when I'm playing. Only afterward when the pressure is on with the news reporters and the whole Cubo Zoan thing, I just wish that would go away."

"Your secret is safe with me," the trainer said. "But I'll be watching for any other signs. We don't know what the effects your condition will cause you and we have to be careful."

Like everyone else, the trainer had not been told the details surrounding the circumstances of Francine's athletic prowess. He was as much in the dark as everyone else as to what side effects Francine could experience. No one in the world knew that answer as no one had lived through what she had experienced to have any long-term side effects.

There was a slight knock on the door to their room. The trainer helped Francine clean her face and then opened the door. Francine's coach, Camille, stepped in and registered something wasn't right.

"What's up?" she asked. "Why the tears?" Her job was to keep on top of Francine's mental as well as physical health. If there was any glitch in the hunt for success, it was her job to straighten things out.

"Nothing. We just had some scar tissue to work out on Francine's right ankle. It takes extra manipulation to get her full flexibility back," the trainer lied.

"Yeah, Camille. Hurts like hell breaking that scar tissue," Francine said joining in the conspiracy.

"OK, you tell me if anything is conflicting you," Camille said. "I come with good news. At least good for us. It seems that Patritsia threw out her elbow in discus practice this morning. That opens up a slot for you as an alternate."

"Great," Francine said, but then rethought the situation. "I mean, is she going to be OK?"

"She'll recover but not in time for this Olympics. If you're going to throw, qualifying is this afternoon. Pack up, we need to hurry," Camille said.

They reached the Olympic Stadium in time to register for the opening rounds of the discus competition. Francine met the Italian throws coach and discussed the situation. Patritsia stood by with her elbow heavily bandaged and in a sling.

The two competitors embraced as Francine offered her condolences. Patritsia wished her replacement well and headed to the stands to watch the competition.

Francine had spent very little time practicing the discus. She had started after the triple jump competition was judged unattainable due to the schedule conflicts. But when it was realized that no slot was available on discus, Francine had stopped.

She would be competing on very little time in the ring. Her competitors, the best in the world, spent every day working on their throwing skills. Francine would have to rely on other attributes to do well today.

The coach helped Francine with the basics of the discus. They went over the proper hold, the release motion and the spin in the ring to obtain maximum velocity. He reminded her to enter and leave only from the back of the ring.

All of it was familiar to Francine from throwing in high school, where she had been part of her school team and had competed in discus as well as javelin and shot-put. The coaches had put her on the 4x100 relay team where she had enjoyed running. Her team had done OK at districts but she had missed out going on to the State Meet. Now she was in the Olympics.

* * *

"Well, sports fans everywhere, here we go. In our continuing coverage of the Olympics here in Rome, we move into day one of what everyone has been waiting for, track and field," the announcer Hugh Godley said.

"Swimming is over with the usual medal haul by the American swimmers. Gymnastics is finished with all those prepubescent girls strutting their stuff."

The producer rolled her eyeballs at her announcer as a warning to keep it family friendly. Hugh ignored her and continued.

"Now we start the power sport of track. And it's anyone's guess who will dominate here over the next week. Will the Jamaicans roll up their competitors in the sprints? Will the Kenyans out kick the Tanzanians in the distance races? And will the Americans squeeze out enough points to remain the overall track and field champion? With me today to answer some of those questions is our favorite French middle distance runner, Steve Fontaine."

"Thanks, Hugh," Steve said. "We certainly do have a great line-up for the viewers all this week. More hours of live competition than any other Olympics. All the big names are here and they appear healthy for this once-every-four-year event. So, let's run down our line-up."

"Wait a minute, Steverino. My old eyes may be playing tricks on me but I see a developing story out there in the discus ring. I know this is only the prelims, but I see on my sheet that the Italians have an alternate for one of their injured throwers." Hugh pointed out the updated info to his partner.

Steve rolled his eyes toward the producer at being called Steverino. Trying to inject a more sophisticated French tone to the broadcast, Steve offered, "Yes Hugh. I noted that change earlier. That comes late but I think the effect will be minimal. The injured thrower as well as the

279

remaining Italian thrower have PRs well below the main competitors. I can assure you that the top ten are quite safe."

"I wouldn't be so sure, my Gallic friend. I've seen this McDowell woman compete before. I'm here to tell you, she's a human dynamo. We should be reevaluating the field as we speak."

Steve grimaced at the French reference. *Where do they get these bourgeois announcers?* he thought. "Well, Hugh. I checked the record. Ms. McDowell hasn't thrown competitively since high school. And she didn't even qualify to compete at her Colorado state meet. She would have to be Superwoman to come in here and compete with the Germans. They've owned this sport for the last ten years."

"Well, speak of the devil and here she comes! Your favorite German thrower and defending World Champion is stepping up now. Let's see how this first flight goes?" Hugh said.

Helga walked around the net and stepped into the ring. She looked down the field as if registering in her brain where she would place the discus. She turned her back and swung her arm out behind her, the discus clutched tightly.

With a quick first step, she swung her massive body around once and then twice. With her rotation at its maximum, she whipped her arm across her chest and let the discus fly. She continued her spin and caught herself before she hit the board on the front of the ring. She spun around to watch her flight.

The ground crew ran quickly to the spot the discus first hit the ground and pushed an electronic measuring device into the spot. The distance registered on the electronic board next to the ring: 70.22 meters.

Steve jumped on the distance, "A good first throw for our World Champion. Oh look, our high school star is throwing right behind her. Let's see how Ms. McDowell responds to the challenge."

Hugh didn't offer any smart remarks at his color man's taunts. He just matter-of-factly reported what was happening in the discus ring.

Francine stepped around the net and into the ring. She could tell her nerves were the better of her today. While she had played a lot of tennis and volleyball the last six months, she was suddenly aware that her discus skills were suspect.

As she stared down the field trying to pull her emotions together, the Italian partisans started a chant. Much had been written on the Francine case and whether she would get to compete in track. With their hero now in the ring, they were looking forward to an Italian competing against the Germans.

Francine wound up her spin and snapped her arm out to release the discus. The metal object flew out of her hand and into the protective net. Only Francine's incredibly fast reflexes kept her from being clonked in the head by the ricochet. The crowd groaned as Francine picked herself up off the ground and stepped forward out of the ring, thus defaulting herself for the throw.

Steve was ready, "Not a pretty one to start for our high school wannabe. Maybe she's very good in tennis and volleyball, but I think she might not be up to the big girl challenge here today."

He got a foul look from his partner at his glib comments. The female producer cut the announcers off and switched to an ad.

Hugh took the opportunity to make things interesting. "So, my French buddy. Care to make a little wager on the outcome of this event? You get Helga and I get the high schooler."

"But of course, Mr. Godley. I'll be happy to take your British money. Pounds, I believe you people still use, isn't it? Are they still exchangeable for real money?"

"Oh no, my fine fellow gastronomic. I wouldn't dream of soiling your hand with something so gauche as money. No, my bet is the winner picks the meal, the loser eats and pays."

"Wonderful, I can taste my truffles now. I will delight in watching my fine English friend choke down a plate of Normandy's finest." Steve relished the idea.

"No, no my friend. Bangers and beans. No sir. There'll be no dirty mushrooms for the likes of you after this. And stewed tomatoes with chutney," Hugh added.

Steve tried not to blanche, at the idea of losing and suffering through British cooking. His interest in Helga's performance suddenly doubled.

* * *

Helga continued to build on her first distance on her subsequent throws. With three attempts each, each thrower tried to move on to the next round.

Francine improved measurably on her first throw in that at least it got out of the ring without hitting her. She continued to hold last place in her flight as she struggled to get her timing down. Trying to coordinate the foot spin with her arm swing and tie it all in with the hand release for optimum power was eluding her. The Italian coach was waiting for her by the railing off the main track. The local supporters had grown very quiet as Francine struggled with her throws.

"Francine, relax. Close your eyes and let your body do the work. You're thinking too much. One time it's the feet that are fine. The next time you forget your feet but your arm is great. Then you forget your release. Let it all work together."

"I'm trying, but it just doesn't want to work all at the same time," Francine answered, frustration visible on her face.

The coach thought of an answer. The competitors continued throwing as the two stood away from the cage. Soon Helga was standing in the ready position for her last throw. That meant Francine would get her last chance to qualify.

Finally, her coach hit on an idea. "Francine, you play tennis. The whole world knows that. When you go out there, just think of a good low ground stroke. Its almost the same motion. Just without the foot spin or hand release. Just think tennis and stroke it."

Francine turned to see Helga step into the ring as she jogged back and picked up her discus. She closed her eyes and did as her coach suggested. Taking some practice ground strokes with the discus in her hands, she added a few foot steps to it.

Francine opened her eyes as the crowd came to life. Helga walked out of the ring smiling. The reader board rotated and announced the distance. The roar of the crowd increased when it announced a throw of 72.16 meters.

Francine stepped toward the ring as Helga brushed by her. In a low voice, the big German looked down and said, "Stick with those other sports little one. This is a real woman's sport out here."

It was all Francine could do to not respond to the insult. She stepped into the ring and closed her eyes. Imagining herself from above, she lined up in the start position. She swung her arm in good tennis ground stroke fashion and then pulled it back behind her.

Still with her eyes closed, Francine quickly spun her feet, her body following. Her ground stroke kicked in and then her hand release. Opening her eyes as she came to a stop behind the penalty board, she searched for her discus and only caught it as it hit the grass.

The Italian crowd sensed that it had been a good throw and cheered, hoping that more noise would move the mark further. The blank board rotated in place, waiting for the official measurement. The digital reader finally lit up and the crowd went crazy.

Francine had just moved up to fourth place in her flight. With three women left to throw for their chance to advance, Francine sat down on the grass and waited. She pulled on her sports pants and jacket to stay warm.

Sitting with her legs drawn up and her head resting on her knees, she watched as each thrower stepped into the ring. Each time her fourth place spot held. But as she sat and tried to clear her mind, she reached for her water bottle to wet her dry mouth.

The bottle fell out of her hand and hit her in the foot. Her hand tremor returned as she quickly grabbed it with her other hand. No one could tell as she felt the uncontrollable shaking continue.

The shaking didn't stop until the last thrower had been eliminated from the competition. Francine had squeaked into the next round. She would have to do better tomorrow to reach her dream. Her right hand continued its tremor in her pants pocket as she marched off the field.

Chapter 26

Canberra, Australia

The Australian national capital city was not on the tourist route. Built in the middle of nowhere --- which is saying a lot, considering it's Australia --- Canberra was not often visited by even Australians. Located about halfway between Melbourne and Sydney, the capital acted as sort of a referee between the two biggest cities in the country.

Lately, Sydney was more famous in the world. But at the beginning of the 20th century, Melbourne was the star that everyone knew. And Melbourne clung tenaciously to the Australian Open Tennis Championship as its star event.

Canberra, as the national capital, acted as the final arbitrator for all Australia. And the Federal government had come down hard on the entire country over the McDowell problem. And it was a massive problem to the Australian bureaucrats. Already, nine crazy foreigners had arrived in the country and had proceeded to get themselves killed trying to replicate the McDowell effect.

Dr. Keith Mountain, from the Ministry of Health, sat at his desk and stared out at the verdant country beyond the buildings. Still a back-water in Australian life, the city remained small with open country close. Keith longed to be back out in his native bush country and away from this headache of tourists killing themselves.

His secretary buzzed the intercom to announce that someone was in the outer office who wished to see him. While highly unusual for strangers to just walk in without an appointment, it wasn't totally unheard of here. And if it wasn't important, his secretary would have diverted the stranger elsewhere.

He waited for his visitor to be escorted into his office when a rather attractive woman was led in and shown a seat by his desk. Dressed in appropriate clothing but with sandals on her feet, her bleached out blonde hair and dark tan fit with many that spent their time in the Australian sun.

"Keith Mountain at your service mum."

'Thank you for seeing me. I'm Lynn Randwick. I've come all the way from Coral Bay in Western Australia."

"It must be important then. You've certainly come a long way. What's on your mind?" Keith asked.

Keith knew Coral Bay as the site of the McDowell event. It had also been in the news reports lately with tourists dying from their stupid attempts at athletic fame..

"My boyfriend is Tony Smythe."

The name hit Mountain like a billabong filled with lead shot. He knew from the extensive reports of the McDowell incident that here was the girlfriend of the man who had rescued Ms. McDowell from certain death. "I am familiar with Mr. Smythe. Does this involve the McDowell affair?"

"Then you should know that Tony left last week on a jet out of Perth for Zurich, Switzerland. And he didn't have a pot to piss in for money. I should know since I've been carrying him on our rent for the past few months," Lynn said. "The tourist crowd that he relies on for business is way down since this whole thing. Except for the nut jobs who show up asking how they can get those superhuman skills. The more they die trying the fewer regular tourists show."

"So Mr. Smythe is traveling to Europe and I assume he hasn't retuned yet. You are concerned about what, exactly?"

"I saw his ticket before he left. He flew first class. And I checked where he was staying once he reached Zurich. The hotel is nicer than anything in all of Australia. Someone is picking up the tab on all this. And I thought you might want to find out who that mystery someone is," Lynn said.

"I believe we do, Ms. Randwick. I'll make inquires through our embassy in Bern and see what we find out. In the meantime, are you staying in Canberra? I will call to upgrade your accommodations, at government expense of course. And when you head back to Coral Bay, it will be our treat."

Lynn smiled. Keith Mountain smiled back. *I think I know who is behind this Smythe thing,* he thought. He was about to put the full weight of the Australian government behind confirming his thoughts.

* * *

Francine had made it through the second flight of discus competitors. She was number 12 out of sixteen in the final round. Her fellow Italian team mate had just made the cut at number sixteen. Unfortunately, Francine was receiving some bad press from the Italian papers.

Expecting a better position for their star athlete, her twelfth place standing wasn't going down well with many in the press. And Helga continued her taunts and intimidations. Whenever Francine walked by, Helga made it a point to brush her competitor, sometimes forcefully.

But discus had to wait. Next on Francine's tight schedule was her gold medal match against Svetlana Treschenko. The Russian had bested Selena Roberts in the semi-finals so once again, Francine would not see her main rival in a major tennis event.

The bad feelings established at their last meeting carried over to the Olympics. Svetlana threw Russian trash talk at Francine whenever she got the chance. More and more the accusation of cheating met Francine wherever she went. And the Russian poured fuel on that fire at every opportunity.

Camille worked with Francine to control the damage. Camille explained that Svetlana had no answers to Francine's power game and was only attempting to throw her concentration off before the big match. Unfortunately, it worked. Francine came out flat and unfocused and proceeded to lose the first set 6-4.

The second match was more in Francine's favor as she tried to clear her mind of everything but tennis. She squeaked out a win 7-6. The Olympic gold medal would be settled in a tie breaker.

But that left the Italian Women's Volleyball Team standing in the arena without their star player. Phones went to work as the head of the Italian Olympic Committee tried to solve their rapidly approaching problem.

Francine knew she had to clear her mind of any distractions and concentrate on the third and final tennis set. The volleyball team would have to wait till she was finished with tennis. Then she would see about the next sport.

Francine walked to the baseline for the first serve of the deciding match. She took a couple practice swings before bouncing the ball. Throwing the ball high, she popped onto her toes and caught the ball on its descent.

The ball streaked across the net in a now standard Francine power serve. Svetlana had seen this type of serve before and still couldn't handle it. The ball bounced on the court and then hit the back wall with a resounding boom. The speed indicator registered 249 km/h. The local Romans cheered at the ace.

Svetlana scowled at her opponent. The next one blew by her also. And the next. And then the next. The two competitors walked to their benches for a change over. Svetlana purposely bumped into Francine as they walked around the net in opposite directions.

The crowd hissed at the insult. They grew louder as Svetlana prepared to serve. The chair umpire called for quiet.

Svetlana's serve was easily handled by the quicker player as Francine put all her strength into the return. The ball flew back across the net and caught the opposite corner of the court for a point. The crowd loved it.

After Francine broke Svetlana's serve once, the rest of the match slid over to the typical Francine drumming.

The crowd continued to display its opinion of the bad Russian manners. The more the crowd heckled, the worse Svetlana's game became.

Francine closed her out 6-0. Shaking hands at the net, Francine looked around for her escape. She had a volleyball team waiting and needed to exit quickly.

She left her tennis gear as she ran off the court. Camille was waiting at the exit and directed her out of the building. They both spotted her grandfather Lorenzo standing in an open area just off the main tennis courts.

An Alitalia helicopter was sitting with its rotors turning. Lorenzo motioned the two toward the open back door. Jumping in, Francine buckled in just as the pilot lifted off the ground. She just had time to see the throngs of well-wishers that had gathered on the hillside to watch the large Jumbotron screen the Olympic Committee had set up.

Camille handed her the uniform of the Italian volleyball team and Francine quickly changed. Her sweaty tennis outfit was stuffed into a bag and passed to her grandfather, which he carefully placed by his feet.

The pilot pointed at the headphones he wore to indicate that everyone should put their set on. Francine reached up and retrieved her set from the clip holding them to the ceiling. Putting them on, she heard the local sports broadcast from the volleyball game.

"Frank, have you ever seen anything like this?" a voice said.

"No, Hugh," a second voice said. "But the Russians did kill the lights in that famous gold medal basketball game between the United States and Russia.

After the break, the Russians came back and won. That was the year the Americans refused their silver medals in protest. And don't forget the Super Bowl where the lights went out" a second voice said.

"Well, there you have it from our announcer, Frank Buck," the first voice said. "He should know about how these things happen. Just to recap, the first game went badly for the Italians as the United States rolled to a crushing victory. Then halfway through the second match, when the Italians seemed on the verge of suffering a second resounding defeat, the lights went out."

The second voice jumped in, "And I'll guarantee that the lights won't be fixed until the Italian's star player arrives from her gold medal winning performance at the tennis center. Hold on, I can hear the helicopter now."

"Well, I have no idea where they're going to land. I haven't seen any helipads inside the Olympic Village, have you?"

"Ah Hugh, we're here in Italy, remember? I think the Italians will work it out."

Francine turned her focus away from the announcers coming over her headphones and looked out the helicopter window. Below her lay the main piazza just outside the Olympic Arena. Designed as a gathering place for visitors and athletes to sit and relax, it was now full of security personnel.

A square of uniformed officers were standing holding a rope that cordoned off the center of the piazza. The normal crowd had been moved aside to allow a clear spot to land. The pilot carefully lowered onto the ground.

A Rome Olympic Committee official opened the door and held it open for Francine and Camille.

Jumping out, the crowd roared its approval over the whine of the jet engine copter. As they hit the arena's entrance door, the pilot lifted off and the security quickly dispersed into the crowd. Soon, everyone was settled back into their spots to watch the Jumbotron that had been installed on the outside of the arena.

When Italy reached the gold medal round, tickets to the volleyball match became the hottest ticket in Rome. A large crowd had gathered outside the arena just to be near the site of what they hoped would be an Italian victory celebration. Now that their star player had arrived, the excitement doubled.

Francine joined her team standing by the sidelines in the dim emergency lighting. Her teammates gathered around her and they all wrapped their arms around each other. Slowly the arena lights began to come on. Being mercury vapor lights, it would take about ten minutes for them to get fully charged.

The American head coach who had been complaining the whole time finally threw out to the Up Ref, "About time! I guess we can get going now that all the Italians are here."

The Up Ref, being from Germany, ignored the comment and stood looking straight ahead. There would be no comment on how the Italians ran their Olympics.

The Italian head coach moved into the circle formed by his players. He knelt down on one knee and looked up. With Francine present, he switched to English.

"OK, we know what we have to do. We're down by 12 in this match. Play one point at a time. We can get back in this. Now, on three."

"One, two, three," the team all chanted in unison, and then ripped, "Roma."

They broke their huddle and took up their positions on the court. Francine moved to the scorer's table so she could be substituted as soon as play was resumed.

Entering the game to a rousing ovation from the local fans and a smattering of boos from the opposition, she ignored it all. Her game face was on as she looked at her Setter. Cha Cha, as the team had nicknamed her, was staring back at Francine. The Setter nodded that Francine should be ready in her back court position.

The ball would be coming Francine's way. Unfortunately, the American players all knew who was going to get the ball. The big front row for the United States all stared at Francine. *They will be keying off me,* Francine thought. *Just one point and I move up to the front row.*

The American team got the signal from the Up Ref and the ball came in hard away from Francine. Her teammate moved out of the way so Francine could quickly slide in under and pass a perfect ball to Cha Cha.

Francine took off and leaped at the ten foot line just as a quick set sprang up in front of her. Before the Americans could react, Francine just nudged the ball slightly as she flew toward the net. The ball left her fingers on her right hand, floated the short distance to the top of the net, hit the tape and rolled down the net.

The American Libero dove for the errant ball but only managed to catch enough to hit it under the net. Point Italy. The Italians rotated and Francine moved to her Outside Hitter position. The Americans countered with a substitution, bringing in a back row Setter. The regular Setter was replaced on the front row with a 6'4" Middle Blocker.

With three women over 6' 3" now facing off against 5' 6" Francine, they would be able to throw a roof of arms over her and stuff her down. Francine walked over to just behind her Middle Blocker they called Po Po. Francine tapped Po Po in the back and whispered something to her.

At 6' 5", Po Po was the tallest player on the Italian side. Francine had noticed in their short time practicing together that Po Po had phenomenal hands and timing for a big player. Normally tall players lack the quickness and mobility of the smaller players.

Francine and Po Po had worked on a play that might overcome the height of the Americans. Francine then turned to her Libero and with Po Po blocking her hand signs from the opposition, she motioned with her thumb toward the right side. The Libero nodded that she understood and raised her eyebrow to Cha Cha. A slight tilt of the head toward the right side went unnoticed by the Americans.

The Italians served the ball and the Americans dug a good high one. Their Setter moved slightly under it and did a quick set to the Middle. The American Middle swung and Po Po caught enough of it so the Italian Libero could easily handle it.

But instead of passing the ball to the right where the Setter waited, she passed the ball to her left where Francine stood. As the ball floated down, Francine took off on her approach and leaped up to meet the ball. At the same time, keyed off of Francine, all three American front row players shifted to cover the anticipated outside hit.

Francine still had a touch to give, so faked a swing, brought two hands up and did a sideways set to Po Po. The Italian middle easily jumped up, placed her two hands just at the top of the net and gently redirected the ball straight down onto the American side.

Again the opposing Libero didn't even come close to digging the ball as she slid in from the back row on her stomach. Point Italy. The fans roared their approval and took up the chant, "Roma, Roma, Roma."

The American coach jumped off the bench and yelled at his players. But the next point went the same way. The three Americans all committed to a Francine hit only to be beat by a Po Po ball dump. Twice more the ball repeated itself. Francine would continue the play until the Americans were forced to adjust.

The key was the Italian Libero handling the ball with enough control to get it into position for Francine to handle it. The Americans adjusted their offense so that now their hits would be cross court, avoiding the Libero. But Francine was patrolling the Italian right back for such shots.

By the rules, she couldn't pass to herself, so Francine passed the ball to Cha Cha. But instead of moving to the outside, Francine flashed to the middle for a quick set. With the ball snapped across the top of the net rather than up in a high arc, it was easily touched by a leaping Francine and redirected straight down.

The American blockers hadn't moved quickly enough to get into a good position and had missed their opportunity. Point Italy. With the American blockers now confused over where the ball would be attacked from, they spread out.

It was time for Francine to go to work on the outside. Receiving the next ball and having only two tall players in front of her, she hit away. With her exceptional hand-eye coordination, she proceeded to hit off the blockers' hands, the ball bouncing out of bounds each time.

Even when the Americans had the timing down and created the roof of four arms across the net that would smother other players, Francine's skill set overcame it. She hit to intentionally strike one of the opposing players arms or hands. The ricochet flew out of bounds.

Francine was using the player's bodies as a back board. If the Americans hadn't been there with their outstretched arms, the way Francine was hitting, all of her balls would sail up into the stands for American points.

To rub the lesson in, Francine didn't even jump for the ball. Instead, she let it float down to her standing on the court. She proceeded to smash a winner off the arms strutted completely over her. The resulting ball had been aimed almost straight up at the time, but bounced off and went out of bounds just feet from Francine's position.

Again the American coach jumped up and screamed at his players. He moved his arms together to indicate that he wanted those balls directed into the court, not out. The players looked at him and rolled their eyes.

The Italians finished out the game, making up the twelve point deficit before Francine arrived and won by eight. The match was now tied up, one game apiece.

The two teams switched courts and as they did a player that had been on the Nebraska team walked by Francine and shoulder-bumped her. They had played against each other in the NCAA playoffs and the bad blood that had developed was reignited.

As the players lined up before start of play, the Nebraska player stood in the back row and made threatening gestures at Francine. Francine ignored the taunts as she waited for the Down Ref to set the rotation.

Play resumed and the ref rolled Francine the ball for first serve. She bounced the ball a few times and then looked at the opposing team. She checked her coach and he was showing five fingers to indicate where he wanted the serve to be placed.

Francine walked back from the baseline and bounced the ball a few more times. Then throwing the ball up and away from her, she ran to catch up with it. Leaping from behind the baseline, Francine flew over the back court, focused on the falling ball.

But unlike most jump serves, Francine hadn't put any spin on this one. The consequence of a non-rotating ball was that when Francine hit the ball with a flat hand, the ball flew forward with no spin. A floater serve is the hardest type of serve to handle because the aerodynamics of a non-rotating ball effects its flight. The ball wobbled from side to side as it crossed the net. The Nebraska player jumped to set her platform for serve receive.

But as she was about to make contact, the ball moved slightly and ricocheted off her two arms up into the stands. Three more jump floaters were mishandled and the Nebraska player was substituted out of the game.

Like a good baseball pitcher, Francine changed up her serve. With the Libero from the last game back in, she would be ready for serve receive. Francine switched to her specialty, the net ball.

Standing at the baseline, Francine hit a hard floater that was carefully aimed at the top of the net. The ball streaked in, hit the tape, stopped any forward motion and dutifully dropped down the net. The American players all dove trying to get to the ball as the ball hit the court. Point Italy.

* * *

"Unbelievable," commented Frank Buck, color announcer for ZBC Sports Network.

"I've seen this before, ladies and gentlemen," Hugh Godley added. "Ms. McDowell ate up the competition at the NCCA Women's Volleyball Championship a short 10 months ago. And to think the American coach decided that he didn't have room for her on his team. Amazing."

"There she goes again. The Americans seem out of rhythm in this game. Whenever they get what could be a momentum changer, our star Italian changes the dynamics. Ms. McDowell certainly has the skill set to get it done."

The two announcers watched and described a textbook case in how to play volleyball as Francine almost held a clinic on the sport. The points continued to flow the Italians way as the Americans scraped for each point. Soon the game was over.

"We take a break with the games set at Italy 2, America 1. We'll be back for the fourth game in a minute. But first, a word from our sponsor," Hugh said.

An ad for Zeus Sports featuring Francine playing her multiple sports came on. As the ad ran, Frank and Hugh compared notes on other news from the Olympics. One was a shocker. The producer flashed the finger that they were back on and they dropped the bomb shell.

Hugh was ready. "Incredible turn of events in tennis. We have just received news that the Russian tennis coach has filed a protest over Francine McDowell's victory over Svetlana Trenschenko. It seems that Ms. McDowell, in her haste to get to her volleyball match here, did not submit to the required drug testing."

Frank added, "Hugh, that's huge. With this whole WADC thing clinging to everything Ms. McDowell does these days, this will be one more nail that Cubo Zoan will use to hammer Ms. McDowell's coffin, I'm afraid."

"The teams are coming out of the locker room. Do you think our star player has gotten the word of this development?"

* * *

Francine's coach had gotten the word and purposely kept it from her in the locker room. This was no

300

time to be distracted from the play at hand. But taking the court changed all that.

With the United States serving first, the Nebraska player was back on the court. Francine was lined up at front right so she would be the first Italian server once they won side out. The Nebraska player broke the news.

"Hey cheater, how do you like that you lost your tennis gold medal?"

Francine looked at her coach for answers. His response was quick. "Francine, focus, play volleyball, win. Nothing else matters right now."

So there is something to what the woman from Nebraska was saying then, she thought. She was still thinking about it after the American ran up a 5-0 lead on the Italians. The Italian coach called a time out.

"Francine, get your head in the game," he said.

"But what is going on with tennis? Am I losing my gold medal there?" she asked.

Her coach yelled over the crowd noise, "You'll lose your medal here if you keep thinking about other stuff. That will all sort itself out later. We are here now." He screamed 'now' to get his point across.

Francine looked at her fellow players and they were all trying to energize her. They formed their circle and began the chant, "Roma, Roma, Roma."

The crowd joined in. The noise grew as the Up Ref whistled for the game to resume.

Francine was ready and focused. She passed a good ball to Cha Cha who did a quick set to Po Po. The big Middle lightly touched the ball and directed it down onto the opposing court. Point Italy, finally.

Once refocused, the American chances at winning the gold medal diminished. With each Francine hit those chances grew dimmer. When Francine rotated into the back row and the service position, those chances stopped. With multiple weapons at her call, Francine eviscerated the American defense.

When the opposing team set a defense for a fast jump serve, Francine placed a high floater that dropped into the front court. When the United States adjusted for a flat serve, Francine would throw up a spinning jump serve that arrived like a dropping fast ball.

The match ended in a whimper as Italy rolled to victory three games to one. The local partisan crowd both in the arena and outside on the piazza went wild. After the consolatory handshake by the team members, the medals were awarded.

This would be Francine's first medal since she hadn't stuck around for the tennis ceremony. And now with the Russian protest, she wondered if she would even receive it.

But the volleyball officials made sure that after the medal ceremony all the players were escorted to the medical facilities for testing. Francine provided the samples as the Olympic Committee required. She would have to wait to see what the decision was on the Russian protest.

Chapter 27

Rome, Italy

"And furthermore, this whole McDowell controversy has been highlighted by the Russian protest over the utter disregard of Olympic rules requiring anti-doping tests to medal winners," Cubo Zoan continued. He was holding a press conference at the Roman Coliseum.

Using Rome's most famous landmark for a backdrop, Cubo was taking his life in his hands being in public and accusing the star of Italian sports of cheating. It fit with his disdain for all things Italian that had marked his life as well his father's life.

The crowd that had gathered hissed their displeasure at the speaker, but Zoan continued, "The World Anti-Doping Council continues its investigation of this woman and her inhuman skills. We can only wonder how such an unknown can step onto the worlds biggest stage and dominate in three sports."

Slurs were now coming his way from the more vocal members of the crowd. The television cameras panned across the crowd for the viewers back home.

Zoan finished up. "WADC is close to issuing a ruling in Ms. McDowell's case and I can assure sports fans everywhere that it will set the athletic world on its head. I can't comment further on our ongoing investigation."

"What a dick," someone yelled from the crowd as Zoan walked off toward the Arch of Constantine and a waiting car. He was whisked away as the crowd surged to catch up to him.

* * *

Lorenzo quickly turned off the television that had just carried the Zoan broadcast. His granddaughter poked her head around the corner from the kitchen to look at the now blank screen.

"Grandfather, what was that man talking about? Are they really going to rule on my case?" Francine asked.

"None of your concern. You have your discus competition today. That should be all that you are thinking about. Now, go back in the kitchen with your grandmother. Let others worry about all the rest for you."

Francine dutifully returned to the kitchen and her grandmother cooking pasta. Dewey walked in commenting on the wonderful smell. Francine took him aside.

"Dad, what's going to happen with this whole Zoan thing?"

Dewey looked at his daughter. He wasn't sure what to say since everything was still up in the air. The last two days since Francine's tennis victory had seen the International Olympic Committee consider the Russian protest over Francine missing her drug test.

The Italian Organizing Committee that was running the Rome Olympics had made numerous efforts to find out which way the International Committee was leaning. They had been rebuffed each time. The International Committee was still miffed at the locals and their handling of the Olympic Arena lights episode.

The Americans were still complaining about the stoppage in play because of the lights. They had not filed a protest over the incident but rumors were running rampant that they had discussed such a move.

Dewey finally answered, "Honey, all of this is out of our control. Today is your last competition. Focus on that and leave the rest outside the stadium."

* * *

Hugh Godley, ZBC Announcer Extraordinaire, was in the sky box that hovered over Olympic Stadium. From his perch high above the field, he used binoculars to keep track of competitors as the last day of track and field took place.

The Rome Olympics was winding down toward the closing ceremony. The normal heroes had emerged. The swimmer that won a slew of medals had had his day. The women gymnasts from the United States had once again stolen the hearts of viewers everywhere.

The Jamaican sprinters in both women's and men's events had continued their dominance. A surprise was that the Americans were holding a close lead in the medal count. But the world continued to catch up in producing world-class athletes. American colleges and universities might still be the training ground of the world's athletes but in international competition, it was wide open.

Except in discus, where the Germans had dominated in both the women's and the men's event. Gone were the days of questionable sex issues when the big East German 'women' took home all the medals.

Now, the Germans relied on excellent conditioning and superb coaching to continue their reign. Into this arena strode a 5' 6" American competing for the Italian team.

Hugh caught sight of the young woman walking in with her fellow competitors and said, "Well partner, here comes our star Italian. Is she going to pull off what no one in history has ever done?"

"Hugh, she's already done that," Steve Fontaine said. "No one has ever won a gold medal in two separate sports in the same Olympics before. To win a third would be beyond historical, it would be miraculous. And in this city of miracles, I'm not sure there's room for one more."

Hugh chuckled at his partner. He still had his bet riding on Francine and he intended to collect. He had spent his quiet times concocting the most disgusting British meal he could think of to force down the smart Frenchman's throat. He had to put up with his Gallic superiority and couldn't wait for the games to be over. *Maybe I can get them to hire an American color person next time,* he thought. *How they ever came up with a Frenchman is beyond me?* he thought.

"Well, we're about to find out. The competitors are taking their warm-up throws now. But we need to switch our attention to the 800 meter final at the moment," Hugh offered. At any track meet, multiple events were happening simultaneously and the Olympics were no different. They would have to wait to see the discus competition.

* * *

Francine was busy with her warm-up routine by the edge of the discus area when Helga walked up to her.

"Ready to cheat your way to a medal today?" the big German woman said.

"No, Herr Helga. I don't use any substances to enhance my abilities," Francine said. "But if I remember right, the German's perfected the art of doping. Your private parts fall off from the injections yet?"

The German thrower scowled at the insult and walked away. Francine returned to her stretches. As she bent over to pick up her water bottle, a twinge shot through her right hand. The water bottle dropped to the grass, her right hand trembling.

She grabbed it with her left hand and tried to stop the shakes. As she stood there, her fellow Italian thrower walked up to wish her luck. As teammates, they could encourage each other as they competed.

The woman noticed Francine's right hand shaking. "Is everything OK?"

"Yeah, just a little nervous, I guess," she said. She didn't think her teammate bought the excuse.

The officials opened the competition and first up was the other Italian. Francine watched her teammate get a respectable throw in and walk back to their little area. Francine waited for the next two throwers before she was called.

Picking up her discus, she had to hold it in her left hand to keep it from falling. Clutching the discus with two hands, she walked into the ring.

With her right hand still shaking, she took her position in the ring and readied herself. Her feet moved as her body spun into the windup. Her extended arm swung with the spin and at the right moment she whipped her arm to send the discus flying.

Except nothing came out. The discus rattled around the net from where Francine had dropped it just as she had started her wind up. She jumped out of the way as the discus rolled toward her. She landed in front of the foul line.

"Foul," yelled the official watching. "No distance. Next."

Francine bent down to pick up her discus but this time used her left hand. Her right continued to shake noticeably. She walked back to her waiting teammate and collapsed on the grass. A tear formed and rolled down her cheek.

"Francine, what happened? You dropped before you even started your move. And look at your hand!" the Italian said.

Francine needed no help in realizing her right hand was going into spasms. She clutched it to her chest to try and stop the shaking. Tears rolled down her cheeks.

Helga walked over to her competitor with a smirk on her face. Instantly she was met by a fiery wild-eyed Italian discus thrower.

Francine's teammate hissed, "You come any closer, Kraut, I scratch your eyes out."

Helga stopped at the threat as if she knew the Italian woman meant it and retreated back to her little patch of sod. Francine opened her teary eyes and looked at her teammate with gratitude.

"Grazie," she squeaked.

"What are you going to do? You can't throw like that," the teammate said.

Francine closed her eyes. She knew her teammate was trying to be helpful, but stating the obvious wasn't helping her. She had to think. *Relax*, she thought. *The trainer had said that stress caused the tremors.*

Francine pulled out her music and tried to relax under her headphones. But all too soon, her teammate returned from her second throw and shook Francine. Her time to throw was approaching and she needed to ready herself.

The official called for the next thrower and Francine picked up the discus with her left hand. As she walked toward the ring, all the other competitors looked as her right hand shook. The tremors had not gone away.

Taking her position in the ring, she tried to place the discus in her right hand. The fingers gripped and held. She wound up and twisted to the throw. Her feet rotated and her body spun and her arm whipped, but her hand only held on long enough to release a wobbly disc that fluttered limply out and dropped to the ground.

Francine heard the big German roar with laughter at the ten meter distance. The discus lay in the grass just outside the ring. The officials that retrieved each discus started to walk the long distance in to gather up the device when Francine stepped over the board.

"Foul," the official said.

Francine felt the stares and heard the laughter as she headed back to her spot to wait. There were four more throws for each competitor. She had to come up with an answer in that short amount of time.

Tears returned as she lay on the grass trying to relax her hand. But the spasms continued unabated. She couldn't beat a middle schooler with a throw, never mind compete in the Olympics. Her embarrassment grew as she waited.

The board showed Helga leading the competition with two other Germans in second and third place. Her teammate wasn't last only because Francine had yet to put up any distance.

"Francine, your coach is over by the fence. She wanted me to get you."

Francine walked over to a worried looking Camille. Camille looked down as Francine held her right hand to hide its shaking.

"Your hand," Camille uttered. "How long have you had this?"

"The trainer noticed it last week. I didn't say anything since it comes and goes. It just didn't need to show up now," a frustrated thrower announced to her coach.

"Is there anything medically we can do to calm it down? Ice, heat, something?"

"I've tried all those, and more. Nothing works. It just has to work itself out. What am I going to do?" Francine asked, her frustration evident.

After a brief discussion, Francine had to return for her next throw. Her competitors were waiting to exalt in her failure once more as her right hand was obviously not responding.

"Pass," Francine announced to the official. He marked down a pass on the score card.

Her teammate was waiting when she returned to her spot. "Francine, what are you doing? A pass? You have to put up a distance or you'll be out of the competition."

"I can wait and give my hand time. It has to settle down soon."

But it didn't calm. So Francine passed again on her next turn in the ring. Meanwhile, Helga was extending her lead with each throw as she consistently built on each attempt. The other two Germans stayed right behind her as they separated themselves from the other 13 throwers. It was looking like an all-German medal ceremony.

* * *

"I can taste those truffles now Hugh. Cooked to perfection with some anchovies, maybe a brie sauce over the whole plate of them," Steve Fontaine, former French Olympic runner and ZBC Sports color personality, piled on.

Hugh gagged at the thought of the French food he would be eating if his star didn't figure out how to get the discus past the 20 meter mark. Never mind the 73.40 meter distance that the leading German had set.

"Steverino, we are at the last round of throws. Ms. McDowell will have to pull a miracle, as you said, out of her Roman pouch to win this one today," Hugh said.

"Here comes her Italian teammate," Steve said. "The two of them have been busy over there in the down time working on something. I don't know what they have planned, but a Roman miracle will be performed here if this makes it to an Italian winning."

"If the Pope is watching, and I'm sure he is like all good Italians, he better get the sacraments ready to declare a miracle. St. Francine will earn her sainthood if she can pull it off." The producer shook her head at the cheeky announcer. The ratings showed the viewers loved it.

The competitors in front of Francine took their turns at increasing their distances. But none came close to challenging the leaders. The three Germans sat and watched as their lock on the medals continued. They could feel the ribbons around their necks as they sat and waited.

"Francine McDowell," the official called. The Italian partisans in the huge stadium came to life as Francine stepped forward for her turn. They had quietly gone comatose as their star struggled and passed on each throw till now.

This was their last chance to will their athlete on to greatness. The cheers carried around the stadium as other events were ongoing. Athletes who were waiting for their event all turned their attention to what was about to happen in the discus ring.

Francine took up a position facing down the field. She stood for a long time as Hugh studied her in his binoculars. The crowd hushed as Francine slowly backed up to her start position. But she did it holding the discus in her left hand while she wound herself into position backwards.

"I don't believe this! She's going to attempt to throw left-handed," Steve announced. "Her bio states she always threw right-handed. And she plays right-handed in tennis and volleyball. Unbelievable!"

"Hold on to those vestments, sports fans. You're about to witness a miracle before your very eyes," Hugh added.

The crowd reacted when they realized what Francine was about to attempt. The murmurs of everyone commenting at once broke the silence.

Francine took her first step to the right and spun her body. With her eyes closed tight, she continued her spin and added her arm whip. At the perfect time, her arm reached its maximum speed and the discus flew out of her left hand.

The crowd knew almost at once it was going to be a huge throw as the discus sailed out toward the waiting officials. They scrambled to back up as the discus bounced off the ground and stopped. It was a great throw and the crowd cheered its approval.

The mark was going to be close. The cheers changed quickly to silence as everyone waited while the official stuck his digital reader in Francine's mark. The blank readerboard rotated waiting for the distance to appear.

Francine carefully stepped out of the back of the ring and walked free of the net. Her teammate jumped into Francine's arms screaming. They both turned just as the stadium went crazy. Francine had set a mark .25 meters past Helga's leading score.

"St. Francine has done it! I would never have believed it if I hadn't been here watching the whole time. The Vatican will be working overtime tonight getting things ready for her induction, I can assure you," Hugh said. "My Gallic friend, what do you think of those apples?"

Steve, the color guy, just sat in stunned silence. His open mouth said it all.

Hugh jumped into the dead air time. "Just what I thought, a Frenchman speechless. That says it all, my friends out there in TV land. Oh to have been here and witnessed it first hand is just so much sweeter." His mouth watered as he thought of his bangers.

Finally Steve reached reality. "Don't forget, the three Germans still have their final throw, my British reprobate."

Hugh ignored the insult. *Maybe we can get an Aussie track person to do color next time,* he thought. *I'd even take a Kiwi over this frog,* he thought.

"I wouldn't want to be any one of them if they beat out Italy's star. Remember, they still have to get out of the country after this is over. If you think English football fans are rowdy and violent, I can only imagine what the Italians will do if these Germans knock off their hero," Hugh offered.

"Mr. Godley, are you suggesting what I think you're suggesting?" the Frenchman asked.

In your ear Frenchie, Hugh thought. Hugh held back what he really wanted to say for once in his life. He switched tacks, "OK, here comes the first German that has a chance to tempt fate."

The former third place and the second place thrower took their opportunity and didn't change the standings. Helga would be the final thrower. She had a silver medal and she held the gold in her own hands.

Francine's throw was under the world record currently held by Helga, so it was possible to reverse the fortunes.

Helga stepped into the ring to catcalls and boos from the extremely partisan crowd. They had a winner they liked and they were doing everything possible to rattle the German. Helga ignored the crowd and stepped into her throw.

Spinning and releasing, the discus flew out. The crowd stopped and held its breath as the distance grew. Finally hitting earth, the officials ran to mark the distance. Still holding back waiting for the board to light up, the crowd sat.

The explosion shook the stadium as the distance placed Helga in second place. Francine had won her third gold medal in three different sports. Her teammate grabbed Francine and lifted her high. The crowd responded as their cheers lifted Francine higher.

* * *

On the medal stand, Francine didn't even notice that her right hand was back to normal until she shook hands with the official as she bent over to receive her medal. She stared down at her now fully functional extremity in frustration.

Helga, standing next to her with her silver medal, broke her mood. The German reached over to shake Francine's hand and commented, "It's all good now, yes."

Francine returned the hand shake and added, "Yes, it's good now."

"Well, I would hate to see you throw with your good hand then. Maybe you keep throwing with your off hand, ja."

The three waved for the photographers as they were led off for drug testing by the Olympic Committee.

Chapter 28

Evergreen, Colorado

The decision on Francine's leaving the tennis venue to compete in volleyball and thus missing the required drug test for medal winners was announced the last day of the Olympics. The International Olympic Committee ruled that since Francine had a drug test immediately after her volleyball win, that was sufficiently close to her tennis win to qualify her for both.

The Russians continued to complain and the International Committee clarified its decision. They had determined that since no one had ever attempted doing multiple sports at a single Olympics that the rules had not been written for such cases.

When a swimmer or a track competitor competed in multiple events in their sports, the testing had been postponed to allow the competitor to race to their next event. Testing was done soon after.

The Americans continued to grumble about the lights going out in a strategically critical part of their volleyball match. The Italians responded that things happen all the time and that the Americans hadn't come close to beating the Italians after play was resumed. It would continue to be a sore subject between the two countries' teams.

No one filed a protest on Francine's use of her left arm in the discus. The German coach just shook his head many times and continued to mutter, "Was zum Teufel," but he never protested.

The Roman celebration was still continuing when the McDowell's slipped out of Fiumicino Airport bound for Atlanta. From there, they caught a flight to Denver where they were met by a gaggle of television reporters and wild fans.

Francine's foray into Italian athletics was quickly forgotten as their favorite daughter came home to her home state. It was only after they were settled in their home in Evergreen that some normalcy returned.

Camille was still with the family as she worked with Francine to get her focused on the US Open. They had a couple short weeks to be prepared to face one of the toughest competitions in women's tennis.

They also had to find some answers to Francine's hand tremors. If the shakes struck during the US Open, she might have the same problems as she had in her discus competition.

Francine's personnel physician, Dr. Mike Turpin, made a call to his colleague in Perth, Australia. Dr. Coleman had been Francine's doctor during her initial treatment from the sea snake bite and the box jellyfish sting. He would be their local expert on the aftereffects of the 'stite'.

"Francine, I'm afraid I have no good news from Dr. Coleman. It's just as we surmised," Dr. Turpin said. "No one has been in your situation ever before so he has no suggestions as to what you might expect for reactions."

"Nothing? He doesn't have any ideas?" Camille asked.

"Nothing but the obvious," Dr. Turpin added. "That Francine is alive at all is a miracle. He commented on the nine dead people that have tried to replicate Francine's condition by being bitten and stung. Enough information on what happened to Francine has leaked out to make that information very dangerous."

"So hand tremors could be a reaction to the 'stite'?" Camille said.

"We shouldn't be surprised at anything. But the question I have is, do we continue on?" Dr. Turpin asked.

"Hold on. We're not stopping now. I'm so close. If I can win the US Open I'll have my Golden Slam," Francine injected.

"But you've already accomplished what no other athlete has ever done," Dr. Turpin said. "Isn't that enough? Think of what could be happening to your body."

Dewey had heard enough. He asked everyone else to leave so he could talk to his daughter alone. He had noticed the strain come over Francine's face as the talk turned to further effects of her Australian adventure.

"What do you want to do, honey?" Dewey asked. "Ignore all the could bes and what ifs."

"Dad, the 'stite' may kick in tonight and kill me in my sleep. It might wait a week, or a year. I don't know what's going to happen."

Dewey blanched at his daughters fatalistic talk. He still felt enormous guilt over what had happened in Coral Bay. To lose her now would be too much for him and his wife.

Francine had her answer set before he could respond. "If I'm going to suffer the effects of the 'stite'

319

sometime, so be it. But right now I'm healthy and I have my phenomenal skills still. I intend to use them until God decides otherwise."

Dewey hugged his daughter and called the rest of her team back into the room. "It's decided. Let's get ready to win the US Open."

* * *

"Karl, my old friend, am I glad to see you again," Hugh Godley said.

The ZBC Sports Network was at the US Open and Karl was the anointed color personality. "Yes Hugh, good to be back with you after your sojourn to Frenchy land. How was the stewed tomatoes?"

Hugh laughed at the reference to the bet he had made with Steve Fontaine, track personality for ZBC Sports. After winning the bet that Francine would win the discus competition, Hugh had laid on the worse British breakfast he could think of for his French food snob.

"I think he's still trying to wash it down with a good Beaujolis," Hugh added. *But I do like French wines*, he thought.

"Good, and I'm glad to hear that ZBC Sports has added that great Kenyan runner to its announcing lineup. I'm sure Bolo Xapatu will add great color to your next track event," Frank said.

"Yes, he may have six Olympic gold medals in distance running but his English accent is what gets me going. And we enjoy the same foods together. He studied at Oxford you know. Brilliant man, credit to his race," Hugh said unabashedly.

The producer waved her hand at her non-politically correct announcer. Karl picked up on the warning.

"Looks like they want to cut to a commercial. So, the finals when we return."

The monitor flipped to an ad. Once again Zeus sports was there with Francine throwing the discus with her left hand. The commercial had almost become a cult classic. The ad ended with a picture of Francine and the Zeus moniker below her image, "Because You Can."

* * *

Sitting watching the ad with a giant smile on his face was the CEO and President of Zeus Sports, Stan Day. Sitting beside him was his main competitor, Al Garbarino of Athena Athletes. Business rivals, they were fast friends out of the corporate offices.

They were both guests of the New York Tennis Club at the US Open. Ensconced in the private sky box looking down on the court, they watched as Francine McDowell and Selena Roberts warmed up for the women's final.

"You know, it's just not fair. You sponsor both players in the championship today. We need to work on evening things out, my friend," Al joked.

"Oh, and your Svetlana hasn't been chewing up the competition this past year? It's only right that I get a turn," Stan shot back.

"Have you been around my rising star? Her Russian manners are something else. I'd be glad to trade her to you, for say, one of yours. I think Italians should be represented by an Italian company, don't you?" Garbarino referred to Francine's continuing to represent Italy in her athletic endeavors.

"Well, she talks like an American in my mind. I don't care what some nincompoop on the US Olympic Committee did to make my star bolt for Italy. But I sell shoes there too. And have they flown off the rack since Rome," Stan added.

Garbarino stewed at his friend for a minute and then laughed. Life was too precious to linger on who was selling more shoes. Tomorrow was a new day and maybe he would have the superstar under contract then. *And then we'll see how my American friend likes the competition,* he thought.

Stan Day broke his friend's day dream. "They've warmed up. We'll see who comes out on top."

* * *

Hugh set the stage for the women's final. "Finally, we have these two meet. Francine has never played Selena in open competition."

Karl jumped in, "In any competition. Luck of the draw always kept them apart. And injuries over the last year had kept Selena out of the finals. But she has looked healthy this tournament as she marched through her competition without dropping a set. In fact, no one even came close. Svetlana came closest in one set but losing 6-3."

"You're right. Selena definitely has her big power serve going and her base line game is where we always remember it. She will be formable today," Hugh added.

"On the other side of the net we have St. Francine," Karl said. "Her miracle at Rome only solidified her standing as one of the greatest athletes in history, if not the greatest. But can she keep the pressure in check and focus on the game today? She has struggled this tournament which is very unlike her."

Hugh jumped in, "Any wager that you'd care to make?"

The producer switched to a commercial to avoid any improprieties. Announcers weren't supposed to take sides.

Off the air, Hugh kept at it. "What do you say?"

"Hugh, as a good German, I love bangers," Karl said. "We just call them bratwurst.. And they taste better then your British swill. But if you want to go for it, I think McDowell has run out of gas. Whatever did its thing to get her to the heights she's been at is running out. You saw that against the German throwers at the Olympics. She had to throw left-handed. Her right hand was toast. She can't play left handed tennis at this level. So you have a bet."

Hugh smiled briefly at his partner's acceptance of the bet on the outcome. He too was concerned about his favorite player and her chances. But he'd never back down to any German. Then he almost lost his lunch when the German said, "Hope you like pickled pig's tongue. My mom makes the best. And that clove smell when they're cooking makes your eyes water just waiting to slide them into your mouth."

Hugh was still recovering from the image of pickled pig's tongues when the producer gave him the cue.

"OK my Teutonic friend. I think we have an understanding of what's at stake here today. It's American vs. American, sort of. It's the match everyone in tennis has waited for all year. And we here at ZBC Sports will bring every grunt and groan live. But first a word from our sponsor."

The monitor switched to the ubiquitous Zeus Sports ad that dominated the airwaves of late. It had been updated with successive images of Francine receiving her three gold medals with short clips of each discipline she had won in. At the end the required ending clip once again demanded, 'Because You Can'.

Karl grumbled off camera as he expressed his displeasure at seeing the ad for the umpteenth time. Hugh eyeballed his partner to express his displeasure at 'dissing' one of the network's bread and butter companies. Ads paid his salary and Hugh was focused on keeping those revenue streams coming towards him.

The monitor switched back to the announcers. Hugh said, "We have the warm-ups done and the preliminaries finished. Its Francine's serve to start."

On the court, Francine bounced the tennis ball several times and threw it high straight up. She leaned back as her racket was extended behind her head. As the ball reached the apex of its flight, it descended back toward Francine. She smashed the ball and ran to her spot on the court.

"A well-hit ball to start. I'm not seeing any right hand shaking problem in that one, Karl," Hugh said.

"No, she's been holding serve very steady in spite of her struggles these past two weeks. Selena got a piece of it but couldn't control the return. 15-Love, McDowell," Karl added.

The match went back and forth as each player held serve. The dominance that Francine had shown in the past just wasn't overpowering her opponent today. At 6-5 with Selena serving to tie, Francine stumbled on a bullet of a serve. She came up limping.

"Uh, oh. We are seeing a limp in Francine after that tumble. Let's check the replay," Hugh offered. "Yes, right there, she rolled her ankle after that shot attempting to get back to the baseline."

Karl jumped on this development. "She appears to be attempting to walk it off. But she is favoring her right ankle. That's the same ankle she injured in high school and was a concern at the Australian Open. This could be a huge development."

From their view, Francine appeared to be trying to work her ankle to continue play. She walked around to the baseline and gathered herself for Selena's serve. It was a hard serve to the outside. Francine's opponent was testing her lateral movement. Francine quickly got the ball and hit a shot down the line for a winner.

Hugh jumped at the winner. "Doesn't appear to be any lasting effects. That was a well-played ball that seems to have stunned Selena. I'm sure she was thinking she had a winner."

"But will she try it again or play it safe? Maybe an easier serve and then volley would be a better idea here. Get Francine moving back and forth with cross-court shots and really test that ankle," Karl advised.

As if Selena had been listening, the next serve was right at Francine. It was returned and Selena went to work forcing the ball from side to side. Francine sprinted back and forth on the baseline to run down each shot. She finally hit a cross-court that was tight on the sideline for a winner.

The next two shots pressed Francine but she eventually worked them to where she could hit a winner each time. Breaking Selena's serve finally, Francine won the last game to win the set 7-5.

"The first set belongs to Francine," Hugh said.

"Its not over yet," Karl added quickly.

* * *

Francine advised the chair umpire that she needed medical attention and the tournament doctor and trainer were brought out. Removing her tennis shoe on her right foot, the doctor examined the ankle for injury. Swelling was evident as he felt for any obvious injuries. Francine winced as he prodded and hit the tender spot.

The doctor advised, "I don't feel anything broken. But I'd have to X-ray it to confirm."

"Tape ii up tight," she instructed the trainer.

"I have to warn you that if something is broken in there, you could be doing permanent damage to yourself," the doctor warned.

The trainer was hesitating taping and Francine told him again, "Tape it."

The trainer bent over and began his taping job. The doctor stood up and watched in silence.

Francine offered something as he watched, "It's the US Open final. If I win, I have my Golden Slam. If I default and walk off the court, I may never have another chance."

A tear formed in her right eye as the pain from the tape squeezing her ankle shot up through her body. Her grimace announced her state to the watching world.

The trainer put her shoe back on with some difficulty due to the thickness of the tape. He pulled at the laces as he cinched them up tight. He offered his hand as Francine carefully stood up and tested her right ankle.

The painkiller the trainer rubbed on seemed to help but she still could feel the discomfort. She stepped out on the court and did some small jumps. *It works, but I'm not sure for how long*, she thought.

As she crossed by the net as the two players went to their respective sides of the court, Selena kept her expression very professional. There was no question of concern or any taunting. Francine knew it was all business today. Their friendship that had been developing between the two African-American players was left at court's edge.

Francine waited for Selena's serve. She started her small foot dance as her opponent swung back to hit the ball. As the racket started its forward movement, Francine's dance exploded into rapid movement.

With her feet already moving prior to the ball even crossing the net, her quick reaction time sprinted to get to the ball. Francine reached the outside ball and snapped a down-the-line winner. Selena's expression didn't change losing the first point.

Francine knew that the longer the match went, the less chance she had of winning it. Her ankle would slowly get worse with more pounding. A quick finish was called for, but that wouldn't be easy with a healthy Selena across the net.

But the first set went Francine's way as she broke her opponent's serve. The next sets were traded back and forth as each player kept their serve going. At 4-4, Francine stepped up to the baseline and readied herself. Her return game had been working well for her and she had accumulated her normal high percentages of winners.

Francine moved to serve and as she did her right leg slipped slightly. As she stumbled from the misstep, the ball flew out straight at her opponent. Selena handled it easily but her cross-court return missed. *Point*, she thought. The crowd roared its approval at the continued splendid play of both players. But for Francine, panic was overtaking her.

As she stopped in place and bent over, she could feel her right leg begin to go into spasms. She bore down more weight on it in an attempt to keep it under control. From afar, it just looked like she was resting her injured ankle.

But she knew this was different. It was the same shaking that had got to her when she was competing in the discus at the Olympics. But this time it was her leg that was trembling, not her hand. She fought the wave of panic as she tried to quell her muscles.

A small twitch remained as she walked to the baseline to await Selena's serve. *Had she seen the shaking?* she thought. *How much longer do I have before my leg gives out?*

She stood by the back board and looked up into the stands where Camille sat. Their looks met and Francine knew her coach had seen it. Camille's expression tried to install confidence to finish out quickly.

Selena drove a hard ball down the center, just catching the line for a great serve. Francine charged and caught the ball. She took off as much power and returned a relatively soft ball. Selena moved to intercept as she readied herself for an overhead smash.

Francine almost drug her right leg with her as she rushed to the net and got ready. As Selena looked up at the falling ball, she drew her racket back. She crushed the ball toward the opposite side of the net with such force that the ball would ricochet off the hard court into the stands.

Except standing in the exact right spot, Francine snapped her racket to intercept the ball and redirected it back across the net to a perfectly placed corner shot. The crowd went nuts in its appreciation of what could only be described as a miracle shot.

Winning the set, the score stood at 5-4. *If I can hold serve once more, it will be over*, Francine thought.

Francine threw down a tough serve, but Selena connected with it and returned a crosscourt shot. Francine willed her legs to move. Her left leg cooperated but her right leg didn't. It acted like it wasn't even connected to her body. As she stumbled badly and missed the return, the crowd gasped.

Francine fought for control just to not fall on the court. Her right leg visibly shook. She bent over again and pushed down on her leg with both arms. The shaking refused to stop.

She hobbled back to the baseline and took three balls from one of the ball boys. She knocked one ball off her racket gently back to him. She tested her left leg and it was working normally. *Four points and I can finish this,* she thought.

She took a deep breath and shifted her weight to her left leg. Her right shook in place as she tossed the ball. Raising up on her toes, she smashed a ball with all the strength she could. The ball streaked toward the outside and blew by a scrambling Selena.

One down, three to go, she thought. Selena adjusted her position slightly to take the corner away from Francine's serve. Francine proceeded to burn a serve down the middle that just caught the center service line. Selena tried to recover, but the ball just missed her racket.

Two to go, Francine thought. She tossed her ball and felt the twinge as she brought her racket forward. Hitting the ball awkwardly, the ball drove itself into the net. The racket flew out of her hands and bounced off the court. The noise of the racket shattering startled the crowd.

Francine held her right hand as the spasms hit her. Her right leg continued its shaking as she walked over to her bag to retrieve a new racket. Her right hand refused to grip the plastic wrap on her new racket. She reverted to shoving the racket under her right arm.

With it secured tightly, she pulled the plastic off with her left hand. She hobbled back to the baseline and held out her right hand for a ball. As the ball boy bounced an easy ball to her, she moved to grab it. Her right hand refused to work and the ball bounced off her hand.

The ball boy scooped up the errant ball and walked over to Francine. He carefully placed two balls in her right hand. Francine struggled to close her hand around them.

"Here, Ms. McDowell, let me help you."

Francine smiled at him for his kindness, but she noticed the right side of her mouth wasn't responding. The boy looked at her contorted face. An expression of concern registered on his face.

"Thank you," Francine slurred out. She turned to face her opponent and tried to think. *Two more points is all*, she thought.

The crowd was stone silent as they witnessed Francine's struggle with control. She had difficulty just standing on the baseline and holding her racket.

* * *

"She's finished. Toast as they say," Karl said from the broadcaster's booth. "It's almost painful to watch."

Hugh Godley watched in silence. For once in his life he was speechless. He shook himself to make sure he was really witnessing the self-destruction of a fellow human being. The entire stadium held their breath as Francine readied to serve.

"Hugh, the officials need to stop this. That young lady out there is in serious trouble. Her body is shutting down on her," Karl said.

Hugh remained quiet along with everyone else. He watched and waited. *What would his star athlete do?* he wondered. *To be so close, and now what?*

Francine answered the questions by dropping a ball onto the court. As it bounced off the court, with the racket in her left hand, she sliced down on the ball. The slice, from Hugh's perspective, was almost like she had attempted to hit the ball with the edge of her racket, but missed.

The dramatic downward movement had the desired results. The new strings dug into the ball and forced a violent spin on the ball's motion. With just enough angle to move the ball toward the net, the incredible spin made sure the ball would barely clear the net before dying. The ball dropped harmlessly onto the opposite side of the court.

A sluggish Selena crashed forward in a vain attempt to get to the ball. She would have made it if the ball had bounced. But instead, the ball hit the court and just rolled away, the spin taking all of the upward motion out of the ball.

"Unbelievable!" yelled Hugh, finally finding his voice. "Have you ever seen a shot like that my Lederhosen friend?"

Now it was Karl who was speechless. Hugh filled the airtime.

"No, I didn't think so."

Finally recovering, Karl jumped in, "But now we are at match point. The pressure is on. Can she do the trick shot and get away with it again?"

On the court, Francine was getting ready to show the world if she could. She stood by the backboard and allowed the ball boy to hand her two balls. She nodded to him in her still crooked smile and turned to face Selena.

Standing fifteen feet behind the baseline, she readied herself. Selena watched her quizzically.

"What's this? A serve from the back stop?" Karl said.

Hugh watched intently. *It is a bit strange*, he thought.

Francine bent over and pushed on her right leg. From above, it appeared she was massaging her muscles. As the crowd waited, she continued to work her leg. Then she worked on her right hand.

Finally appearing ready, she bounced a ball with her right hand. It seemed to be working slightly as she then threw it up and out toward the middle of the court.

Hugh held his breath for what he thought might be coming. *But how could she?* he thought. He had seen this many times, but it had been on a volleyball court, not a tennis court.

Francine raced to catch up with the ball and seemed to have both legs finally working. Her left hand held her racket as she leaped at the baseline. Her momentum carried her up and forward as she flew over the baseline.

Suspended above the back court, she located the falling ball. Timed to perfection, she swung with all her strength and caught the ball at the apex of her jump. With the hit a good ten feet inside the baseline and a good nine feet above the court, the downward angle of the ball hit just past the net on the opposite side.

Selena jumped to try and get the ball as it ricocheted over her head and into the stands. The crowd jumped to its feet in celebration. But as Francine landed and took two steps, she collapsed on the court. Her body immediately went into convulsions.

US Open officials rushed to lend assistance. The official US Open doctor ran out on the court and inserted a pen in her mouth to keep Francine from biting her tongue.

Francine's personal physician, Dr. Turpin, climbed down from the family box and ran to his patient. Soon a gurney appeared from the tunnel and Francine was placed upon it. She was quickly wheeled off and disappeared down the side tunnel. Ambulance sirens carried to the stadium as the crowd sat in stunned silence.

"Ladies and gentlemen. You have just witnessed the most courageous act of sports I've ever witnessed in my career. Probably in all the annals of sports. We can only pray that Ms. McDowell is OK."

Chapter 29

New York, New York

"Members of the press, this is why we are so strident in rooting out all instances of athletes taking performance-enhancing drugs," Cubo Zoan said. "That Francine McDowell is in a hospital as we speak fighting for her life is proof enough that the sports world needs to wake up to the excesses that are taking place. All in the name of winning, athletes like Ms. McDowell put their lives on the line so corporate sports titans can make more millions. Things have to change now. We can't let Ms. McDowell's sacrifice be in vain."

Two days had passed since Francine had won the US Open. Two days of controversy and innuendo as everyone involved with professional sports tried to deflect the public outcry. The Francine vs. Selena match had been the highest rated television sports program in a long time.

And now, from around the world, concern and anger flowed toward New York City and the hospital that held Francine. But it was misdirected as Francine had been put into an induced coma, loaded on a Boeing 757 outfitted with the latest medical equipment and personnel and was just now landing in Perth, Australia.

She would be admitted under a false name and placed under the care of her original physician, Dr. Coleman. The Western Australian medical expert was as close as anyone to knowing what had happened to Francine. He also knew the best options on treatment.

Cubo Zoan was unaware that he was in the wrong city. It didn't matter. New York had the big media outlets that would assure his crusade would reach the world. Francine was just a convenient tag line to emote sympathy. With public sympathy came political power.

Politicians would be pressured to change the rules on sports to protect innocent lives. And the World Anti-Doping Committee, and Cubo Zoan, Director, in particular, would be ready to accept the job of oversight.

As the press conference continued, Zoan stated that he would take questions. The press all clamored for answers.

"Is WADC now ready to strip Ms. McDowell of her ill-gotten medals in light of the past two days?" one reporter asked.

Cubo quickly jumped to answer as if this had been a plant. "Yes, in light of the events we've all witnessed and the findings that WADC has made concerning Ms. McDowell's enhanced performance, I can state we have recommended to both governing bodies of track and tennis that she be stripped of her wins. And further that all her awards be returned so that the proper winner might be recognized. The ones who don't cheat."

"Strong words, Mr. Zoan," Hugh Godley said. "Is WADC ready to release its findings?"

"As you know, the Australian government has been very concerned that the consequences of Ms. McDowell's event be kept from public scrutiny. We will honor that request and have marked our report for internal use only," Zoan answered.

"How convenient," Hugh redirected. "No prying eyes to challenge your findings. No breath of fresh air, so to speak, so the public will know the truth."

Cubo was ready, "Again, the Australian government is very adamant about this subject. To do anything otherwise would invite their response. Mr. Godley, maybe you should direct your inquiries to the Australian Embassy."

Cubo smiled inside. Thank God for the stupid Aussies and their law sealing everything concerning McDowell. *And thank you to all those dopes that keep going to Australia and dying trying to get the McDowell effect,* he thought. *Makes my job so much easier.*

Life was going well for Zoan as more sports were in discussion with WADC for providing testing and supervision to their sports. He was on his way to controlling all the major sports.

The U.S. Senator from New York had that same day given a press conference where he stated he would be introducing legislation requiring the NFL, Major League Baseball and the NBA to all submit their players to WADC oversight.

And in Europe, the big plum was about to drop. The FIFA World Soccer Cup was ready to sign with WADC. Cubo Zoan was already envisioning himself in a new McLaren sports car that he had his eye set on. There would be no Ferrari or Lamborghini exotic car in his life. No Italian car would do. It could only be a British or German sports car.

And that beach house in Rio would finally be his. He could dump his apartment and move to the water finally. St. Moritz held his interest, but he wanted that connection to his home in Brazil. *And those beautiful, scantily clad women on the beach*, he thought. *Not those bundled Swiss babes he had to deal with in St. Moritz.*

Chapter 30

Melbourne, Australia

The ensuing four months after the US Open had seen Cubo's predictions come true. The IAAF met and voted to disqualify Francine from her Olympic win in the discus. The following month the ITF met and similarly stripped Francine of her four Grand Slam wins along with her Olympic Gold Medal in tennis.

The FIVB, governing body for volleyball, continued to hold out against the World Anti-Doping Committee's strong-arm tactics. Its governing board met and reconfirmed Italy's Olympic win in Women's Volleyball. Against the continued whining of the United States coach, FIVB passed a resolution recognizing Francine McDowell's accomplishments both in college and with the Italians. That had brought Cubo Zoan out preaching. He chastised volleyball for its 'head in the sand' attitude toward cheating players.

News of Francine's transfer to an Australian hospital had faded as no personal sightings had been made since her collapse at Arthur Ashe Stadium in Flushing Meadows. The staff at King's Hospital in Perth guarded the privacy of their star patient from all comers.

While Dewey and Anna Maria made the daily trek across the street from their borrowed apartment to visit their daughter, even the local news people joined in the conspiracy. Francine's parents were treated with special behavior as the McDowell family became Perth's guest.

But the sports world continued. As the Australian Open began competition, the usual big names were in attendance. Selena Roberts was expected to take the number one spot away from Svetlana. With Francine stripped of her wins, Svetlana had been elevated to number one.

But a healthy Selena was crushing her opponents leading up to Melbourne. With the Russian and the American on opposite sides of the bracket, they were expected to march through the competition. The betting money was on the two of them meeting in the final.

After two weeks, the final that was expected was set. Selena would play Svetlana for the Grand Slam win and a number one ranking. The whole Francine era seemed to be forgotten from just a short four months before.

For one ZBC Sports announcer, the world wasn't the same. He had witnessed some of the greatest competition in his life, and what remained paled in comparison. It showed in his broadcasts as rumors buzzed that he might be replaced. During the morning Sports Center Show, the two sportscasters discussed the upcoming finals that would be held that afternoon.

"So Hugh, we are set for the first Grand Slam without our Ms. McDowell," Karl said. The rumors included the whisper that Karl Mahr was slated to take over the top spot. Karl pushed his partner, "I don't know about you, but I'm excited to see a healthy Selena back in form."

Hugh hung his head down and didn't bite on the lead in. The producer waved her hand at her former top announcer to get some life into him. He had been dogging it the whole tournament and the ratings were slipping badly. *I don't care*, Hugh thought.

As the producer cut to a commercial, Karl leaned toward his partner. The smell of alcohol on Hugh's breath made him back up.

"My friend, you need to snap out of it. There is life after Francine," Karl said.

"Is there? I'm not so sure," Hugh offered. "That woman gave it her all. Literally left it all on the court. And then those bastards strip her of her accomplishments. Its just not right."

"Well, you can take it up with that Zoan creep if you want. Word is he's arriving today for the finals. Seems he's here to celebrate his cleansing of the cheaters from sports," Karl said.

"Well, I'd like to ---" Hugh mumbled before being cut off. The monitor flicked to a new ad as the pre-game show continued.

* * *

The Singapore Airlines Boeing 747 Jumbo jet settled down onto the runway at Melbourne's Tullamarine International Airport. Sitting up front in First Class, Cubo Zoan finished his French Champagne. As he drained his glass, he looked out the window as the ground came into view.

The day was already hot outside and the glare off the pavement blinded him slightly. He turned away and his eyes adjusted to the serene interior of the big jet.

Reaching the gate, the flight personnel let the First Class people off prior to the hordes in the economy section. With over four hundred passengers on the flight from Singapore, Australian Customs would soon be flooded.

Zoan quickly walked off the plane and headed toward baggage claim. He gathered up his fine grain leather bag and examined it for abuse by the airlines. Seeing none, he sprinted toward Customs to beat the mass of humanity just reaching the baggage carousel.

Handing over his Brazilian passport, the Customs official opened it to his picture and identification. He placed the opened document over the glass as a digital reader scanned across it. Working the computer, the official looked up at the visitor standing in front of him.

Looking down to confirm what the computer was telling him, he hit a key to notify his superior that someone tagged by the computer had arrived. He looked busy as Cubo waited impatiently. Soon a man in a suit arrived escorted by two armed policemen.

"Mr. Zoan, please come with me," the suited man said. He took Cubo's passport from the Australian Customs Official and began to walk off.

Cubo started to hesitate until the two policemen stepped in behind him and waited. Zoan followed the man in the suit. The four walked out of the Customs area and took a side door that the suited man opened with a security card.

Once behind the door, the four followed a corridor and climbed a set of stairs. Windows looked down over the International Lounge and Cubo could see people milling around oblivious to his existence. He stared at them before the corridor turned and he was led away from the windows.

Placed into a windowless room, one policeman stood guard inside as the other one stood outside the door The man in the suit had disappeared. Zoan was perplexed as to why he was being kept in the room.

"So, do you know why I'm here?" he asked the policeman.

There was no answer as the large man stood with his arms held easy in front of him. Unlike officers from other former British possessions, this Australian police officer carried a gun on his belt along with other weapons for subduing criminals. Cubo studied the mute man for some kind of answer.

Soon, the door opened. A different man in a suit walked in and sat down at the table opposite Cubo

"Mr. Zoan, do you know why we have detained you?" the man asked.

"I think this is an outrage. I have no idea why I'm being held, but I can assure you, my staff was meeting me today. They will miss me right about now. I'm quite sure they will be contacting the Brazilian Embassy as we sit here," Cubo said.

"Does the name Tony Smythe mean anything to you?" the man asked.

Cubo froze. *The Australian that had been wined and dined in Zurich and pumped for information,* he thought. The man who had witnessed the McDowell woman's attack and knew all the details. *Certainly I know him,* Cubo thought. *But I'm not opening my mouth.*

Hearing no answer forthcoming from his silent subject, the man asked, "Perhaps the name Lynn Randwick rings a bell?"

Who the hell is that? Cubo thought. "Never heard of her."

"But mum on Tony Smythe. Sure that you've never crossed paths with that name?"

Cubo sat mute. He knew the Australians had gone after people who had talked too openly about the McDowell event. He had learned that some had received jail sentences. Being a sophisticated fellow, Cubo thought, *I think I'll wait for my embassy to go to work here.*

"Staying silent then Mr. Zoan? Wise decision," the man said. "But I'd like you to meet someone who has been dying to talk to you."

The man left the room and soon returned. "Let me introduce the Dr. Keith Mountain, of our Ministry of Health for Her Majesty's Australian Government."

Cubo looked blankly at the new man in his suit. He didn't offer his hand but sat still as he waited.

"Mr. Zoan, I've been waiting for this day," Dr. Mountain said. "You have been up to no good where it concerns our Ms. McDowell and her adventure here in Australia. Perhaps I should update you since you have time to kill until your embassy arrives."

The doctor let his statement sink in. He continued, "First, when Ms. Lynn Randwick informed us that her boyfriend had flown on an all-expense paid trip to

Switzerland, we contacted our embassy in Bern. Unknown to you, our man there contacted your stooge, Mr. Tony Smythe. We reminded him of the Australian law on Ms. McDowell's accident and told him if he intended to ever return home a free man, he had better cooperate."

Cubo's expression shifted a bit and the health official picked up the pressure.

"It seems the friendly female companion you made sure he met his first night had wrung much of the information out of the slightly inebriated Smythe. The compromising pictures that you had taken of their little soirée that night certainly would have done the trick. Blackmail is such a sordid business."

Zoan was now noticeably agitated as Dr. Mountain continued.

"Fortunately, national governments have much more to raise the stakes with than blackmail. Since nine people have now attempted to recreate Ms. McDowell's life-altering experience, nine deaths have resulted. Reminding Mr. Smythe that he could be charged as an accessory to those deaths brought instant cooperation. Am I reaching you yet, Mr. Zoan?"

Zoan pursed his lips and held firm. *I will wait for my embassy to come to save me from all this,* he thought.

"So, when you met with Mr. Smythe the next evening, you must have thought how cooperative he was. Unfortunately for you, in reality he was really wearing a wire. We have the whole conversation recorded and he is safely back in Coral Bay waiting to testify at your trial," Mountain said.

Cubo blanched at the thought of a trial and all that would be brought out. His expression registered with the Australian officials.

"Now, you can just wait here for your embassy to contact us," Dr. Mountain said. "In the meantime, we are drawing up nine manslaughter charges against you for the deaths of those bent on greatness. But I wouldn't put too much stock in your nation's help. The last two victims of the risky business of duplicating Ms. McDowell's experience were Brazilian. The last one was just a week ago. Seems your government is quite upset about the whole affair."

Cubo sank into his chair. His body went limp in recognition of what was about to happen to him.

* * *

"Well, this news might perk you up, Hugh," Karl offered. "Seems that passengers getting off the flight from Singapore reported that Australian officials escorted our old friend Cubo Zoan away. The police were in attendance and he hasn't been seen since this morning."

Hugh smiled at the news. *That certainly helps my disposition if that guy takes it in the teeth*, he thought. As the producer grabbed the kill switch, Hugh said, "What a dick. What goes around, comes around, I think the saying goes."

"And now a word from our sponsor," Karl quickly injected.

An ad came on for Zeus Sports that featured a healthy Francine plying her sports. Hugh watched the monitor intently as the ad ran. It was a highlight of her accomplishments and as usual, ended with the phrase on the screen, 'Because You Can'.

Karl had a slip of paper in his hands when the cameras returned live to their position. Hugh took the lead.

"We have our women's finals right now. All the hype is done and two challengers are ready to get things going," Hugh said.

There was a quiet spot while Karl handed the slip of paper over to his partner. Hugh read the news silently. A smile broke out on his face at what he read.

"Ladies and gentleman, the Australian Open Committee just handed us news of a special ceremony that will happen just before start of play. We turn the mic over to our Open announcer at Center Court."

The TV cameras switched to a man in a white suit, a white fedora on his head, standing at the net. As Selena and Svetlana waited impatiently for this change in schedule, the announcer clicked on his microphone.

"Good afternoon. Before we start play to determine this year's Australian Open Champion in Women's Tennis, I wish to welcome a very special guest to today's match. At the invitation of our Prime Minster, will you all welcome last year's winner, Ms. Francine McDowell."

The crowd all rose as one and cheered for the player who had been adopted by all Australia as one of their own. From the tunnel by the special boxes, Francine stepped carefully out toward the crowd. Using a walker, she stopped. She reached for her dad's arm to steady her as she stepped around her walker.

The two walked arm and arm up the short flight of stairs to the Prime Minister's box seat. Anna Maria followed closely behind as Francine's walker was removed by tournament staff.

She shook the Prime Minister's hand and then stood and waved to her adoring fans. They returned the adoration they felt toward this American-turned-Italian all by a twist of fate in Australia. That she was in public for the first time spoke volumes as to the progress she was making getting her normal life back.

Even Svetlana stood and clapped for her former antagonist, along with Selena. As Francine took her seat, the match got under way. The two competitors went head to head under the watchful eye of Francine.

Selena came out on top in two sets. When Francine was invited down to award the trophies, she begged off so as to not distract from the competitor's victory. Only the insistence of Selena got her and her dad to center court.

Francine disappeared just as quickly back to Perth to carry on her rehabilitation. With her exposure in Melbourne, the press was a little more insistent on news of her health. Dewey and Anna Maria held impromptu press talks on their walks around Perth, and it soon became known that Francine was progressing nicely back to health. The gifts of athletic excellence were gone, but not the spirit.

It was six months later that Francine's spirits took a huge lift. With Cubo Zoan among the missing, locked up in an Australian prison with a twenty-year sentence, the WADC had searched for a new director.

The news conference announcing the new director also held important news. First was the announcement that the former director had overstepped the bounds of evidence investigation in collecting information on athletes. And second was that with the generosity of Zeus Sports Apparel and Athena Athletic Wear, a very sizable donation had been made to set up a multimillion-dollar research facility to find the proper tests to determine if an athlete was cheating.

The new research facility would be located in Perth, Australia and would be run by Dr. Coleman, formerly of the King's Hospital. No longer would innuendo and hearsay rule in determining the guilt or innocence of athletes.

Soon afterward, very quietly, on a Friday afternoon in the summer, both the ITF and IAAF announced the reinstatement of Francine McDowell in both tennis and track. Her medals and records were reestablished and her previous charges were expunged as the World Anti-Doping Committee apologized for the past transgression of its former director.

* * *

In a very hot jail outside Darwin in the Northern Territories, a prisoner sat, sweating, in a cut down orange jump suit. The air conditioner, which frequently broke, was nonfunctional as the tropical sun blistered the old concrete building. All the prisoners had cut the sleeves and legs off their suits as they sat in the common room. The prisoner and his fellow inmates watched the news on the rec room's lone television.

As news of Francine's reinstatement in both tennis and track was announced, a commotion in the back interrupted the report.

"Hey, bloody hell! I'm trying to watch this. It's about that crazy American woman that got zapped over in Coral Bay. If you blokes don't stuff it, I'll bloody well come back there and bugger the bunch of you," an inmate yelled. Since he was the acknowledged leader of the toughest gang in the prison, the quiet was instant. "That's better."

The TV report went on and explained the McDowell affair, leaving out details of her attack in Coral Bay. Footage of Francine's exceptional athletic skills were reviewed before discussing her redemption in the eyes of the official sports world.

As the extended news report continued, one prisoner grew more agitated. The prisoner rubbed the stubble on his head where once long flowing locks fell down. Sitting by himself, he sulked. He had made no friends in his short time in jail, and drew stares from the other prisoners at his strange behavior.

The report finished with recent video of Ms. McDowell along with her parents and personal coach all running on the beach on Rottnest Island off the coast near Fremantle. The reporter seemed generally happy to be reporting that Ms. McDowell had fully recovered from her recent brush with death.

The agitated prisoner stood up, walked over to the television and kicked in the screen. He screamed in rage as the glass from the old cathode ray tube set flew across the room. The TV set sputtered in sparks.

"Zoan, that will get you thirty days in solitary for destruction of government property," a guard yelled.

The End

Acknowledgements

First I would thank Timothy Johns, my tireless editor. Though he works hard that my writing is presentable, place no blame on him for the final product. That all rests with me.

My good friend and fellow writers, Larry Stoddard! and Jeanne Crownover are always there with encouragement and comments.

My proof readers offer valuable feedback at different phases as my draft is put together. Dick Martin, Marsha Wiles, Tiffany Martin, Barbara Foster, John Briggs and Rod Gravelly have all kept me from straying too far off on tangents.

Charlie Cremeans was instrumental at the beginning of my writing in offering words of advice, support and encouragement.

John Ewing was an early supporter who didn't get to see the final product. His wife Bertha Ewing was invaluable as a listener as I read out loud to her on one of my many edit jobs.

Finding Morwenna Rakestraw to do the cover layout was a relief.

Mitch Press of World Book has offered his wisdom from his family's years in the book business. While not all encouraging, his guidance as publishing transforms in the digital age has been invaluable.

Lastly, my wife deserves much credit for supporting my life as a writer.

Dear Reader,

Thank you for your selection of reading material. I hope this book measured up to your expectations. The most critical part for a new author is getting the word out to other readers.

I would appreciate your help in spreading the word. There are three important things you can do. You need to understand the importance of the first one to my becoming a successful writer. Amazon.com is huge in the new book publishing era. So please:

1.   Go to Amazon.com and leave a review
2.   Tell a friend about this book
3.   Tell your social network about this book.

The more positive reviews that are made in various places will help readers find me.

Again, thanks for your support.

W.B. Martin

And check out my website at wbmartinauthor.com